HAYNER PLD/ALTON SQUARE

DARK
PROPHECY

also by anthony e. zuiker

LEVEL 26: Dark Origins

DARK PROPHECY

a level 26 thriller
featuring steve dark

anthony e. zuiker

with **Duane Swierczynski**

DUTTON

DUTTON

Published by Penguin Group (USA) Inc.
375 Hudson Street, New York, New York 10014, U.S.A.
Penguin Group (Canada), 90 Eglinton Avenue East, Suite 700, Toronto, Ontario M4P 2Y3, Canada (a division of Pearson Penguin Canada Inc.); Penguin Books Ltd, 80 Strand, London WC2R 0RL, England; Penguin Ireland, 25 St Stephen's Green, Dublin 2, Ireland (a division of Penguin Books Ltd); Penguin Group (Australia), 250 Camberwell Road, Camberwell, Victoria 3124, Australia (a division of Pearson Australia Group Pty Ltd); Penguin Books India Pvt Ltd, 11 Community Centre, Panchsheel Park, New Delhi—110 017, India; Penguin Group (NZ), 67 Apollo Drive, Rosedale, North Shore 0632, New Zealand (a division of Pearson New Zealand Ltd); Penguin Books (South Africa) (Pty) Ltd, 24 Sturdee Avenue, Rosebank, Johannesburg 2196, South Africa

Penguin Books Ltd, Registered Offices: 80 Strand, London WC2R 0RL, England

Published by Dutton, a member of Penguin Group (USA) Inc.

First printing, October 2010
1   3   5   7   9   10   8   6   4   2

Ⓩ REGISTERED TRADEMARK—MARCA REGISTRADA

LIBRARY OF CONGRESS CATALOGING-IN-PUBLICATION DATA
has been applied for.

ISBN 978-0-525-95185-8

Printed in the United States of America

Tarot Card Creative Direction: John Paine
Tarot Card Illustrations: Damion Poulter

PUBLISHER'S NOTE

This book is a work of fiction. Names, characters, places, and incidents either are the product of the author's imagination or are used fictitiously, and any resemblance to actual persons, living or dead, business establishments, events, or locales is entirely coincidental.

To my mother, Diana, this one's for you . . .

DARK
PROPHECY

It is well-known among law enforcement personnel that murderers can be categorized as belonging to one of twenty-five levels of evil, from the naïve opportunists starting out at Level 1 to the organized, premeditated torture-murderers who inhabit Level 25.

What almost no one knows is that a new category of killer has emerged. And only one man is capable of stopping them.

His targets:
Level 26 killers.

His methods:
Whatever it takes.

His name:
Steve Dark.

PROLOGUE

Rome, Italy

As Steve Dark pulled the latex mask out of the water, it seemed to be laughing at him.

The barren eyeholes stared back, as if in wide-eyed mock surprise. *Who, me? Do this?* The zipper mouth twisted around the edges to imply a cruel sneer. The rest of the suit hung wet and limp from Dark's hands, as if it were the skin of a lizard that had long since scampered off to points unknown. The details were familiar; the same zippers, the same stitching. The suit seemed identical to the one the diabolical Sqweegel had worn, only this version was completely black.

Tom Riggins caught up with Dark, put a hand on his shoulder. "It's not him," he said.

"I know," Dark said quietly.

"I'm serious. You and I watched that son of a bitch burn. This is just someone fucking around. A copycat. You know that, right?"

Dark nodded. "Let's get this thing bagged."

Hours before, there had been instant panic—Special Circs was rushed to Rome, an international task force was formed. Somebody poisoned the Trevi Fountain in Rome, killing dozens of people, and

5

that unknown subject had left something strange floating in the cyanide-laced waters. The scene was right out of Hieronymus Bosch—hundreds of pink bodies, a soul-sickening stench. Scores of ambulances, fire trucks, and police cars were shoehorned in the main road. Worried onlookers clogged every alley and side street.

A Roman *polizia* van had escorted Dark and his team to a cleared section a few yards away from the fountain. Uniformed officers lifted the orange crime-scene tape for Dark as he ducked under and then helped clear his way to the famed fountain. The bottom was almost completely empty, except for gold and silver Euro coins and a quarter inch of water—poisoned water, lapping at the bottoms of Dark's shoes.

Huddled around the drain area were five Roman cops standing broad shoulder to broad shoulder, blocking the view from onlookers. Dark's escort whistled, and they parted.

When he first saw the black, rubbery mass floating in the water, Dark stopped dead in his tracks. He had to will himself to take several deep breaths before approaching, his mind reeling, his veins suddenly pumping ice water.

In that one horrible moment, Dark was fooled into thinking that maybe, *somehow*, the Level 26 serial killer had survived. The rational part of Dark's mind knew that was impossible. Dark had chopped up his body with an axe, and he had watched the spindly parts burn in a crematory oven. Still, seeing the suit, and its mocking countenance, was enough to flip Dark's mind over to the irrational side.

The team found a lab in Rome. It was a far cry from the one Dark was used to back at Special Circs in Virginia, but the basic tools were there. Dark swabbed the suit for DNA, then ran the sample through. As he waited, Dark sipped bitter, lukewarm coffee and tried to keep his mind focused. But the brain in his skull was like a trapped animal, and it refused to settle down. He kept running through the nightmare events of the past few weeks. He kept seeing flashes of his infant daughter, now in the care of a complete stranger back in the United States. He kept seeing flashes of Sibby, the love of his life, smiling at him. A smile he would ever only see in his dreams.

Finally, the DNA results came in, and they sparked a CODIS hit back in the United States—Las Vegas, in connection with a cold case.

Dark braced himself for everything from a copycat to a reincarnation. Someone who had followed the case, had gotten off on it, and decided to follow in Sqweegel's footsteps. This was nothing new. The original Zodiac had many admirers who picked up his techniques over the years—taunting the police with letters, killing lovers in isolated locations. The killer had captured the public imagination, and there were those who wanted to take advantage of that.

And now this seemed to be the case with Sqweegel. There had been no serial killer like him in recorded history. Sqweegel, a contortionist madman who kept his body encased in a forensic-proof murder suit, left no traces behind unless he *wanted* them left behind. He could hide in the smallest of crevices and wait with inhuman patience until his victim was distracted or asleep. Then Sqweegel would crawl out of his hidey-hole and attack with a savagery that belied his size and build. He had been obsessed with punishing humans for perceived sins and saw himself as a cleansing agent on the soul of the world. And he had fixated on Dark—the manhunter who spent years tracking him. To Sqweegel, Dark required the ultimate punishment.

Maybe this was an acolyte, trying to follow in his master's creepy footsteps.

But after Dark and his Special Circs team returned to the U.S., there were no more incidents. No forensic-proof suits left behind, no puzzles, no taunts. No unsolved murders that came even close to Sqweegel's MO.

No more bodies.

No threats.

Nothing even close to the horrors that Sqweegel had perpetrated.

Until . . .

five years later

I

the hanged man

To watch Steve Dark's personal tarot card reading,
please log in to Level26.com and
enter the code: hanged.

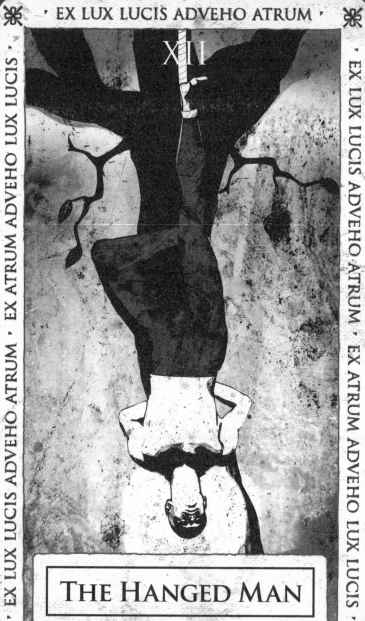

EX LUX LUCIS ADVEHO ATRUM

XII

THE HANGED MAN

Chapel Hill, North Carolina

About five minutes into the torture session, Martin Green realized he was going to die.

Green's body was hanging upside down—one end of a rope tied tight around his right ankle, the other end secured to a light fixture in the ceiling of his own basement. At least, he presumed it was a light fixture. He had his basement finished a few years ago, and there was nothing else up there to secure a rope. And since his assailant had knotted a dirty, oily rag across his eyes, he had no way of visually confirming this.

A light fixture would be good. Maybe his weight would be too much. Maybe he'd snap free. Maybe then he could figure out how to get out of this insane predicament.

At first Green thought it was just a home invasion. Admittedly, he was an ideal target. Single guy, living in a large house. All they had to do was pick up his pattern, then strike. Friends told him he should think about security, considering who Green was and what he did. Green had shrugged it off. He was a behind-the-scenes guy. Ninety-nine-point-nine percent of the country didn't even know he anthony e. zuiker

existed, and even those who *did* know him had no real understanding of his work. Why would he need a security team? Now that need was abundantly clear.

Green had read enough to know what to do in this situation:

Give the invader what he wants.

"The safe's in my bedroom," Green said. "Behind the Chagall. I can give you the combin—"

A rough hand forced open his jaws, shoved a rag in his mouth. A leather belt cut across Green's cheeks. Little hairs were ripped from the back of his neck as the belt was buckled, then fastened tight. Too tight.

Goddamn it, Green tried to yell. *I can't give you what you want if I can't talk.*

All that came out of his mouth was an angry muffle.

As he snorted mucus and cold sweat up his nose, Green realized that maybe whoever was down here with him didn't want the combination to his safe, or even the fake Chagall that hung in front of it. So what the hell did he want?

Then he heard the *snip-snip*-snipping of scissors—his pant legs being shorn from his body.

And then felt the first cut from the razor, up along the inside of Green's naked thigh, a hot river of blood trickling down to his crotch.

Not more than thirty minutes ago, Green had been savoring his last sip of single malt, slapping the American Express Black on the bar top, fishing around in his pocket for the valet stub. Green was proud of himself for pulling the plug now. He had a morning think-tank session in D.C., and he would be opening his eyes at an obscene hour to catch a plane. Better to cut it short now, clock in a few hours of good rest.

The valet pulled up with the Bentley. Green eased himself behind the wheel and gunned it down the street, feeling a pleasant alcoholic blur. Not too much, not too little, either. Just right.

By the time he pulled up to the driveway of his $3.5 million, eight-bedroom house, Green was feeling adequately sleepy. Which was good. He liked having his days unfold just right—the perfect blend of exercise, work, play, food, and drink. Tonight, Green was looking forward to sliding into his thousand-thread-count Egyptian cotton sheets and enjoying the pleasant sensation of his mind simply clicking off. Not passing out from exhaustion or booze. Not staying awake because he was too wired from the day's events, either.

Then Green opened his front door and flicked the light switch . . . and nothing happened. He cursed, then flicked the switch again and again. Still nothing. The power was out. Green took a few steps into his vestibule then froze. Even in the dim light, he could see that someone had yanked open drawers, knocked paintings off the walls, pushed furniture aside.

Green was instantly queasy. Someone—some *stranger*—had been inside his house.

He fought the urge to turn around and flee the premises immediately. He couldn't be a chickenshit about this—he had to see what had happened, what these sons of bitches had stolen from him.

This wasn't supposed to happen. Just last year Green had installed a wildly expensive security system to prevent just this sort of thing.

He walked over to the wall-mounted security panel. The unit appeared dead—even though it had a dedicated power line. Had the backup battery had been disabled, or malfunctioned? He pressed ENGAGE. Nothing.

Okay, you idiot. Get out.

Get out *now*.

Then Green heard a noise, coming from his kitchen—something like a cabinet door *snicking* shut. There was only one thing worse than being burglarized, Green realized. And that was coming home in the *middle* of a burglary.

Green quickly fished the cell phone out of his jacket pocket and pressed nine with his thumb, taking slow, careful steps back toward the front door when . . .

He froze.

His muscles felt as if they wanted to snap free from his tendons. His joints locked in place. Green opened his mouth to scream, but couldn't. Even if he were able to make his vocal cords work, his nearest neighbor would be too far away to hear. His eyesight blurred. The entire house seemed to tilt on its axis. Part of his mind screamed *Stop it! Stop it already!* but the thought stayed frozen in his mind, no louder than a whisper.

Green felt himself being pulled to the ground, dragged across the floor toward the cellar door. The world went upside down.

And then he woke up, hanging from his basement ceiling.

Again, he must have passed out. The last thing he remembered . . . the scissors?

His leg.

Oh God, his leg.

What worried him most was the fact that he couldn't feel his legs. Either of them. Not the rope cutting into his right ankle, not the fabric of his pants. Nothing.

Something tugged at the belt on his face. The wet rag popped out of his mouth. Green choked for a second, gathered up double lungfuls of oxygen, then screamed. The sound blasting out of his mouth wasn't so much meant to communicate as it was to sonically assault his torturer. With his limbs bound, what else could he do?

Green screamed again before something flat and hard chopped him in his Adam's apple. His cry turned into a pained choke.

"Shhh," a voice said.

Even though he was shivering and couldn't feel his damn legs, the removal of the ball gag gave Green a ray of hope. Maybe this was just a robber who wanted to put a scare into him. *Well, you know what? It's working, buddy. I'm absolutely petrified. And even though you cut the living shit out of my leg, I'm willing to let bygones be bygones. Take my money. Take whatever you want. Just go.*

After he coughed a few times, Green recovered his voice.

"You win—please just let me go. I swear. I won't tell anybody."

He tried to sense the location of his assailant. Was he behind him? Green thought he heard the wrinkling of material behind him. But his senses were telling him that someone was standing right in front of him, too. Face to face. He could almost feel hot, strong breath on his face.

"Look, I know important people. I don't say that as a threat— I mean I can get you what you want. *Whatever* you want. Just talk to me."

There—movement—behind him. Green tried to twist himself around. Not that he could see anything, but it gave him the smallest glimmer of control of the situation. He may be dangling from his basement ceiling, but at least he could rotate to sort of face his attacker.

Still, he tried to plead his way out of the situation.

"Please. Tell me what I can do to make you happy."

Instead of a reply, his assailant sprayed something on Green's face. Instantly, it felt like his face was on fire, ravaging his skin one layer at a time. Green had never felt anything like it, couldn't even catch his breath to scream.

Then a crinkly bag slipped over his head.

Someone spoke to him. Through the bag it was little more than a whisper, but Green could have sworn he heard the word—

this

—right before he inhaled, and the burning sensation spread to his lungs, which was when Martin Green knew for sure he was about to die.

chapter 1

S teve Dark snapped awake, rolled out of bed, dropped to the floor.

Landing silently on his fingertips and toes, he stayed frozen in place and listened. Traffic hummed on nearby Sunset. Someone laughed, drunkenly. There was the faint *click-clack* of high heels on concrete. A car horn, muted and distant. Normal L.A. night sounds. Nothing out of the ordinary.

But still . . .

Supporting himself on fingertips and toes, Dark slowly crept through the house, keeping to the shadows, listening intently. The only sounds he could discern were the soft popping of his joints as he moved. Dark recovered his fifteen-round Glock 22 from its concealed space beneath the floorboards, then stood up on the balls of his feet. He slipped off the safety. He always kept a bullet chambered. The initial sweep took about ten minutes and revealed nothing. He checked the windows and doors, one by one. The front door—secured. Window locks—in place. Security system—on. Invisible window and door tape—unbroken. Not a single entry point had been disturbed.

Dark put himself through this routine so often it was almost becoming rote. Which was a problem. He couldn't let himself become complacent. He should devise another routine. Maybe think up another safeguard.

After slipping on the safety on his Glock, Dark placed it on the couch next to him. Then he opened his laptop and accessed the remote site that stored his video surveillance. Every square foot of his home was covered by pinhole-size, motion-activated cameras. The quality was low-res, but then again, Dark wasn't shooting precious family moments. He merely wanted to detect movement. Dark tapped the ENTER key, and the remote site began to download video from the past six hours that showed any movement whatsoever. When it finished loading, though, it only showed Dark's own movements through the house. Nothing else.

So what had he heard?

Just some stray noise from a nightmare?

Dark checked his watch. 3:21 A.M. Early, even for him. He didn't sleep much, and the loss of two more hours was disappointing. But at least the house was secure.

Wasn't it?

Dark had thought the same thing five years ago, and a monster had still managed to squirm his way into his living space. It had been a different house, with a much cruder security system, but it shouldn't have been so easy. Dark had learned the painful lesson: You could never be too careful. Dark had destroyed the monster with his own hands. Hacked away at his adversary until he resembled a pile on a butcher's table. Watched the pieces burn. Spread the ashes with a metal rake.

Still, the lesson remained: You could never be too careful.

Dark padded his way to the kitchen and flicked on his electric carafe that heated water in about sixty seconds. A coffee would be good. After that . . . he didn't know what. Ever since leaving Special Circs, his days had seemed both shapeless and endless. Four months of limbo.

When he left, he told Riggins he had a lot of unfinished business. Namely, reconnecting with his daughter—who almost didn't recognize her father's voice on the phone.

But Dark had spent most of the summer installing security in his new home, telling himself he couldn't possibly bring his daughter here to visit without it being locked down tight, 100 percent secure. That process felt like battling a hydra. Chop off the head of one potential problem, six more seemed to spring up in its place. Dark did nothing but work on the house, check the Internet for murder stories, and try to sleep.

Five years ago he'd killed a monster. But no matter what he did, he couldn't shake the feeling that another monster was coming after him . . .

So now it was three thirty A.M. and his instant coffee sat cooling in a mug and the sounds of L.A. murmured and there was nothing left to do.

chapter 2

Dark walked into the second bedroom. The primer had been applied to the walls a few weeks ago, but he still needed to ask Sibby what color she'd prefer. She was five now, old enough to make those kinds of decisions. The wooden bed frame sat in the corner, yet to be assembled. Boxes of dolls and doll clothes were piled up in another corner. Dark wanted to surprise her with a roomful of them. She loved dressing them up, making them talk to each other. But they'd sat undisturbed since he purchased them at the Grove a month ago. Nowhere to put the dolls until the walls were finished and the shelves were mounted.

Could he really do this? Be a dad? He'd had so little practice.

Over the years Dark had tried to create some kind of semblance of a normal life when he wasn't working at Special Circs. But it was difficult to act like a father when you were almost never with your daughter. Not long after the Sqweegel nightmare, Dark had sent Sibby to live with her grandparents in Santa Barbara, clear on the other side of the country. It was supposed to be a temporary move. Dark planned on getting out of Special Circs as soon as possible so that he could get his daughter back and start a new life.

Easier said than done. One case blurred into many cases. One year turned into two, three . . . and then five.

The work kept Dark in the game. He was practically addicted to it, never felt more alive than when he was crawling in some killer's brain, trying to out-think him. And despite his best intentions of slowing down and finally stepping off the Special Circs merry-go-round for good, Dark found it nearly impossible.

Until this past June. He'd finally done what he'd long promised and pulled the plug. Part of it was the bureaucracy; Special Circs had increasingly fallen under political sway, and the process frustrated Dark. But mostly Dark wanted his daughter back, safe at home.

A few minutes later Dark was speeding through the nearly empty streets of L.A., cigarette in his mouth, loaded Glock tucked away in his jacket pocket.

Dark didn't have to travel around the world to find evil. It was all around him. In L.A. County alone—where Dark hoped to make a home for his little girl—someone was murdered every thirty-nine hours. A majority of those murders happened during the night, between the hours of eight P.M. and eight A.M., and half of those happened over the weekend. In other words, a night just like this— early Friday morning. Four A.M. People died in South Central, up in the Valley, out in El Monte, as well as in the supposedly "safe" enclaves of Beverly Hills and the Westside and the beaches of Malibu.

He liked to drive at night because he felt the urge to face the danger firsthand. Not read about it. Dark needed to see it. Smell it. Sometimes *touch it*, even though Dark knew he could be arrested for such behavior. But when you see a couple of toughs, pockets hung heavy with weapons, heading into a mini-mart in Pomona, what were you supposed to do? Wait to read about it in a crime roundup in the next day's *L.A. Times*?

At least with Special Circs he had been on the front lines. Along with his boss, Tom Riggins, and his partner, Constance Brielle, Dark had fought evil every day. Monsters may be everywhere, but it somehow felt reassuring to have at least a few of them in your gun sights.

And now?

Now Dark felt like he was caught in some limbo. Not a man-hunter or cop anymore. Not a father. Not fish, not fowl. Some un-born version of the two. Dark knew, deep in his heart, that the only answer was to choose one and forsake the other.

It was time to head back. Blast himself with cold water, snap himself out of these tired old torments. He couldn't very well teach college students with a mind full of garbage.

chapter 3

Special Circs HQ / Quantico, Virginia

Ⅰt was official now; there were too many fucking things on Tom Riggins's desk.

Tiny slips of paper with last names and out-of-state phone numbers scrawled on them. A pair of bullets. An empty plastic container of antacid. A screwdriver. A framed photo of his daughters. File folders upon file folders, stacked like a paper Tower of Babel, all of them jammed with photos and neatly printed descriptions of the most gruesome things people did to each other. Half-consumed cups of coffee.

What Riggins would really love is time to finish one of those cups of coffee. Not that it was any good. The stuff was too strong, with a strange metallic aftertaste he could never figure out. But if Riggins managed to get to the bottom of a single cup of the swill, maybe he'd feel like he actually accomplished something for a change.

Special Circs had started out as something amazing—the most elite violent-crime unit in the world. But years of bureaucracy and muddled directives from above had turned Circs into a shadow of its former self. "Elite" in press release only; now in real danger of becoming just another random fiefdom in the byzantine empire of Homeland Security.

Riggins was thinking about going to the kitchenette, pouring himself a fresh cup, then standing right there at the sink and downing the whole thing, steaming hot, until he saw bottom.

As he stood up to leave, the cell phone on Riggins's desk buzzed. He had to go searching for it, swatting aside file folders and flicking away cigarette ashes. Finally he found it. The name on the screen:

WYCOFF

For a while there, Riggins had reprogrammed the phone to display KING ASSHOLE whenever the secretary of defense called. After a few weeks, Riggins changed it back. Not because he was worried that Wycoff would see it. Riggins just felt KING ASSHOLE didn't quite cover it. When he came up with something better, he'd program it in.

Riggins thumbed the cell and pressed it to his ear. "Yeah."

"It's Norman. I've got something for you."

Got something for you. Like they were a group of errand boys with Glocks and Ph.D.'s. Then again, Riggins bitterly noted, for the past five years, that's exactly what they'd been. To the ruin of them all.

"What have you got?" Riggins asked.

"Do you know the name Martin Green?"

"Should I?"

Wycoff huffed—which could either be the sound of annoyance or grim laughter. "Green's part of a high-level economic think tank. Early this morning, somebody killed him."

"Well, that's very sad."

"I'm sending you a few photos via the secure transfer site. Take a look, and get down to the scene in Chapel Hill immediately."

"Who—me? You want me to go down to North Carolina?"

"Immediately, if not sooner. Like I said, I'm sending the files now."

"Come on, Norman, what's this cloak-and-dagger shit? Tell me what this is about. And how this qualifies as a Special Circs case."

Riggins was the head of Special Circs, which had started as an offshoot of the Justice Department's ViCAP—Violent Criminal Apprehension Program. ViCAP was the computerized think tank that tracked and compared serial killings. It was a vital resource for law enforcement. But sometimes, ViCAP tracked cases so violent, so extreme, that local cops or even the FBI weren't quite equipped to handle them. That's when Special Circs would step in.

Norman Wycoff, however, didn't seem to understand the distinction. Even after five years. Not the whole department—just Riggins, Constance Brielle, and Steve Dark. Working off what Wycoff perceived as a "debt." A debt incurred for doing the right thing.

Normally the secretary of defense would have absolutely zero sway over any Justice Department agency. But Wycoff had inserted himself into their biggest case five years ago for personal reasons. And now Riggins, due to a series of circumstances that still made his stomach turn, suddenly found himself as Wycoff's errand boy.

"It's a Special Circs case because I say it is," said Wycoff. "After all this time, are you still too dense to understand that? Green's an important man. He means a lot to certain people in my world. We want you on this. This comes from the highest levels."

Highest levels. Wycoff loved to deploy that phrase, either to deflect potential blame or puff up his own perceived importance.

"Fine," Riggins said. "I'll send someone to check it out."

"No. I want *you* on this, Tom. Personally. I want to be able to tell them I sent the best man for the job down to check it out."

Well, this was new. Usually Wycoff was content to give Riggins an order, then let him assemble the right team to deal with it.

"Right," Riggins said.

"So you'll go?"

"Send me whatever you got," Riggins said, then pushed END.

Riggins waited, looking over all of the crap on his desk, and thought about how easy it would be to sweep it all away with a stiff arm—computer and all. Just watch everything tumble to the ground. Then stand up and walk out into the cool Virginia morning air and forget about chasing monsters for a living.

Just like Steve Dark had.

chapter 4

Usually if there was a *special request*—namely, some dirty bit of business Wycoff wanted done—Riggins would call Dark. It had been part of their "deal" following the Sqweegel case.

Back then, Wycoff agreed to shield Dark from prosecution for killing the suspect known as "Sqweegel." In exchange, Wycoff wanted Dark's exclusive manhunting *services* from time to time. Services, like the tracking and capture of cartel leaders. Fugitive financiers. Double agents. Terror masterminds. Sometimes, the trail ended in death. Funny; Wycoff didn't have a problem with murder in *those* cases.

The secretary of defense thought he had Dark by the balls. If Dark wanted to keep his position at Special Circs—and stay out of prison—he'd run Wycoff's international errands, off the books. There was no way a man like Dark would ever quit the job. It was all he knew, all he had.

Yet, that's exactly what Dark had done, back in June. Riggins remembered that day vividly. He thought Wycoff was going to have a seizure. The man wasn't used to hearing *no*.

"You'll be in solitary confinement before dusk, you arrogant bastard," Wycoff had barked.

"And your career will be over by dawn," Dark had replied. "You don't think I'd do something like this without making certain arrangements, do you?"

Wycoff recoiled as if he'd been slapped on the nose with a rolled-up newspaper. "You have no evidence. Of anything."

"Even you can't be that deluded. I've been elbow deep in your shit for five years, Norman."

Wycoff glanced over at Riggins, who was standing off to the side, enjoying this more than he should. The look he gave was somehow both furious and pleading: *Fuck you, Riggins, for allowing this to happen*. But also: *Riggins, get me out of this*. But Riggins stared back, impassively. Dark was his own man.

Wycoff tried a different tack. "Nobody threatens the government and walks away."

"I'm not threatening the government, Norman. I'm threatening you. Come near me, or my daughter, and you're done."

And just like that, Dark was out.

Wycoff had all kinds of paperwork drawn up and promises exacted—Dark was to have no contact with Special Circs, ever, no how, no fucking way, etc. But Dark hadn't seem too broken up about that.

Which confused Riggins. What the hell was Dark doing?

Dark, who he considered the closest thing to a son, hadn't said a word about it. Riggins had the typical tangle of parental emotions: hurt, worry, anger. But mostly worry.

Not that Dark should fear retribution from Wycoff—fuck that arrogant prick. No, Riggins worried about Dark's sanity. The job seemed to be the only thing that enabled Dark to keep things together. It was also the only way Riggins could keep a careful eye on him. Five years had passed since that awful night when he crossed the line. Five years since Riggins had learned something truly horrible about a man he'd considered to be a son.

Five years of Riggins's silence . . . because for five years, Riggins had kept careful watch over Dark. And now?

Now, Riggins could only wonder what a man like Steve Dark was doing with his time.

Back in the early 1990s—when Dark was hell-bent on earning a spot at Special Circs—Riggins had been in charge of vetting all applicants. Early in the process, Riggins learned Dark had come from a foster family. He went digging. Soon, Riggins wished he hadn't.

Fortunately, Dark remembered hardly any of it—even under polygraph and hypnosis. A fire, when he was a kid. A lot of yelling. Being in his room, alone.

Later, Dark was sent to a loving foster family in California. His new parents, Victor and Laura, thought they would never be able to conceive. They adopted Steve. Not long after, Laura got pregnant. Twin boys. Still, they treated Steve no differently from his younger siblings.

Years later, a monster who came to be known as "Sqweegel" butchered Dark's foster family in the most brutal way Riggins had ever seen. Dark left Special Circs and crawled into seclusion. He only came out when Riggins forced him to—and together, they caught the maniac responsible.

And for the past five years, Dark had been back to work at Special Circs. But it wasn't the same. How could it be? He'd lost his wife and foster family to a monster, and been pushed to the edge of sanity. The only thing that held Dark back from the brink, Riggins thought, was his daughter. Sweet, innocent little Sibby. Whom he never saw.

Now Riggins had a choice. Appease Wycoff, or fuck Wycoff.

The decision didn't take long. He dialed Jeb Paulson's extension. "It's Riggins. Got a minute?"

Riggins had been at Special Circs longer than anybody. He'd

seen eager new recruits—crime scene investigators who were at the top of their games back home—burn up and flame out within months. Sometimes it only took a few weeks. He hoped Paulson wouldn't be one of them.

Riggins wasn't exactly an optimistic man. Life had pressed his face into too many piles of shit for years now. Still, he had some hope for Paulson. He was the best he'd seen since . . . well, if he was honest with himself, since Steve Dark. The two had a lot in common. The brains. The intuition. The no-nonsense approach to their jobs.

Paulson appeared within seconds. "What's up?"

"Agent Paulson, grab your go-bag."

chapter 5

University of California–Los Angeles

T he girl took her time approaching Dark, taking great care to not seem obvious.

Ten minutes into the faculty mixer, she started throwing glances at him. Not a lot. Just enough for him to know she existed. Then she gradually made her way across the conference room, feigning small talk with this professor, that assistant. She lingered at the carving station, where a bored pair of undergrad student workers were robotically slicing up roast beef under a heat lamp. When she pretended to finally notice him it was a fake collision—nudging his shoulder with hers, cheap chardonnay splashing around the plastic cup in her hand. "Oh! So sorry."

"It's okay," Dark said.

A look of fake recognition bloomed in her eyes. "You're Steve Dark, aren't you?"

He nodded.

"You know, I gotta say I'm surprised to see you here," she said. "These things must bore you to death."

Dark lied: "Not at all."

Truth was, he stopped by as a courtesy to the department chair.

If he wanted to keep teaching, he had to at least make an attempt to fit in. The last place on earth he wanted to be was in this stuffy classroom, making small talk. It was like being a returning war vet, used to the cut of the sand and endless hours of patrol and the pounding of heavy artillery—suddenly dropped back into the civilian population. But that's what the university expected of its teachers. Even the part-time adjuncts, like Dark.

So Dark had positioned himself in a corner near the door, counting down the minutes until he could leave, when he saw this girl, making her awkward approach. Most of the faculty ignored him, seeming vaguely annoyed by his presence. Was a member of the department actually going to *speak* to him? Dark had seen her around the halls—her name was Blake, or something like that. Grad student and teaching assistant, here at UCLA on a full ride. Tall, fiery red hair, a spray of freckles across her nose and cheekbones. She often wore knee-high boots—the kind that looked vaguely professional, but could also fit the dress code at any SoCal S and M parlor.

"Come on," Blake said now, smiling. "This must be like watching paint dry compared to your old job."

"It's a welcome break, believe me."

"Well I *don't* believe you, Mr. Dark. I've read a lot about you. I've taught you, in fact. Studied the kinds of monsters you've chased. And while I'm sure some of the students here give you a run for your money, there's no comparison, is there?"

Blake smiled as she talked. Her eyes lit up—hungry for details. *Go on*, her eyes said. *Shock me with something.*

The truth was, Dark thought teaching was strange. The last time he'd stood in front of a classroom was when he'd briefed a room full of cops in Florida. An organized group of elementary school teachers had sexually molested dozens of five- and six-year-olds. The predators ensured the children's silence by teaching them a lesson about death—taking classroom pets and slitting their throats before the kids' stunned eyes, telling them: *This is what death is. If you tell any-body what we do here, we'll do the same to your parents.*

Is that the kind of detail Blake wanted to hear? Would that pass for polite faculty-mixer conversation?

Instead Dark told her: "I like it here."

Still, teaching had a surprising side effect: It forced him to ana-lyze what he used to do for living. For years he'd operated on in-stinct. Sure, he'd had training—first the police academy, then Special Circs. Dark had studied forensics until he was mumbling about blood splatter patterns in his sleep. But the textbook stuff had no real impact on how he caught killers. When he accepted the adjunct gig at UCLA, and sat down to write his first syllabus, Dark was forced to ask himself: *How do I go about catching monsters?*

In the classroom, just a few hours ago, he told his students: It's not about finding that one magic clue that will crack open the case. It's about listening to the story the clues are telling. If you can't solve a case, that means you don't have enough of the story yet.

Dark knew Blake's story right away. At the start of the faculty mixer she had been wearing an emerald engagement ring. Now the fourth finger on her left hand was bare, leaving a band just a shade lighter than the rest of her creamy skin. Soon, Blake would look for a pretense to meet with him in private—a request for help on a paper, or something.

"What brought you here, if you don't mind me asking?" she asked.

Dark glanced over at the meat-carving station and recited the canned answer he'd come up with a few months ago. "One day I re-alized I'd been chasing monsters for close to twenty years, and maybe it was time to start seeing what I'd missed."

Most people wanted a pat, easy answer. They didn't want to think about what Dark did for a living. What it had done to his soul.

Like the fact that when he looked over at the undergrad cutting the meat, focusing on the gleaming blade dancing across flesh, all Dark could think about were the countless bodies he'd seen carved up in the same way. Men. Women. Children. Too many children. The butchers he'd chased didn't care . . .

Stop it, he told himself. You're not thinking like a normal human being.

You're in a school, for fuck's sake.

Dark was at UCLA as an adjunct—teaching an upper-level course in their criminal justice department. From elite manhunter to undergrad lecturer, all in the span of a few months. The university claimed to be thrilled to have him, but most of the criminology faculty dismissed his presence as a desperate publicity stunt. Dark was still infamous from the Sqweegel case five years ago, and the two would be forever associated in the public mind. Even the student paper had taken a jab at him, suggesting his students add a "full-body condom" to their order at the campus bookstore. *Otherwise, he'll grade your DNA*, the joke went.

"Would you have some time later this evening?" Blake asked now. "I do have something I wanted to run by you—if it's not too much of an imposition."

"What kind of something?"

"For my doctorate. I promise, just a few minutes of your time. Dinner's on me."

Dinner now. She was really stomping her boot down on the accelerator. Dark wondered if she'd already made up an excuse for her fiancé, or if she'd step aside and make one up on the spot. As she waited, Blake twirled her fingers around her hair, made her lips look the tiniest bit fuller, opened her eyes slightly wider. Dark wished he couldn't read people so easily.

"Dinner's out," Dark said. "But I do have office hours after my twelve thirty this Monday."

Blake started to move as if she didn't hear him. "I'm going to have a little more wine. Care for some?"

Like she was trying to get him drunk at a kegger.

Dark handed her the cup. "Sure." However, it would take a lot more than cheap chardonnay in a paper cup. Dark knew how the afternoon would play out: Ms. Blake here would go home to her fiancé, and he would go home alone. Sometimes, Dark longed to turn off the manhunter part of his brain. Even for a little while. Just drink the wine, give Blake the freak show she wanted, and blank out everything else in a blur of sex and alcohol.

But Dark couldn't. Not with his daughter's half-finished bedroom waiting for him.

chapter 6

As Dark drove home from UCLA he had every intention of calling his daughter up in Santa Barbara and talking to her about paint for her new bedroom. But by the time he pulled up in front of the house, Dark realized he couldn't just *ask* what color. There were thousands of varying shades; Sibby would want to see samples. So that meant going to the store, picking up a handful of paint chip palettes, then driving up to Santa Barbara. He was long overdue for a visit anyway.

Dark keyed into his front door, though, and realized it was probably too late in the evening for that. The faculty mixer had gone on too long; traffic along Wilshire sucked. By the time he made it up to Santa Barbara, his little girl would be getting ready for bed.

So instead, Dark decided to do a little studying in his basement.

Not many California homes have basements. But Dark's home, which he'd purchased in July, was the former home of William Burnett, an infamous 1940s-era surgeon. Infamous, that is, to a handful of people in retirement homes. The rest of L.A. had completely forgotten about him.

Burnett had owned a couple of clubs on the Sunset Strip, kept the LAPD greased, and trafficked in prescription narcotics. Which made him very popular on the strip. However, such schemes rarely last forever. Dr. Burnett's life fell apart when he started taking too many of his own pills and ended up killing a patient on the table when he clamped down on the wrong artery. The investigation lead to a dozen wrongful-death suits, and, finally, criminal charges.

Dark had discovered Burnett's secret basement the first time he was alone in the house. The real estate agent was outside, taking a call; Dark had gone exploring. He wanted a home that could be quickly fortified, sealed up. He'd faced off against too many monsters who liked to hide in crevices.

Dark found something strange in the master bedroom. Ancient scuff marks, stained over and over again until they were almost imperceptible. Dark dropped to all fours, felt between the boards with his fingers. Definitely something off there.

But then the real estate agent walked into the room, and was instantly alarmed. "What are you doing? Is something wrong?"

"Just checking to make sure the floor is level," Dark said. "A house this old, in earthquake country—sometimes the floors can warp."

The agent huffed and hawed about how the house was certified level, and in total compliance with the regulations of the City of West Hollywood. Dark had let it go . . . for the moment.

Later that night, Dark returned, broke in. It wasn't difficult. All real estate agencies used the same chunky lockbox—which was easy to pick. Dark searched the master bedroom for almost an hour before he found it—the secret latch hidden on the side of the closet light switch. Flip the latch, and the faceplate sprung open. Inside, a white plastic button. Press the button, and you heard the thump of a lock opening, under the floorboards. A hatch swung open, leading down to a secret room.

Dr. Burnett, you kinky bastard.

Nobody knew about it. Not the real estate agencies. Probably not even the previous residents, going all the way back to Dr. Burnett, who moved out in the early 1960s. If by "moved out" you mean awaiting arrest, stark naked and sweating, in the middle of your empty home.

Dark went down into the basement. It looked like a medical examiner's office, 1950s style. Steel exam tables with drains. White metal cabinets. Tile floor with a drain. You could hose the room down easily. Dr. Burnett probably kept his stash down here.

But the exam tables?

Dark did more research. According to files buried deep within the LAPD archives, Dr. Burnett was the suspect in at least five prostitute murders in west L.A. and Hollywood during the 1940s and 1950s. Whole bodies were never found. Just parts. Dr. Burnett, a prominent Los Angeleno, was never officially charged. His name was buried in the files. No one knew. No one except Dark.

So of course he had to buy the place.

Dark flipped the latch now, headed downstairs to his research lair. He'd improved the entry system, replacing the worn old floorboards with new pieces of wood, and strengthening the doors and stairs. Yes, he'd told Riggins that he wanted to stop thinking about monsters and murders. Get on with his life.

Truth was, he couldn't.

Dark had two desktop computers and a laptop set up on a slab with a base that used to be the good doctor's old exam table. Three of the walls were lined with forensic books and blue binders— copies of old murder books he liberated from the Special Circs libraries over the years. Every book he'd ever read about serial killers was now on the shelves down here. When Dark had first invited his future wife into his apartment, she'd spied his collection immediately.

You got enough books on serial killers? she'd asked, nervous tremor in her voice.

I used to catch them for a living, Dark had said.

That was not long after the first time he'd quit Special Circs, after his foster family had been murdered. When Dark moved in with Sibby, he put his collection in storage. Over the past few months, however, he'd been pulling it out, one box at a time. He told himself it was to help put together his class syllabus, but he started rereading them, too. Obsessively.

The fourth wall was dominated by the doctor's old desk, and here Dark kept his forensic supplies. There was also a doorway to another small room where Dark kept a small collection of unregistered weapons and other case files. The space, which had seemed so cavernous when he first discovered it, was now drowning in murder files. He was giving serious thought to having more space carved out. The only question was how he could do it undetected. Dark didn't think Riggins would understand what he was doing with a room like this.

chapter 7

Chapel Hill, North Carolina

Jeb Paulson boarded the plane forty minutes after leaving Riggins's office—a land-speed record, he thought. As a Special Circs agent, Paulson knew he had a jet at his disposal. But asking for the plane was the wrong move—there were other cases, other priorities. Riggins was expecting Paulson to figure this out himself. He briefly considered signing out a Bureau SUV and driving it down south—which would take about four hours. Three, if he punched it. But it might be faster to book a cheap, last-minute flight online. He did a search, then booked it from his cell phone on the way to Dulles. He made it through security, flashing his Federal badge, and walked up to the gate, bag in hand, with five minutes to spare.

His wife, Stephanie, loved to tease him for preparing his "go-bag," preprogramming travel sites into his BlackBerry, and keeping a pair of pants and a dress shirt draped over a chair in their bedroom—all *just in case.* "You're not James Bond," she'd said, smiling and poking him in the ribs.

"I know," Paulson would reply. "Sexier, right?"

"Please. You're not even Roger Moore."

"You hurt me, Stephanie. Deep inside."

Paulson paid extra for a seat up front. Last on, first off. Waiting in line, he booked a rental car. In flight, he read everything he could about Martin Green. This was his first real case—solo. He was going to investigate the living shit out of this. Riggins had to know that his faith in Paulson would be rewarded.

You're not a replacement, they told him. Still, Paulson couldn't help but dream.

The legendary Steve Dark had left Special Circs in June. Paulson was sitting at his desk by August. Five years ago, while still at the FBI Academy, Paulson had clipped everything about Dark and the Sqweegel case he could find. Even files he probably wasn't supposed to know existed. The man was fascinating. A born manhunter. Everything Paulson wanted to be—minus the tragic baggage.

But even *that* fascinated Paulson. To know that a man could thrive in an insanely stressful job for nearly two decades? Many men idolized sports stars—especially ones who managed to make a comeback. Paulson idolized Dark in the same way. Because no matter what, Paulson's life couldn't be as fucked up as Dark's. He wouldn't allow it. He'd learn from the man's victories, repeat none of his mistakes. He'd do better.

A while back, Paulson had asked Riggins if they could ever meet up with Dark. You know, unofficially. Over a beer. Riggins had shaken his head and more or less told him no, never gonna happen.

Maybe that would change after Paulson proved himself in this new case.

This case wasn't a serial killing—yet. But it was strange enough for the Chapel Hill homicide detectives to alert the FBI. At the same time, the name "Martin Green" lit up smart phones all over Washington, D.C.—Green was apparently important to a large number of even more important people. The way Paulson understood it, Green was the kind of name you heard in smoke-filled rooms, not on the evening news. And Riggins had chosen Paulson to be his point man. "That means something," Paulson told Stephanie.

"Yeah," Stephanie replied with a mock grimace. "It means you're going to be home very late tonight, and we're not going to have sex."

Paulson knew how lucky he was to be married to Stephanie. She totally got it, totally understood the rigors of his chosen field. Stephanie was in all the way, and he absolutely loved her for it. Even if she did make fun of his go-bag now and again.

Paulson made it to Chapel Hill in record time. Chapel Hill, along with Durham and Raleigh, formed the famous "Research Triangle"—more Ph.D.'s per capita than anywhere else in the country. Green seemed to be the richest and smartest of them all. At least according to the clips Paulson read on the plane. He had to admit, his eyes glazed over a lot of the financial stuff. But one thing was clear: Green was connected.

The lead homicide investigator, a tall, white-haired guy named Hunsicker, met him out in front of the Green house. They shook hands, Hunsicker giving him the up and down, slightly quizzical look in his eyes. Paulson knew what he was thinking. *Is this guy even out of high school?* Paulson had been cursed with a baby face and curly dark hair.

"What do we have?" Paulson asked.

Paulson knew what the crime scene looked like from the photos Riggins had sent him. But it always helped to hear another investigator's take on it.

"Let me show you," said Hunsicker. "Words won't do it justice."

Hunsicker walked him through the entryway. The house was furnished with designer housewares and was professionally maintained, but the inside was a mess. Papers and utensils and clothes strewn everywhere.

"Robbery?" Paulson asked. "Or just made to look like one?"

"No, there's definitely stuff missing," Hunsicker said. "Jewelry, watches, some electronics, some art. Insurance guys have already been out here, and whoever did this got away with a bundle. We also think the vic kept a seriously large amount of cash in a bedroom safe—we found money wrappers and a little logbook. Which may have brought this whole thing. But if you're going to rob somebody, you knock 'em over the head or shoot them. You don't do this to them."

"Show me," Paulson said.

Paulson followed the homicide detective into the basement. He tried to push everything he'd read and seen out of his mind. He wanted to view the crime scene with fresh eyes.

Green was still hanging upside down from the ceiling, his body was suspended by one ankle. His other leg was bent at the knee and tucked behind, his legs making an inverted number four. Both legs appeared to have been flayed, exposing the blood-buttered muscles beneath. Green's hands were tied behind his back. The first thing Paulson notice was the stagecraft. Everything was orchestrated to be appreciated by the viewer walking down this flight of stairs. The grisly tableau was meant to shock. The image was supposed to sear itself onto your mind. This was something you weren't supposed to forget. Something you would be *unable* to forget.

Paulson moved for a closer look. Green's head was badly burned, as if it had been set on fire, then extinguished. Paulson wondered how the killer did that without the rest of the body catching fire. There were no scorch marks anywhere else in the basement. Could you wrap a man's head in some kind of bag, then set it ablaze from the inside?

Maybe Green had been tortured. The robbers knew he had all of that cash hidden away, so they brutalized the man until he coughed up a safe combination.

Paulson made a mental note to take a look at Green's financials. Even with grisly torture-executions, sometimes the best advice was to follow the money.

"What's the time of death?" Paulson asked.

Hunsicker walked around the scene, but looked at everything except Green's body. "Based on body temp, he was killed around midnight. He was last seen at a restaurant a few miles away—we talked to the bartender, and the valet guy. Green left alone. He could have picked someone up, but there's no evidence of anyone else in his car."

"Who found him?" Paulson asked.

"The security company received an alert," Hunsicker said. "The system had been disengaged, and when it came back online, we received a call. You ever see anything like this?"

Thing was, Paulson had. There was something familiar about all of this. He just couldn't bring it to mind right away. It nagged at him. Paulson had to remind himself of the advice he once read: *Keep your mind clear. Don't take mental shortcuts. Let the evidence speak to you.*

Just like Steve Dark.

chapter 8

Johnny Knack always thought there was no thrill like a massive deadline rushing at you, ready to grind you into paste. He was a reporter, a hard-core news dog down to the marrow in his bones. But lately—as much as he hated to admit it—the real rush didn't come from deadlines.

It came from a small pile of hundred dollar bills tucked in a white paper envelope.

Courtesy of his current employers, who apparently had bales of the stuff at hand.

Now you had to be smart with it. You didn't go handing the whole thing over to a cop. No sir, you tease that wad out. Make a big deal of opening that envelope, carefully plucking a single Franklin out from his friends. See, it's not the single Franklin that does the trick—it's the others. The cop thinks, *Shit, this was the easiest hundred I ever made.* And there's plenty more where that came from. One hundred bucks, you were in.

He'd never enjoyed such power.

Even better, Knack worked for a Web news aggregator that was almost always mentioned on tabloid TV. Cops heard that name, and knew they weren't exactly dealing with *The New York Times.* Ethics, shmethics. It was a whole new media playing field, and the Daily Slab floated in that murky Web space between respectability and sleaze. Not quite the Daily Beast or HuffPo, but then again, no Drudge or TMZ.

What the Slab had—and what had attracted Knack to it a year ago—was a borderline psychotic obsession with *scoops.* If it happened anywhere in the world, the Slab wanted to tell you first. And they were willing to hemorrhage cash for the privilege.

The Slab's owner was a former dot.com millionaire who lost it all, earned it back, and decided to make his next fortune in news. He could afford the scoops because his checks were the plumpest. His press kit made a lot of noise about "bombing mainstream media back into the Stone Age." The owner had deep pockets for long-form investigatory pieces, too. Well, long form for the Web at least: a thousand words and up.

Knack had been looking into an exposé of Martin Green—a man who'd miraculously avoided the shit-splatter of the subprime mortgage meltdown a few years ago. In J-school you were taught to put a face to the story. There was no better face of greed than Green.

And the best part: *Nobody fucking knew it!* His editor at the Slab agreed—they loved creating villains as much as scooping mainstream media. Green would be an *amazing* villain.

So Knack had been sniffing around Chapel Hill for the past week, trying to flesh out the bio of a man who worked hard to avoid the spotlight. He had a nice house, but nothing ridiculously flashy. He drank, but not to excess. He was divorced, but these days, who wasn't? No kids. No kinks—as far as Knack could tell.

It was turning out to be a dull story until a little after midnight, when Knack's phone rang and a cop told him Green was dead.

Since then, Knack had been working the scene for hours, but he'd had no luck sneaking behind the yellow tape. The scene had been clamped down sphincter-tight, and not even his envelope of crisp new Franklins could help him out. Which was curious. Green was a player, but he wasn't the freakin' president.

And the clock was ticking.

Knack noticed that the B and E squad was on the scene, too, along with a security company van. *That* was interesting. Green appeared to have died following some kind of break-in. His cop source had gone mute after the first tip, but he had told him over the phone: *This is a weird one.*

Meaning: It wasn't a coronary that took out Green.

It was something else—something *weird.*

At 2:31 A.M., Knack pulled out his BlackBerry, thumbed it for a couple of minutes, then hit SEND. He took the little scrap of official info he had from the cops (namely, that a guy named Martin Green had died in his house in Chapel Hill, North Carolina) and teased it out into a 350-word piece, full of innuendo, questions, outright fabrications. Grounded in hard fact, of course.

The e-mail was opened by the Slab's night editor at 2:36 A.M., and posted on the site by 2:38 EST. Anyone with a phone could read Knack's words instantly. Huzzah, huzzah. Another scoop for the Slab.

Except Knack kind of hated to file the story. Now, even the somnambulant mainstream papers would notice Green, and there went his long-form piece. *Poof.* Now, he'd be competing for a story he'd owned just a few short hours ago.

Knack needed to own Green's murder, no matter what.

chapter 9

Knack sat in his rental car, popped another breath mint, and kicked around the possibilities. Could this be a random home invasion that turned ugly? No way of knowing until he saw the coroner's report, see what was done to poor old Greenie.

But what if it wasn't just a home invasion? What if someone wanted Green dead on purpose? Wanted him dead because he was such an awesome villain?

Nothing Knack had turned up so far pointed in this direction. But that didn't mean it wasn't true.

Knack paced the scene. Every once in a while a cop would give him some shit about moving on, and Knack would show him his courtesy card from the Chapel Hill PD (another gift from his friend on the force). Knack's stomach growled, but he didn't want to risk a five-minute fast-food run. Step away from a scene for even a few minutes, you could miss everything.

Instead, Knack popped more breath mints, and tried to convince his stomach that it was actual food. He used to smoke, but hated how everyone started recoiling from him a couple of years ago. So fucked up. So Knack popped breath mints obsessively. He couldn't stand to finish them, so he would spit them out when they wore down to a tiny pebble. Then he popped another one. Still, people tended to recoil whenever he opened his mouth.

Knack was hanging around the scene, kicking around scenarios, looking for an in, when he saw someone interesting pull up. A young guy—jeans, expensive watch, good shoes, rental car. Almost immediately, he was escorted into the scene like royalty. No FBI vest, no other identifying items. But this guy practically screamed *Fed*.

Oh yeah. Knack needed to find out who the fuck he was, pronto.

Sure, he could try official sources. But that was almost always a supreme waste of time. Instead, Knack walked up to the guy's rental and tried the handle of the passenger door. It was unlocked. Knack loved that—the cock-sure confidence of federal law enforcement officials. Dude pulls up to a crime scene full of cops, why would he bother locking his door?

Knack lowered himself into the seat, popped open the glove box. There it was, just like he thought. The rental agreement. You're supposed to keep them with you, of course, but this guy probably just stuffed it out of sight quick because he'd been in a hurry to get to this crime scene.

Let's see who you are . . .

. . . Mr. Jeb Paulson?

Knack wrote down the name, along with his address and phone number, before stuffing the rental agreement back in the envelope and replacing it in the glove box. He scanned the inside of the car, quick. The vehicle had that new-car smell—something the rental companies sprayed in. Knack had once written a piece about it.

In the backseat was a small duffel bag. File folder sticking out of the side pocket.

Knack looked around. Nobody had noticed him. Yet.

He reached back, grabbed the file folder, flipped it open. Inside were a few pieces about Martin Green—the same pieces Knack had dug up a few weeks ago. But then, in the back, was a little thin slice of gold.

A printout of a crime-scene photo—embedded in an e-mail.

From someone named Tom Riggins, to this mystery man—Paulson. The terse message read:

Review, get down to Chapel Hill.

But the photo. Oh, the photo. Even in black-and-white printout, Knack could see this had been no simple home invasion. Somebody had played around with poor Marty Green. Hung him, skinned him, burned him, and did God knows what else to him. Someone clearly had *fun*.

The scene reminded him of something, but he couldn't place it. Knack had been raised a good Catholic boy, and it looked like the torture of a saint. You had saints who were stabbed in the head. Saints who were flayed alive then tossed into salt mines. Saints who had their eyes and tongues removed and then were forced to eat them. Forget torture-porn flicks. You want the real hard-core stuff, you read *Lives of the Saints*.

So who was the saint of the upside-down torture snuff? If only he'd kept in touch with Sister Marianne. She could help him sort this out in a minute.

Knack suddenly remembered where he was—in the rental car of some unidentified Federal agent of some sort. He gets caught in here, he might be breathing through a hood in a secret Cuban prison later tonight. Keeping the printout in his lap, he gingerly slid the folder back into the duffel bag, stepped out of the car, closed the door. Calmly strolled back toward his own car, wondering where he could find a scanner.

At a local copy shop, waiting for the image to scan, Knack thought about how he could put himself in a position to see what was on that legal pad. In the meantime, he pecked away on a netbook, Googling this mysterious Tom Riggins. Guy turned out to be a lifer at something called Special Circs, which was notable only because it wasn't noted very often. Special Circs seemed to be tied into the FBI, but Riggins's name also popped up in relation to the DOJ. Interesting. So Paulson had to be Special Circs, too. Why had he been summoned to the Green murder?

Within the hour Knack e-mailed a follow-up about Green being the target of a "vigilante death cult" (oooh, yeah, he liked the sound of that) according to "well-placed anonymous sources." He buttressed this assertion with a blind quotes from the local cops, as well as innocuous quotes from friends and neighbors that, with just the right framework, could read as sinister and despairing. For instance:

Green kept to himself—which could also mean he was hiding.

Green drank occasionally—which could also mean he was drowning his guilt in single-malt.

Green was divorced—even his family couldn't stand to be around him. By extension, he deserved to die.

The trick wasn't to say these things overtly. You let the "facts" and the quotes hang out there. Readers were good at connecting their own dots. Readers just wanted a few surface details that would help them categorize a guy like Green and then file it away. It was shorthand for real thinking.

Green = Greedy Money Man = Racked With Guilt Over Something = Green Became the Target of Vigilantes.

Simple.

This "death cult" was designed to provoke a reaction from the Feds. They'd want to know his sources. Well, fellas, tit for motherfucking tat. Besides, Knack had the best thing: the crime-scene photo.

chapter 10

West Hollywood, California

Another night, another panicked wake-up. Another frenzied sweep through the house, checking doors and windows, lingering on his daughter's half-finished room. Another series of hours to kill before dawn.

So Dark surfed through murder stories.

He knew he shouldn't. He had promised himself that he'd pull his mind out of murders. For his daughter's sake, if nothing else. Even reading about this stuff was like an alcoholic just *browsing* at the local liquor store or a heroin addict pricking the crook of his arm with a syringe, you know . . . *just to remember what it felt like.*

Dark knew this.

He read the stories anyway.

The early morning roundup included a mother who killed her husband in a ritzy $3,500-a-night Fort Lauderdale hotel. It had been their anniversary. Her suicide note claimed she'd endured thirteen years of hell. A father in Sacramento had suffocated his two-year-old daughter. Turned himself in. Asked to be put to death immediately. An accountant had been stabbed on a street in Edinburgh,

Scotland. A bandit who claimed his pistol fired accidentally when he held it to the temple of the kid he was robbing. At least eight—no, nine cases of children shooting other children. And this was just since midnight.

There are an estimated 1,423 murders in the world every day. That worked out to a murder every 1.64 seconds. Dark did a daily scan of homicide briefs, which included the cruelest words in the English language: *Bludgeoned. Slashed. Stabbed. Shot. Gutted. Eviscerated.*

But this morning, Dark found one that practically jumped off the screen.

The ritual torture-murder of a man named Martin Green.

Dark quickly read the story—which had been first broken on a gossip Web site called the Slab. The piece was everything Dark hated about modern crime journalism. It was sensationalistic, vaguely sadistic, gruesome, and yet thinly reported. The writer, Johnny Knack, had woven a story using the thinnest of threads. The paucity of details—that's what bugged Dark the most. The stuff he *did* have was misleading and obscured the real story. Most offensive of all, the story had a completely unsupported premise: that a financial adviser named Martin Green had been the targets of a "vigilante death cult."

However, Knack *did* have an exclusive:

A crime-scene photo, right from Special Circs. Or as Knack put it: "High-level sources close to the investigation."

Dark copied the JPEG from the Slab site and dragged it into a piece of presentation software on his desktop. After a few clicks, the image was projected onto the basement's lone bare wall. Dark stood up, killed the lights. The bright image of Martin Green's final moment shined on the white concrete. Nowhere near scale but large enough for Dark to see the smaller details.

The longer Dark stared, the more it became clear body position didn't serve any specific torture purpose. This wasn't like a waterboarding or asphyxiation. The man's body was staged. It was meant to look like *something*. This was a ritual.

Why did your killer do this to you, Mr. Green?

Why did they burn your head, and nothing else?

Why cross your legs like that? An upside-down number 4. Did that number mean something to your killer? To you?

Who *were* you, Martin Green? Just the wrong guy in the wrong place at the wrong hour? Or did our killer choose you for this grim ritual for a specific purpose. Did he find you, study you, hunt you. Then late one night, blindside you . . .

The fact there even *was* a photo amazed Dark. Special Circs took great pains to keep their cases out of the mainstream media. And the photo meant his old friend Tom Riggins had a mole in the department, or at the very least, a greedy support staff member looking to augment his meager government salary. Leaking photos like this wasn't just a firing offense, in Riggins's opinion. This was a torture-slowly-then-put-you-in-Gitmo kind of offense. Dark could imagine Riggins's reaction to something like this. He'd be like a crack-addled shark right about now, making his way through the corridors, sniffing for blood.

Dark found himself reaching for his cell phone, his thumb almost pressing the auto-dial button—number six—which would connect him with Riggins. Then he stopped. Tossed the phone back onto the morgue table.

Riggins had made it clear: no more contact. No conversations, not even a cup of coffee and a hearty discussion of the weather. He and Riggins were through.

chapter 11

The cell buzzed in his pocket. Dark fished it out, recognized the number: his in-laws up in Santa Barbara. A delicate, sweet voice spoke to him: "Hi . . . Daddy?"

It was his little girl, Sibby. Named for her mother, who had died the day their daughter was born. Little Sibby was five years old, but sounded younger on the phone, somehow.

"Hi, baby," Dark said, eyes still on the torture image on his wall. "How are you?"

"I miss you, Daddy."

"I miss you, too, baby. What did you do today?"

"We went on the swings, oh, and then the slide. I went down the slide thirty times!"

"That's good, baby."

"Maybe even fifty!"

"Really," Dark said. "That many."

He knew he should turn away from the wall. Close his eyes. Something, anything. *Pay attention to your daughter, you asshole.* But Dark's eyes refused to move. His mind was waiting for something to snap loose in his mind. Why had the killer chosen to pose Green's body like this? Was there something in the context of the murder scene he was missing? It was frustrating, having access to only a few of the pieces. To do this right, Dark would have to be there. See the body. Smell it. Touch it.

After a while a sweet voice jarred him out of his fugue state.

"Daddy?"

"Huh? What, sweetie."

"Gramma says I have to go to bed now," Sibby said.

Before Dark could respond, there was a soft click. She was gone. Dark leaned back in his chair, crossed his arms, closed his eyes. What was he doing? Why did he *keep doing* this to himself? This was not his case. This was not his business. Sometimes Dark wished he could just turn it off for good. Give himself just six months of being normal. Remind himself what it feels like, and maybe then he'd be okay.

II

the fool

To watch Steve Dark's personal tarot card reading,
please log in to Level26.com and
enter the code: fool.

EX LUX LUCIS ADVEHO ATRUM

O

THE FOOL

Falls Church, Virginia

Jeb Paulson tried to remember where he was—what he was doing. He couldn't. Which frightened the hell out of him. Even after the deepest sleep, his memory always reloaded in an instant. Stranger still was that he could see the star-studded sky, and was breathing in cold night air. There was tacky material under his fingertips. See? Nothing made sense. He wasn't even sure what day it was. The weekend, he thought. Yeah, had to be.

"Up," a voice commanded.

Metal jabbed at the side of his head. The business end of a gun. Paulson started to look in its direction when the harsh voice barked again:

"Don't turn around. Just get up."

Slowly Paulson crawled to his feet. He was shaking all over, like he had a fever. His skin felt tingly.

"Now walk."

The gun jabbed him in a kidney. His muscles were ultrasensitive. Everything felt tender. The slightest touch was agony. He hadn't felt this bad since his last bout with the flu a couple of years ago.

"Keep walking," the voice continued.

As Paulson walked across the tarred roof, he realized where he was. On top of his own apartment building. He recognized the tops of the trees across the street, the telephone lines, and the park beyond. What was he doing up here?

Wait. It was coming back now. Last thing he remembered, he'd taken Sarge, their dog, for a walk. Sunday night, after dinner. He did some of his best thinking on those walks. So yeah, he'd been walking Sarge, and thinking about Martin Green, wondering what was next—trying to anticipate the killer's next move. And then he woke up on the roof . . .

No. That wasn't it. *Something* happened before—Sarge barking, Paulson reaching for the door, hoping he made it back before Stephanie fell asleep.

Oh God. *Stephanie.*

"What do you want?" Paulson asked. "Do you want to talk to me? Is that it? You have something to say in private?"

"Keep walking."

"You know, I'm going to run out of roof soon."

"Stop when you reach the edge," the voice said. "I want to show you something, Agent Paulson."

"And if I don't?"

"I'll shoot you and then go downstairs and pay a visit to Stephanie."

Right at that moment Paulson's blood jumped. He wanted to turn around and just obliterate this bastard for daring to threaten his wife. He'd take a bullet—or three or four if he had to, he didn't care. Paulson needed to stop this fucker *now* before he found himself completely helpless. At his mercy. Unable to save Stephanie.

But that wasn't how a Special Circs agent was supposed to behave. You don't corner the monster. You draw him out. Paulson cursed himself. He was smarter than this. He was letting this asshole push his buttons.

So instead Paulson stepped toward the ledge. As he looked down his stomach fluttered. He'd never been a fan of heights. In fact, he pretty much avoided them whenever possible. But if he was forced, *could* he jump? There was a balcony ledge about ten feet to the right. He'd be falling too fast to grab the railing. But if he gave himself a slight running leap, even a step or two might do it . . .

"What did you want to show me?" Paulson asked.

"Reach into your robe pocket."

Paulson froze. He didn't remember wearing a robe. He looked down to discover he was wearing someone else's clothes. Oh Jesus. What the hell had happened? Who'd done this to him? He'd been out, just walking his dog. The last thing he remembered telling Stephanie was that he'd be right back. How long had he been gone? Stephanie must be sick with worry by now.

Unless this same bastard had gotten to her first . . .

"Do it. Now."

"Okay, okay," Paulson said.

Paulson reached in, preparing for the worst. He felt something hard and rubbery that felt like a plastic wire and immediately his brain screamed *bomb*.

But no—there was something soft and fluttery at the end of the wire. He carefully pinched the wire between his fingers and felt something jab into his thumb pad. By the time he pulled it from his pocket, Paulson knew what the object was.

A white rose.

This set off worse alarm bells than the notion of a *bomb*. It meant his attacker was staging something. He wanted Paulson to hold this rose. Dressed in a robe. On the edge of a roof. All at once, at an instinctual level, he knew who was behind him. Of all the dumb newbie mistakes to make, letting a killer trace you back to your own home! Paulson yelled and turned and—

Something hard shoved him in the back of his right thigh.

His balance was off. Paulson tumbled off the edge. Reached out wildly for something—*anything*. It wasn't until a second later that he was able to scream.

chapter 12

Monday classes were over and Dark had killed enough time with the forensics trades—*The American Journal of Forensic Medicine and Pathology, Science & Justice,* the *International Journal of Legal Medicine,* the *Forensic Science Review*—in the campus library. Blake had turned out to be a no-show; Dark supposed her research paper would somehow be completed without his vital input. It was time to go home.

Dark made his way to the parking garage via the Janss Steps, named for the brothers who sold the land to the university. They were iconic; MLK and JFK once held rallies on these steps. But every time Dark descended them, he couldn't help but think: This would be the perfect place for a murder—something right out of Hitchcock. A slow, desperate tumble you were unable to stop, arms flailing, unforgiving slabs of concrete rushing forward to smash into your spinning body. Sure, it would be in broad daylight, but that was the beauty of it. Too many potential suspects and any potential witnesses were too focused on their own steps to pay much attention to what was happening around them.

There you go again, Dark thought. Murder on your mind. Always.

Can't you just walk down a flight of stairs or watch a college student carve a side of roast beef without your thoughts turning to murder?

About halfway down, a voice called out to him. "Agent Dark?"

Dark turned, instinctively reaching for the Glock that wasn't there. Standing a few steps above him was a woman. She wasn't dressed like a student, and her clothes were too expensive-looking for a faculty member's. Her bright eyes had a look of bemusement in them.

"Don't worry," she said. "I'm not here to attack you. Is there somewhere we can talk?"

Dark shook his head. "I don't think so."

The woman's eyes turned hard and flat. "Don't I look the slightest bit familiar to you, Agent Dark? My name is Lisa Graysmith."

The name was familiar, but Dark couldn't place it. She must have caught him trying, because she quickly added: "You knew my younger sister."

It took Dark another few moments, but then he got it. Graysmith—Julie. Sixteen years old. Captured, tortured, and eventually left to die by a monster Special Circs called "Body Double." This killer's modus operandi was to impersonate someone in the victim's life, temporarily lulling the victim into a false sense of security. A friend, maybe a family member. His disguises were never perfect. They relied too much on broad strokes—a hair style, a mannerism. The victims—usually teenagers, sometimes children—never believed the ruse for more than a few seconds. But that was all Body Double—aka Brian Russell Day—needed.

Julie Graysmith had been his final victim. Dark and the Special Circs team caught him soon after, trying to slip into a crowd at Union Station in D.C. They forced him to reveal Julie's location. But the team was unable to reach her in time.

"I never met her," Dark said.

"I think you knew her more intimately than anybody," Graysmith said, descending the steps. "You tried to save her—and more importantly, you caught her killer. I wanted the chance to thank you."

Dark considered this for a moment. If this woman really was the sister of a victim, she didn't deserve a brush-off. Sometimes the best thing you could do for a grieving family member was simply listen. But grieving relatives sometimes wanted answers you couldn't give. Or they wanted to drag you into some kind of legal action.

Then again, Dark wasn't with Special Circs anymore. There was only so far this woman could drag him.

"There's a place nearby," he said.

Graysmith offered to drive. Dark agreed. It would give him the opportunity to look at her car, which turned out to be a spotless BMW. A high-end rental—he saw the telltale bar code in the windshield, which the agency used to check vehicles in and out of the lot. Once inside the brewpub, the woman claiming to be "Lisa Graysmith" ordered an iced tea. Dark asked for a draft beer. A row of flat-screen TVs displayed sports-highlights shows.

"Thank you for the beer."

Graysmith said, "You left Special Circs in June."

Dark looked at her. Not many people knew about Special Circs, let alone the comings and goings of its agents. The press covered Brian Russell Day's arrest, but never mentioned his nickname nor Special Circs's involvement. Officially, it was the FBI who caught him. Day was awaiting execution in Washington.

Dark sipped his beer, saying nothing.

"You don't have to be coy with me, Agent Dark," Graysmith said. "After that son of a bitch was arrested, I wanted to learn everything I could about the man who caught him. I asked around about you."

"Who did you ask?"

"Let's put it this way. We've probably passed each other in the hall a few times in the last five years."

Was Graysmith trying to tell him she worked for the Defense Department? That she knew about Wycoff, and his secret control of Special Circs?

She leaned forward, placed her fingertips on Dark's hand. "I also know about Wycoff's little eight-pound indiscretion."

Dark took his hand away, picked up his beer, had another swallow. Now she was showing off. Almost nobody knew about Wycoff's illegitimate child. Or its connection to the Sqweegel murders.

"You're giving me peeks at your hand," Dark said, "but I don't even know what game we're playing. If you want something, go ahead and ask. If you're trying to draw something out of me, just ask. Other than that, we can finish our drinks and then we can go."

"You caught Day. You've caught many monsters over the years. You're the best at what you do, and you've stopped. I don't know why, but I think it's a mistake."

"Thank you for your concern," Dark said.

"That's not good enough. You can't quit now."

"What do you mean?"

"I think serial killers are like cancer. If you can catch them early enough, you save lives."

"The FBI does that, Ms. Graysmith."

"Not like you. That's why you left, isn't it? They moved too slow for you, muddled in bureaucracy. They didn't trust your gut—even after all of this time. They kept you playing by their rules, and as a result, lots of innocent people died."

"That was nice. Do you mind if I write that down?"

Graysmith leaned back and smiled. "You're not taking me seriously, and why would you? I'm just some woman you met on the steps at UCLA."

"Not just some woman," Dark said. "You're quite attractive."

"I thought about the various ways I might approach you. I had all kinds of dramatic scenarios built up in my mind."

"Did you."

"I thought you'd appreciate the direct approach most of all. I suppose I was wrong."

"There's nothing direct about this approach, Ms. Graysmith."

"Then here it is. I want to give you the tools you need to catch budding serial killers. Funding, equipment, access—everything. You report to no one. Not even me. That's my offer."

An "offer" that was too good to be true. For all Dark knew, she could be someone Wycoff sent to trap him. Coax him out of retirement just long enough to arrest him.

"No thanks," Dark said. "I'm busy teaching and working on my house."

Graysmith's eyes narrowed slightly, but she quickly recovered. "You're testing me. You want me to come up with some kind of proof that I'm serious, is that it?"

"You don't have to do anything. I'm just going to sit here and finish my beer."

Graysmith smiled, then made her way around the table. She touched Dark's shoulder, squeezing it gently. "See you later."

A few minutes after she left, Dark drained the rest of his beer, then used a napkin to carefully pick up Graysmith's iced-tea glass by the bottom. He dumped a half-glass worth of iced tea into his pint glass, shaking it a few times. Then he pulled a plastic baggie out of his bag—he always carried a few around, out of habit—and tucked the glass into the bag.

What troubled Dark was not Graysmith's offer. It was that he had a hard time reading her *at all*. Clearly, she was as good at reading people as Dark. She sidestepped all of the major tells. She skimmed along on the surface, like an insect on a pond. Dark had no doubt she'd show up later. When she did, he'd be ready.

chapter 13

First, Dark made sure he wasn't followed. That meant an insanely circuitous route up Westwood to Sunset to Coldwater Canyon Drive, through Studio City, back up to Mulholland, then a few shortcuts he knew that led him back down to West Hollywood. If anyone had managed to follow him, well then they deserved to be parked up his ass. After easing the car into his driveway and double-checking the locks, Dark disengaged the security system and recovered his Glock 22 from his hiding spot in the living room. The mag was still full.

Downstairs in his basement lair, Dark pulled the murder book on Brian Russell Day. He fed Julie Graysmith's social into his database, then pulled up family info. Turns out there was one sibling: an older sister. *Alisa.*

Or: "Lisa."

Dark clicked on her social and found that her records were sealed—by order of the Department of Defense. Interesting.

Fortunately, Dark had left himself a backdoor when he worked with some of Wycoff's lackeys a few years ago. He didn't abuse it, which was probably why no one had noticed it yet. Some files popped up. Not much—which meant the bulk of it was probably buried deep, and not even on a computer server anywhere.

But from what Dark could gather, Lisa Graysmith was a member of an organization with ties to DARPA—the defense department's so-called "out there" research division. Got a crazy defense idea dream and a billion dollars? DARPA will figure out a way to make it work. Or come close enough. Dark had read a piece the other day concerning DARPA's efforts to turn soldiers' waste products into tank fuel.

What did she do for DARPA? And what did she mean by "help"?

Dark hated the skullduggery. Five years ago, when Wycoff had started blackmailing him into an endless series of "favors," the government had supplied a babysitter named Brenda Condor to look after Dark's daughter, Sibby. Dark hated leaving his little girl in the hands of a stranger, whose allegiance was represented by a set of paper credentials (easily faked) and a phone call from Wycoff. But what choice did he have? It wasn't as if Dark could pack a diaper bag and bring his infant daughter on an international manhunt.

As it turned out, "Brenda Condor" was more than a babysitter. Wycoff had hired her to keep close tabs on Dark, which meant worming her way into his personal life. Fucking him, being the shoulder he could cry on, whatever it took to keep him together. Dark was an asset; Brenda Condor his handler.

Some guys, they come home early one day to find their partners banging the garden boy. Not Dark. He came home early and caught her making a detailing report to Wycoff.

That, somehow, hurt even more.

Dark kicked her out, then sent baby Sibby to live with her grandparents. It was the toughest thing he'd ever done. The entire flight to Santa Barbara he kept looking at his fellow passengers, wondering who might be watching him. Trailing him. Sibby, meanwhile, was obliviously happy, drooling and playing with a tiny stuffed tiger he'd bought her. No idea she was about to be abandoned for the second time in her short life.

I hope you'll understand someday, little girl.

———

And now, someone who reminded him a lot of "Brenda Condor"—
if that was even the agent's real name—was trying to worm into his
life. He didn't trust her. He also didn't need it.

Dark's life was pretty fucking far from perfect, but it was also un-
complicated. Sibby was with grandparents who doted on her every
move. Dark spent his time driving around, working on the house, or
reading about murders in the lair. The whole reason he'd left Special
Circs was to clear his head of the madness and try to figure out a way
to enter his daughter's life again. So unless this Lisa Graysmith had
a way of bringing people back from the dead, he doubted there was
anything she could do to *help*.

Dark made his way upstairs to wash his face, grab a beer, try to
tune things out for a while.

But she was already sitting on his couch, patiently waiting
for him.

chapter 14

"Want to tell me how you got in here?" Dark asked.

Graysmith crossed one leg over the other and leaned back. She'd changed clothes. If this afternoon she wanted to project the aura of stone-cold professional, now it was laid-back confidence. She wore a designer T-shirt, jeans—casual chic. The kind of clothes Sibby would wear around their old house in Malibu.

"Your security system's good," she said. "And I can tell you've done some of your own modifications. But no offense, it's still kind of Fisher-Price, compared to the systems I'm used to."

"You can stop trying to impress me," Dark said. "I've done my homework. I think I found what you wanted me to find. Your résumé would be a spy's wet dream."

"I just want you to know that I'm serious."

"I am very much taking you seriously."

"I don't think so," Graysmith said. "Nobody ever has, really. They see my smile and think I'm blithe."

Graysmith reached into her bag and pulled out a photo. She placed it on Dark's coffee table. "This was Julie."

Dark nodded without looking down. "I remember what she looked like."

Graysmith smiled ruefully. "Don't worry. I'm not going to tell you a sob story. Julie was a bratty little sister. I was ten years older, so it felt like we grew up in two different homes. My parents were tough on me. They were a lot easier on Julie. It bothered me—it was like she could get away with anything, being out late, drinking, partying. I focused on my work, and figured that Julie and I would get to know each other later, when I didn't think she was a spoiled little brat. Well, I never got that chance."

Dark couldn't help himself. He glanced down at the photo and saw that Graysmith did resemble her younger sister. Same eyes and facial structure. Same small ears, delicate nose.

"Her murder devastated my parents," Graysmith said. "They're filing for divorce now—which is common, I understand. Sometimes you just can't go on after something like this. It takes a uniquely strong-willed individual to keep waking up in the morning after losing a loved one."

The way she looked at Dark seemed to be an invite. *Go on. You've lost your wife in the most horrible way imaginable. Tell me you understand. Tell me you feel my pain.* But Dark refused to take the bait. "And you?" he asked.

"I approached it clinically. It's what I've always done. If you have a problem, you simply bring together the pieces that will solve it."

Dark turned Julie's photo around with his fingertips, then slid it back across the coffee table toward Graysmith. "You think I'm one of those pieces."

"I know you are. You're the best there is. That is not hollow praise. It's a fact."

Dark ignored her. He went to his kitchen, took a bottle of beer from a shelf, uncapped it, tossed the cap into the trash. "I'm not what you're looking for. You should go." He took a long pull of his beer.

"Have you heard about Jeb Paulson yet?"

Dark slowly pulled the beer bottle away from his lips. Paulson was the newest member of the Special Circs team. Dark had worked with him once before, on a case in Philadelphia. Last he had heard, Paulson was his "replacement."

"I just received word that he's dead," Graysmith said. "Seems like it's the second in a series."

"What are you talking about?" Dark asked.

Graysmith lifted a thumb. "Martin Green was first. Special Circs sent Paulson down to the murder scene." Then an index finger. "Now it's Paulson. Whoever this is, he's just getting started."

"How do you know about this?" Dark asked.

"I have people back in D.C. who keep me informed of anything that even remotely seems like a serial killing. Like I told you, I am serious about this."

Many thoughts were racing through Dark's head right now—but most of all, the grisly thought of a Special Circs agent dying. "What happened to Paulson?"

"He was thrown off the roof of his apartment building. Say the word and I'll get you to the crime scene in Virginia within four hours."

"For what?"

"To do what you do best."

"No," Dark said. "Special Circs will be all over this."

"Yeah, but Special Circs is not you. They were never as good as you."

Dark looked away.

Graysmith stood and moved quickly to his side. "This killer's not going to stop. I have the resources to catch him. The money, the tools, the access. The only thing I don't have is a mind like yours. You were born to catch these monsters, Dark, and I don't think you can just walk away from a gift like that. I think you've been waiting for an opportunity like this since June. Well, here I am. No strings attached. I won't direct you. I won't order you. I won't influence your investigations in any way. I'll just fund you, give you the tools you need."

When something seemed too good to be true, it always was.

"So what do you say?" Graysmith asked.

"No," Dark said. "I'm through with that life. You can go now."

"You're lying to yourself. This is what you were born to do."

"Okay, I've tried polite. So how about this: Get the fuck out of my house."

Graysmith stared at him for a moment, almost pleading with her eyes, but then left without a word. She left the photo of her sister, Julie, on the coffee table.

chapter 15

The phone woke Riggins from a hard dead sleep. He'd been enjoying the blissful feeling of not remembering who he was or what he did for a living until he fumbled for his cell, pressed it to his ear, then heard the voice of Constance Brielle—his second-in-command. And then it all came rushing back.

"Tom—it's about Jeb."

Constance speed-talked him through what had happened, and told him Falls Church PD had sealed off the scene for them. Before Riggins even had a chance to react or respond, Constance said she'd be by within a few minutes. Riggins let the receiver fall from his fingers, feeling a burn of rage and hurt and confusion. It quickly consumed the pleasant narcotic effects of sleep.

Not another one. Not so soon. This was insane. This whole job was insane. And Riggins considered himself insane for staying in it so long. He couldn't help but wonder if he was the kiss of death. Work with me—die or go crazy soon after. Jeb Paulson had been with Special Circs what—a month or two?

What really troubled Riggins was Wycoff. As usual, he'd played his cards so close to his vest they were practically tucked up inside his cold, black heart. What did he know? Why had Wycoff insisted that Riggins go down to Chapel Hill personally? Did that son of a bitch know that whoever went down there would become this psycho's new target?

Riggins stood up. He was wearing boxers and a ribbed T-shirt. He needed to find his shoes. If a man's going stomping around a crime scene in the middle of the night, he needs his shoes. But the thought of Wycoff enraged him.

Get a hold of yourself Tom, he thought. You're almost smashing through the guard rails and headed into Paranoiaville. *Population: One (Everyone Else Is Out to Get You)*. Wycoff's a prick, but he's not indirect. If he wanted Riggins dead, he'd send his goon squad after him. They'd take him somewhere quiet, then slam some poison into his veins and that would be it. And maybe that wouldn't be so bad, considering.

Still—Wycoff wasn't telling him everything. And Riggins couldn't escape the fact that he'd essentially sent the new kid down south to die.

All too soon, Constance called again. "I'm outside. You ready?"

"Yeah," Riggins lied. His pants were barely up around his waist, and he was pretty sure he was out of clean shirts. Amazing what you forget when you're clocking hundred-hour work weeks because there's no one waiting for you at home. Riggins found the least offensive shirt, clipped his sidearm to his belt, slipped into his shoes, and made it out of his apartment.

Constance, of course, looked gorgeous. "You okay, Riggins?"

"Sure."

Except he was pretty damn far from okay. Part of him prayed he was still dreaming, and that this was a nightmare.

They set out for Falls Church, on the edge of the D.C. border— about a forty-five-minute drive. The way Constance was riding the accelerator, it'd be more like thirty.

———

Constance Brielle couldn't drive fast enough. The name that kept flashing through her mind like a twitchy neon sign was *Steve Dark, Steve Dark, Steve Dark*. But this was not about Steve. This was about poor Jeb Paulson.

At first she'd been a real bitch to Jeb. There was a quiet cockiness about him, as if his place at the table was a foregone conclusion. She hated that. You had to earn that. You didn't just walk in and expect the shorthand to be explained, the in-jokes decoded for you. Nobody had done that with Constance, Christ knows. But soon Constance realized that it was nothing more than a defense mechanism. Jeb sought her out. He'd quietly pick her brain about a few things. No stupid questions. Good questions—stuff Constance didn't think to ask back in her first few weeks at Special Circs. Soon, she realized that she was falling into a kind of mentor role with Jeb. Just like Steve Dark had assumed a mentor role with her.

Well, okay. Constance had kind of pushed Dark into that role.

With Jeb, though, it had become welcome. It meant, in some strange way, that she'd graduated. She'd lasted longer than almost anybody at Special Circs—the burnout rate was unreal—and now she was second only to Riggins. And now Jeb was gone.

It didn't make any sense. Just like it didn't make sense when Steve's family had been attacked at random.

Constance wasn't going to let history repeat itself. It was too late to save Jeb. But it wasn't too late to stop the monster. Her foot stomped down on the accelerator.

chapter 16

A uniformed officer escorted Riggins and Constance to the scene, which had been quickly obscured from the street with yellow tape and tarps. On his cell phone on the way there, Riggins had laid down the law: total media blackout. Nobody sees shit. *And no cops say shit,* Riggins warned, *or I'll have them fucking killed.*

Targeting a Special Circs team member meant the killer wanted attention. Well, fuck you, Riggins thought. You're not going to see shit about this in the papers.

Paulson's body was past the apartment complex's front lawn resting on concrete. Riggins and Constance looked down at their fallen colleague. His limbs were twisted in unnatural angles. In his right hand was a white rose. There was also, strangely, a feather tucked in his brown hair. "Fuck," Riggins muttered. He had sent the boy down to Chapel Hill to that murder scene. God help me if the killer saw him and followed him back here, he thought.

"Do you think it's him?" Constance said, seeming to read his mind.

"Who?"

"Whoever killed Green. The body was staged, just like Chapel Hill. Jeb was there on Saturday."

Riggins looked at Paulson's broken body. "I don't know."

But deep down he did. There was really no other explanation for it. Riggins had sent yet another young man racing off to his doom. What if he'd listened to Wycoff and traveled down to Chapel Hill? Would that be him on the ground, bones shattered and lifeless eyes staring at absolutely nothing? That would have been so much better. Riggins had nothing keeping him in this world. Jeb Paulson, on the other hand, had everything. Unlimited potential, snuffed out in a matter of seconds.

There was commotion a few flights up—panicked cries for a medic. Riggins and Constance looked at each other, then rushed into the building.

One of the Falls Church cops was down in the middle of the hallway—moaning, half-conscious. His body trembled slightly. It was strange to see such a stocky guy down on the ground, curled up like a baby. A medic rushed to his side, lifted his head slightly to place a towel beneath, turned him on his side and lifted his chin slightly so his airway would be clear. Two other medics quickly joined him and grabbed his arms and legs to keep him stable enough to be moved to an ambulance.

"Where was he?" barked Riggins. "What happened?"

The nearest cop told him: "Right here next to me. We were coming out of the apartment and *bam*, he just went down."

"Something airborne?" Constance asked. "Something he touched?"

"No idea," Riggins said. "Nobody move. Don't touch a damn thing."

It occurred to Riggins that maybe this killer wasn't just targeting

Paulson. Maybe the idea was to take out a young member of Special Circs—knowing that senior members would rush to the scene, eager to avenge their own. And then, you spring the trap . . .

"You," Riggins said, pointing at the cop who'd watched his partner fall. "Tell me exactly what happened."

The cop retraced his every step out loud, from arriving at the scene to checking the Paulson apartment, room by room, closet by closet, to stepping outside for a breath of fresh air.

". . . and then Jon pushed the door open a little, and the next thing I know, he's down."

"The door," Riggins said. Something had knocked Jeb Paulson out so hard that he didn't notice being dragged to a roof and eventually pushed off the top to his own death. Had to be something on the door.

Constance went to the door, crouched down. "Riggins, there's some kind of viscous fluid on this knob."

"Okay, let's bag a sample, then do the same with this guy's hands. Then we cut the rest and get it over to Banner. I need somebody with a saw up here. *Now.*"

chapter 17

Special Circs HQ / Quantico, Virginia

A few years ago, if you had died a violent and mysterious death in L.A., whatever they didn't bury or divide among your heirs ended up in Josh Banner's trace analysis lab.

Since then, Banner had gone global.

Banner had helped Special Circs track down Sqweegel. Riggins wasn't a man to forget favors. The moment a spot opened up, he asked Banner to join them full-time at Special Circs in D.C. And he loved it. Specifically, Banner loved being surrounded by evidence. It wasn't subject to human emotions or whims. Evidence was merely pieces of a story you had to put back together again. And Special Circs afforded him the chance to work on the best puzzles in the world. Of course, the key to staying sane in a job like this was blocking out the fact that these puzzle "pieces" were actually broken pieces of someone's life. And that the only reason they ended up here was because that person had died in one of the most horrible ways imaginable.

But Banner had grown up learning how to compartmentalize. It's how he solved problems. It's how he kept his head together. Well, that and comic books.

This time, however, it was difficult. Because on the table in front of him was the sawn-off doorknob of a colleague and a friend. First day on the job, Paulson had stuck his head in Banner's lair and said: "Tell me everything about what you do." This was remarkable. There were Special Circs staffers who'd gone a few years without even asking Banner's first name. Paulson, meanwhile, had treated him like a forensics god. They'd hung out quite a bit, over sandwiches and beers. Sometimes talking shop, sometimes just joking around.

Banner had been a guest in Paulson's apartment. He'd kissed Paulson's wife on the cheek and shook Paulson's hand and said his good-byes, dinner was awesome, thanks so much for having me over and then he'd touched this very doorknob and closed the door behind him.

Banner examined it now, carefully wiping a swab over its metal surface. From here, he would use a machine to separate the elements. Again, another puzzle to solve.

But solve this, and Banner would be helping to find Jeb's killer.

He worked late into the night and almost didn't hear Riggins enter the lab. "What've you got, Banner?"

"A weaponized form of *Datura stramonium*."

Riggins stared at Banner, waiting him out. They went through this every time. It was almost a dance. Banner would tease, wait for Riggins to ask the question. This time Riggins didn't take the bait.

"Sorry," Banner said, caving quickly. "It's also called Jimson Weed, angel's trumpet, or devil's weed. Which is a weird contradiction, if you think about."

Riggins waited.

Banner continued. "Ordinarily, it's just alkaloid that's absorbed through your mucous membranes. Some people smoke or eat it for the hallucinogenic-type effects. But the form on this doorknob is something I've never seen before. It can be absorbed through the skin, and it works within seconds, causing paralysis and cardiovascular collapse. Which explains why Jeb and the police officer were knocked out just by touching it."

"Is this crap difficult to find?"

"In its natural state, no. But this stuff was definitely engineered."

"Who'd have access to something like this?"

"Military, I guess. But you can't rule out private labs or universities."

Riggins thought about it. Their killer had either brains or access—possibly both. "Did any of this stuff turn up at the Green house?"

"No," Banner said. "But something else did. A nasty aerosolized agent called Kolokol-1. A whiff of that stuff and you're out in three seconds."

"It sounds familiar."

"Reportedly, the Russian Spetsnaz used it on Chechens back in 2002. It's a derivative of the potent opiodids fentanyl, which is dissolved in halthane . . ."

But Riggins wasn't paying attention. He muttered to himself, "Two different chemicals. Both used to knock out the victims. Why?"

chapter 18

Washington, D.C.

Knack knew how to get important people on the phone. It wasn't too difficult. You just made it sound like you've already called a thousand times before, that you had some insanely urgent business, and unless they connect you *right this fucking second* you're going to totally. Lose. Your. Shit. It was a tone of voice Knack had perfected over the past few years.

However, this tone didn't seem to work at Special Circs. "I'll transfer you to the press office," a calm voice said.

"No, no, honey, I don't want the friggin' press office, I want—"

"Hold on. Your call is being transferred."

"Fuck."

Knack thumbed the END key. Press officers were absolutely useless to members of the press. He had to try something else.

Wait. He had Paulson's office number from the rental agreement. Some small part of him was disturbed to be calling a dead man's phone number. Then again, that small part of him wasn't the one on deadline. Knack punched in the number. The line rang twice, then there was a *click*. Yes! He was being transferred, just as he predicted. But to whom? The line clicked again.

"Riggins."

Bingo.

"Agent Riggins? Jon Knack from the Slab. Just one quick thing—"

"Good-bye."

Knack had to act fast. He unleashed the next four words in a frenzied burst:

"I know about Paulson."

There was pause on the line. Riggins was cracking the window open slightly. Knack leaped through it.

"This is the second one, isn't it? Look, I know Paulson was in Chapel Hill. He was investigating the Martin Green murder. Now he's gone. You don't think this is coincidence do you?"

"No comment," Riggins said.

"Isn't it highly unusual for a serial killer to be targeting law enforcement?"

"No comment."

"Last time this happened was with Steve Dark, wasn't it?"

Knack heard a grumble. He'd hit a nerve there.

"Honestly, Knack? Just between you and me?"

"Yeah?"

"Shove it up your *highly unusual* ass."

Knack hadn't expected Riggins to confirm anything. But his reaction said it all. There were many kinds of non-denial denials. He opened up his laptop and started writing his story. Now he had a serious update, with "confirmation" from sources deep inside Special Circs. Riggins hadn't given any such thing, but he wouldn't come out to deny it, either. Sometimes getting a source on the phone for a "no comment" was all you needed.

Besides, Knack had Paulson at the scene of the first murder. Now Paulson was dead. It begged the questions: Was this a cover-up? Or the start of something big?

chapter 19

D ark opened his laptop. The Slab had a Paulson story online—
posted just a few minutes ago.

The update mentioned that Paulson had a wife—
Stephanie Paulson (née West), twenty-four. An elementary school
teacher who followed her sweetheart down from Philadelphia. She'd
been in the process of applying for a job in the D.C. school district,
where she thought she'd make the most difference. Knack painted
Stephanie as a bright, selfless woman. Exactly the kind of person
you'd have to be to put up with a partner working for Special Circs.
They had been married exactly thirteen months. There was no
quote from Stephanie, but Knack had been able to track down college friends via a social networking site who filled in the details.

The piece teased the oddities of the crime scene—the fact that
Paulson "may have" been found with a flower in his hand, and
stepped off the roof of his own apartment building. "Police sources"
claimed that there were no ligature marks, no bruises, no sign of co-
ercion of any kind.

Knack claimed to have a source "deep inside" Special Circs, which
was troubling if true. Nobody in Special Circs ever talked to the

press. If Riggins had ever caught an agent talking to a reporter, he'd have that agent skinned and salt-dipped before giving him the boot.

Walking to his kitchen, Dark played around the pieces in his mind—trying to figure out what the killer was trying to say.

Dark poured himself a glass of water and drank about half of it before he realized it tasted flat. Metallic. He didn't want water. He dumped the rest in the sink and went to the fridge for a beer, twisted off the cap. He needed more details. Green's murder—based on the photo that had accompanied Knack's first story—had been elaborately staged. Presumably, the killer had plenty of time to conceive, arrange, then execute such a display. But was Paulson's murder staged in a similar way?

There was only one way he could find out.

"Riggins."

"It's me," Dark said.

There was a pained-sounding sigh, as if someone had perforated one of Riggins's lungs with a piece of jagged glass.

"Just one question," Dark said. "You owe me that, at least."

"Let's not do this. I don't know what you think you're doing, but—"

"Cut me a break. You know exactly why I'm calling."

"I don't care why you're calling. We're through."

"Look, Riggins. I know I'm not supposed to be involved anymore. But maybe I can help. Unofficially. Just between you and me. This is friends and family, you know? I can't get this case out of my mind, and I might as well do some good."

"No. You said you wanted out, well, you're out. I shouldn't even be having this conversation."

"Let me see the murder book on Paulson. I can help."

"You're unbelievable."

"Okay, fine. Just answer a few quick things."

"You shouldn't be thinking about this stuff at all. Why don't you go out and enjoy some of that California sunshine you wanted so badly? In fact, why don't you go spend some time with your daughter? She might appreciate seeing your face."

Riggins could turn ugly when he wanted to. He was either just being nasty to get him off the phone, or he was really trying to piss Dark off.

"Riggins, come on."

"No discussing the case with outsiders. You're an outsider. That's the way you wanted it, right? Don't call me. Enjoy the sunshine."

The line went dead.

Dark thought about calling Constance, but quickly pushed the thought out of his head. His relationship with Riggins was one thing. Constance was another mess entirely.

In the horrible months after Sibby's murder, Constance had been there for him. But it was too much, too soon. First it was dinners. Then long sessions of just sitting there, filling the empty hours together. She tried to replace Sibby, thinking that she could bring Dark back from the brink just a little bit. Dark didn't want a replacement for Sibby. He didn't want anything at all, except to do his job.

The thing was, Constance would probably open up the murder book for him. But that would open the door again. Dark was capable of many loathsome acts, but not that.

Then it occurred to him—how to get those details. He picked up his wallet, pulled out a credit card.

chapter 20

Dark hadn't flown since his last Special Circs mission. For close to five years, he'd been shuttled to all corners of the world at a moment's notice. There were some days when his body clock was so scrambled he had a hard time telling dawn from dusk—and had to wait and watch the sun to see what it would do. Dark had grown to hate flying so much that when he pulled the plug, he rented a car and drove I-40 all the way to L.A., forty-seven hours straight, with stops only for gas and food.

The move to L.A. put him closer to his daughter. L.A. was also a city Dark could lose himself in—a city he knew better than any other. A dozen cities stitched together by mountains and ribbons of asphalt and crime and sunshine and sex and dreams. A city he used to consider home.

Now Dark was preparing to leave it again. He approached the LAX baggage check counter, slid his driver's license into the slot, and waited. Entered the first three letters of his destination. Waited again. Then . . . nothing.

Within seconds, two uniformed LAX security guards were flanking him. "Could you step to the side, Mr. Dark?"

"Why?"

"Just step to the side."

Half an hour later Dark was still sitting at a chipped conference room table in a stuffy, locked room. Nobody told him why he had been detained, but Dark figured it out for himself. Someone, probably Wycoff, had put him on a watch list. He tries to fly anywhere, alarm bells go off. Two uniformed guards escort him to a windowless room. Indefinitely.

Finally, a man in a navy blue suit walked in, manila folder in his hand. An airline logo was embroidered on the breast pocket of his jacket.

"Sorry to keep you waiting."

"Did I miss my plane?" Dark asked, knowing full well that his flight to D.C. was long gone.

"We'll get to that."

The man walked around the table, pulled out a chair, but stopped short of sitting down.

"I understand you're a retired FBI agent?"

Dark nodded.

"Which field office?"

"If you know I'm a former FBI agent," Dark said, "then you'd already know."

The man nodded, then casually flipped open the manila folder and rifled through a few pages, raised his eyebrows a few times. After a while Dark realized who this guy was: a professional time waster. Someone to keep Dark on edge until the person who was really in charge showed up.

So Dark shut down. Said nothing. Wondered how long this would take.

Another forty-five minutes, as it turned out. After fifteen minutes of an awkward, one-sided interview, the time waster was summoned out of the room. When he returned a half hour later, Dark was told he was free to go. No apologies, no further comment. Dark stood up and walked out of the room. He passed through a series of winding hallways until he was back inside the main terminal.

Where Lisa Graysmith was waiting for him.

"Sorry that took so long," she said. "Sometimes the wheels of Homeland Security turn more slowly than I'd like."

"Right," Dark said. "I'm supposed to think you just sprung me."

"Yes. Because I did."

"You probably put me on a no-fly list to begin with."

Graysmith smirked. "Paranoid much?"

Dark said nothing.

She walked toward him and extended a flimsy airline packet. "Here. You're on the next flight to D.C., nonstop, first class. I would have booked something private, but I didn't want to waste any more of your time transporting you to another airport. Next time."

Dark looked down at the tickets in her hand. Part of him wanted to turn around and leave. Go back to his house. Finish painting his daughter's bedroom. Finishing getting on with his life. You quit this bullshit, he told himself. So be a man and *stay* quit.

Instead, he took the ticket from Graysmith's hand. "This changes nothing," Dark said.

"Of course," she replied.

Dark tried to sleep on the flight, but that was a futile task. He hardly slept at home. Why would he be able to relax in a tin can 35,000 feet in the air? Dark thought about Graysmith. She claimed she could get him any details he wanted, access, everything. But he'd just spent the past five years under Wycoff's thumb. He wasn't eager to slip under someone else's. So why was he doing this, flying across the country to investigate a murder? Why couldn't he leave it to Riggins and the rest of Special Circs? What was wrong with him, anyway?

Dark had no real answer for that.

A few hours later, Dark was retrieving his small overnight bag from the overhead bin and making his way up the aisle. It was already evening. He hated the hours he lost going east.

There, waiting in the terminal, was Constance Brielle.

Constance thought she'd be immune to it by now.

But there was that telltale sting, whenever she looked at Steve Dark. The body naturally adapts to negative stimuli, doesn't it? You press a button and receive an electric shock often enough, eventually your body's going to get the idea that *hey, maybe you shouldn't do that*. Why couldn't that be the case with Steve Dark?

A call came from someone in Wycoff's office; Dark's name popped up on a watch list. Riggins had asked Constance to meet him at the airport.

"If I go, I'm going to end up punching him in his fucking face," Riggins had said.

"What makes you think I won't do the same?" Constance had asked.

"I don't," Riggins said. "I'm hoping you'll hit him harder, actually."

They joked with each other, in that usual grim Special Circs way, but the pain beneath was real. When Dark left, he'd abandoned both of them. Now he wanted back in? This day, of all days?

But Constance knew better than to blur the line between personal crap and the job. The job was simple: She was to put Dark back on a plane to L.A. immediately. If he refused to go, then she'd arrest him. And you know what? She probably *would* punch him in the face if he tried to resist. There she went again; blurring the line.

Just get him out of here, Constance told herself.

Dark walked right up to her. "I guess you're here to ask me to go home."

"Not asking," Constance said, holding up a paper ticket. "You're on the late to Burbank by way of Phoenix."

"The government won't even spring for nonstop to LAX?"

"It's the next available flight."

"You take it. Weather's nice in L.A. this time of year. You won't have to put up with the Santa Anas for another few weeks."

"Don't make me do this, Steve."

"Don't get in my way, Constance. This has nothing to do with you."

When he tried to move past her, Constance grabbed his wrist. Squeezed it tight. Pulled it in. Put her face close to his.

"I know why you're doing this. Riggins thinks you're just trying to piss him off. But I know you better than that, Steve. You think history's repeating itself."

"You don't know what you're talking about, Constance. Let go of me."

"Well, it's not. We'll get it under control. Go back to your life."

Dark sighed. For a moment, she thought he was giving up. Instead he twisted his hand and reversed the hold. A second later sharp pain was racing up Constance's arm. She started to reach for her cuffs, but hesitated.

"Besides, she's not at the apartment anymore," Constance said. "She's under guard."

There was a moment of surprise on Dark's face. You had to be quick to catch it. Constance knew she'd hit a nerve. Riggins thought this was about Dark feeling guilty—thinking Paulson had taken his place, and gotten himself killed for it. Constance knew better.

"Stay out of my way," Dark said.

Then he let go of her arm and stormed down the terminal.

Constance added, under her breath: "She's not Sibby."

chapter 21

Falls Church, Virginia

Constance had been right—Stephanie Paulson was nowhere near her apartment. She was staying with her college roommate, Emily McKenney, who also taught in the D.C. school district and had an apartment in Georgetown.

Dark watched them from across the street. Paulson and McKenney were in a diner. He couldn't hear their conversation, but the body language was clear. *C'mon, eat something. Drink something. You don't have to figure out everything tonight, you just have to eat something. Jeb wouldn't want this. He'd want you to eat the blueberry muffin in front of you.*

It wasn't so long ago that Dark would look at food and be repulsed by the sight of it. What use was food, if you couldn't enjoy it with the one you loved? Every type of food reminded him of Sibby. It had been one of the many ways she'd expressed her love for him. Every meal was a kiss. Without her, eating was simply a physical process. Converting calories into energy. Might as well slip an IV needle into his arm, get it over with that way.

McKenney put her hands to her friend's face, forced her to look up. McKenney smiled. A big, gorgeous, friendly smile that said:

I'm with you, I'm not going anywhere, I'm going to continue to be with you.

But Stephanie's look was blank. She saw her friend, she nodded to acknowledge her words, but they meant nothing.

Because Jeb wasn't here, and he would never be back.

Dark had come here to speak to Stephanie. But now that he was standing across the street, he couldn't bring himself to intrude on her grief. What was he supposed to say—*Oh yeah, I used to work in the job that's just killed your husband. And guess what? A maniac killed my spouse, too.*

It was absurd.

When his daughter was just a baby, Dark felt like he'd have some time to get his mind right, then return to become a real father to her. Nobody remembered anything before they were two years old . . . maybe even three, right? Dark only remembered little scary fragments of his own early childhood. Flashes no more real than a dream. The more Special Circs cases Dark worked, the more he told himself: *There will be time.*

The years had slid by fast, though. Now his baby girl was five years old. What must she be thinking? Especially when he couldn't even pay attention long enough to tell her good night, and that he loved her?

Everyone Dark had ever loved had been taken away. His birth parents. Henry. His adoptive parents—and, worst of all, that had been Dark's fault. His mother. His father. His nine-year-old brothers, all lined up, shoulder to shoulder, mouths taped shut, and shot execution style. All because Dark had pursued a monster. Same with Sibby, the love of his life. Dark had gone after the same monster, trying to set things right, and the monster had taken her away, too.

Dark's worst fear was that his daughter would be next.

97

III

three of cups

To watch Steve Dark's personal tarot card reading,
please log in to Level26.com and
enter the code: cups.

EX LUX LUCIS ADVEHO ATRUM

III

THREE OF CUPS

West Philadelphia, Pennsylvania

The stranger had been watching the women for an hour now. They laughed loud, nudging each other's shoulders, and had one thing on the agenda: getting drunk. Which was going to make this easy.

He made eye contact with the one on the end—the small blonde who looked like an actress. She'd probably been told that a million times. The look on her face dared him. *Go ahead. Try something. I'm not interested. I'm defiant.*

Raising his hand, the stranger curled his index finger. Come here.

There was the hint of a smile on the blonde's face, but she pretended to ignore the stranger and turned her attention back to her friends. That was fine. The stranger was patient. There was plenty of time.

When the blonde looked over again—of course she was going to look over again, it was part of the game—the stranger wiggled his finger. *Come on. Come over here.*

The blonde's mouth twisted into a pout; her eyes narrowed into a look of annoyance. *You want me?* her eyes asked. You come over here. Again, she looked away.

She couldn't fully ignore the stranger, though. He was too ruggedly handsome to be completely dismissed. And while she may have grown up being told she resembled a particular actress, she was just a facsimile. Her nose was bigger than the real thing; her lips not as full. And she knew it.

When she looked again, the stranger smiled innocently and wiggled his finger again.

She flashed a churlish smile. *Okay, asshole. Have it your way.*

Now confident, the stranger turned his back on her and raised his hand as if ordering another drink. Within a few seconds the stranger sensed her behind him. Then he felt her small fingertips lightly tapping his shoulder.

"So? What's so important that I had to come all the way over here?"

The stranger spun around and grinned.

"I just knew that if I fingered you long enough, you'd come."

The effect was priceless, the stranger thought. As if he'd slapped her across the face. The surprise and shock caught her off guard. No one speaks to *her* this way. She's a girl with class. She's a fucking graduate student, for fuck's sake! The blonde seemed like she couldn't decide whether to throw a drink in the stranger's face or knee him in the balls or just ignore him all together.

She chose the third option. Tried to, anyway.

The stranger kept flashing his grin, full intensity, as she rejoined her friends, leaned over, whispered her version of the exchange. The stranger wondered if she'd quoted him verbatim, or invented something more cruel. She looked over at him, utter hate in her eyes, but he didn't flinch.

Soon she convinced her friends to join her in the ladies' room. They carried their drinks with them.

It was almost time to begin.

———

What a fucking asshole!

As she sat back down, Kate Hale chastised herself. Why the hell had she gone over to that jerk? Because she was an idiot, that's why. She was also more than a little drunk.

But she deserved it. The first few weeks of grad school— absolutely crushing. She looked forward to fall break, the chance to catch up on papers. First things first, though. Tonight was about getting all dressed up and downing martinis with her friends. She wasn't going to let some thickneck moron ruin that.

"Forget about it, honey," said Donna, who stood in front of the mirror and checked her eyebrows and smoothed the wrinkles on her blue dress. "A place like this, you're going to have a high asshole factor. We should have gone to Old City."

Johnette, meanwhile, ducked into a stall. Johnette wasn't big on martinis. She'd been nursing the same vodka and orange all night. Blow was her thing. She'd welcome the opportunity to hit the ladies' room.

"This is 2010, though, right?" Kate asked. "Does that guy know pickup lines like that died around the turn of the century?"

"It's Philadelphia. What can I say? You grow up here, you get used to it."

"I should have picked a school closer to home."

Donna smiled. "Then you and I wouldn't be here, drinking beers, blowing off steam, and fending off lame pickup lines from Alpha Chi thicknecks. Look. Don't let it ruin your night. We're here to celebrate."

Monday Night Drink Fests were a ritual for Kate and her two best friends. See, Monday was the one night you really shouldn't drink your face off, which is exactly why they did it. Because they could afford to suffer through a hangover on a Tuesday since they were still in school. They wouldn't have the luxury of Monday Night Drink Fests a year from now.

Kate couldn't help herself. A grin broke out across her pretty face, too.

"World domination."

"World domi-fuckin-nation, baby!" Donna yelled.

"Yeeee-hah."

"And we could be dominating more if Johnette would finish powdering her nose," Donna said, exaggerating each word.

Kate giggled. "Johnette?"

Nothing.

The women exchanged glances. Johnette had done this before. Jacked herself higher and higher until she just . . . crashed. Wouldn't be the first time on a toilet, either. But no, Johnette insisted. She didn't have a problem. It was a performance enhancer. How the hell else do you think she made it through undergrad with a sky-high GPA?

"Johnette, honey," cooed Donna. "Come on."

Kate sighed, then stepped over to the stall door.

"Seriously, girl. Enough's enough."

Nothing.

"Hell . . . oooo?" she said, nudging the stall door open.

Johnette was indeed sitting on the toilet. Her dead eyes stared up at Kate. A red cord had been wrapped around her neck so tightly it dug into the flesh, bunching it up.

An icy numb blasted through Kate's body. She took a step backward. The ground felt like jelly. This wasn't happening. This couldn't be happening. The sinks were behind her. Kate reached a hand behind her to steady herself. She looked over at Donna—Donna was always the stronger of the two of them.

Donna wasn't there.

"Donna?" Kate shrieked. "Oh God, Donna, please . . ."

Then Kate felt the cord around her own neck. Hands pressed her shoulders, guiding her down to her knees. There was a full-length mirror next to the door, so she was able to see herself.

And the person standing behind her.

Kate regained consciousness for a few seconds.

Not long, really. But it was enough time to see what was happening around her. She was frightened to find herself standing, somehow. How could she be supporting her own weight? Her limbs felt numb, her head spinning. Kate blinked tears out of her eyes, tried to focus. Donna was standing, too, just a few feet away. Her eyes were wide and her mouth flapping open and shut, like she was trying to scream but no sound could be forced from her throat. Kate tried to speak, too. She wanted to tell Donna they'd be okay, that she didn't know what was going on, but she swore she would make it okay, whatever it was.

And then the stranger moved behind Donna. Placed the gleaming blade of the knife under her chin. Held a martini glass in front of her chest. The hand with the knife jerked to the right—almost too fast to watch.

Blood spluttered from the gash across Donna's throat, running down her chest and into the glass.

Somehow Kate found the strength to push an anguished scream out of her mouth.

"WHY? WHY ARE YOU DOING THIS?"

The stranger looked at her, smiled.

He ducked under Donna's outstretched arm—God, how could she just be standing there, arms out, after someone cut her throat—and took three steps, bringing him nose to nose with Kate. The knife was still in his hand.

"This is not about you," the stranger said. "This is about what you would have become."

Kate tried to cry out again but the stranger was too fast. One second she could feel the cold, sticky blade against her own throat.

And the next second she couldn't scream at all.

chapter 22

Washington, D.C.

Around one in the morning Dark managed to find a cheap room near the Capitol building. He'd brought very little with him: a change of shirt, a notepad, his laptop. He knew he should eat something, so he bought a turkey sandwich and a six-pack at an all-night deli. He couldn't remember the last time he'd eaten something.

Sipping the beer, he thought about Stephanie Paulson. Dark couldn't ignore the parallels. Paulson had gone after a monster, too. Only, the monster had cut him down quickly. Why had Riggins sent him down to Chapel Hill alone? Usually, you sent a small team. Two agents, at least. Dark had been the only one who could get away with the lone wolf routine. Was Paulson trying to follow his lead? Insisted on doing it solo?

Stop it, Dark told himself. *This is not about you. Put your mind on the case. Figure out how Paulson's death is connected with Martin Green's.*

The first was a complicated torture-murder. The killer had to have scouted the scene in advance—for instance, he had to know that the ceiling could support Green's body weight. By contrast, Paulson's death seemed less studied. Almost spur of the moment. No torture. Just a push.

But if it was indeed the same killer, Paulson's death was meant to send some kind of message. Why throw Paulson off his own roof? Why not shoot him, or snap his neck, or run him down with a car for that matter? No, this murder had also been planned out in advance. The killer had to lure Paulson up to his own roof. Or incapacitate him, then bring him to the roof. Revive him. Convince him to step to the edge. Push him. It was too elaborate.

As Dark racked his brain for connections between the two, his cell phone buzzed. A text from Graysmith:

IT HAPPENED AGAIN CALL ME

Twenty minutes later a car picked him up outside the hotel. It had been the fastest check-in/checkout the dull-eyed clerk at the front desk had ever seen. "Something wrong with the room? Sir?" Dark ignored him. There was nothing wrong with the room. There was probably something wrong with his head.

Graysmith had told him that less than an hour ago, Philly PD had been summoned to a triple slaying in a sports bar in West Philly, near the Wharton School of Business. Three women, tortured, throats slit, in a locked bathroom. Their bodies had also been "arranged."

Now, Graysmith had said, was their chance. She could get him to the crime scene immediately, full access, where he could work the scene—before Special Circs even roused someone out of bed. How? Dark had asked. You let me worry about that, Graysmith had said.

Dark decided that, at the very least, it was a chance to see if Graysmith was full of shit or not.

The car brought him to a private airfield where a Gulfstream jet was waiting. The best thing about owning your own plane? You don't have to deal with any FAA security checks. He was airborne within minutes of stepping onto the plane. The only other passenger: a woman in a business suit. Dark assumed she was just hitching a ride on the Secret Government Agency express until she stood up and asked if she could get Dark anything to drink.

"No, thanks," Dark said.

The plane cut through the air like its tail was on fire—faster than most commercial travel was allowed, especially over U.S. soil.

It wasn't just the buzz of the plane. Dark was amazed how alive he felt, even after a full day of travel. Maybe this *was* what he was meant to do. It was a compulsion like no other. If he wasn't chasing predators, Dark knew he might as well just lie down and stop breathing.

But if that was true, where did that leave his daughter?

The plane landed at Philadelphia International not more than twenty minutes later. The twinkling skyline of the city was hazy in the distance. Dark thought about Philadelphia. If this *was* the killer's next stop, why? Was it because Stephanie Paulson was originally from Philadelphia? Maybe this was part of a pattern. Green to Jeb Paulson. Paulson to his wife? Would someone in her family be next? Some other arcane connection?

Within minutes Dark was transferred to another car. It was approximately ten miles to West Philly, the driver informed him— they should be arriving in five. On the way, Dark's cell buzzed against his inner thigh. He fished the phone out of his pocket. It was Graysmith. Never mind that it was the middle of the night. She sounded wide awake.

"I see you're en route to the crime scene," she said. "Got everything you need?"

"You said I'd have access," Dark said.

"Sending it to your phone right now. Just show the lead investigator your screen. Name's Lankford. He'll let you in."

chapter 23

Without the people, noise, or music, the bar looked like an empty stage. The room was full of props, but no one to inhabit them. The stark houselights highlighted every imperfection—scratches in the wood, dust on the light fixtures, stains on the fabric. In a place like this, you'd only consider drinking or eating if the lights were low.

The bodies had been discovered an hour before closing. After the first screams, a bouncer ran back to the ladies' room to find it locked, a key snapped off inside the mechanism. Once he had finally managed to pry open the door and saw what was inside, the bouncer couldn't help it. He'd screamed, too. Panicked patrons fled the bar. The tables were still littered with half-full pint glasses, uneaten chicken wings. Some had even left jackets, and in one case, a pair of high-heeled shoes. If it was a set, Dark thought, then it was as if the actors had been fired mid-production, and told to leave everything where it was.

Graysmith's magic cell-phone credentials had worked. When Dark showed it to Lankford, the lead investigator, he was quickly guided back to the scene of the crime. Two patrolmen were posted as guards, but otherwise they let Dark have his way with the scene.

Which was unreal. How many jurisdictional battles had he fought over the years? How many fights after access to evidence— even with his Special Circs creds in hand?

Dark began to examine the blood-soaked crime scene. First things first—even though the tangle of ropes and bodies in the middle of the room screamed for attention. Dark knew better. He checked every possible entrance (two transoms), hiding place (supply closet, toilet tanks), and crevice (wooden baseboard enclosure) before he turned his attention back to the bodies, ducking under ropes as he searched. There was always the possibility that whoever did this was still here. Waiting. Watching.

He'd learned that the hard way, five years ago.

Finally Dark began to take in the scene, which looked like a marionette show from hell. The bodies of the three young women— Kate Hale, Johnette Rickards, and Donna Moore, according the driver's licenses left in their purses—were arranged with thin ropes and cords fixed to overhead pipes and the supports of the bathroom stalls. A first set of ropes ran from around their necks and up to the ceiling. A few inches below, each woman's throat was slit. Quickly, forcefully. Three more ropes ran from their upraised wrists, also up to the ceiling. A final set of ropes bound their waists, securing them horizontally in place. Their hands, still holding their cocktail glasses, were half-filled with blood. The tile floor below them was slick with blood, too.

The killer hadn't worried about making a mess. He wasn't a Black Dahlia–style surgeon/slasher, eager to drain his victims of blood then lovingly washing and scrubbing the corpse. No, this killer was more concerned with the scene he was creating.

The cocktail glasses, Dark thought. They're holding them upright. Would have been far easier to string them up without having to worry about the glasses. Hell, it would have been easier to snap their necks and move on. What did the glasses signify? Why fill them with the victims' blood? Why target three girls at once? Why not just one?

Killers made choices. Every choice meant something.

Dark pulled out his cell phone, opened the camera app, looked at the screen. Wait. The angle was wrong. Dark took a step back, then over, positioning himself behind the victim in a pink dress. Now the match was perfect, down to the color of ropes. When viewed at the proper angle, they blended into the background. The three victims almost appeared to be alive, lifting their three drinks in a mock celebration of cheer.

Three.

The number wedged itself in Dark's brain and refused to be shaken loose. The number was the key to this scene. He knew it. Why three?

Dark snapped some quick photos on his phone, but didn't go overboard. Unless Graysmith was bullshitting him, he'd have complete access to the Philly PD's forensics reports anyway. Dark had to admit there was a certain exhilaration knowing that he wouldn't have to catalogue this stuff himself. He was free to stay focused on the big picture—to figure out what these crime scenes were saying.

And who was saying it.

The lead investigator, Lankford, stopped him on the way. "Agent Dark? We have something."

Lankford brought him around to a tiny office off the main bar. There was a small black-and-white video monitor, cued up and ready. The setup was crude—VHS recorder, black-and-white camera. But it was better than nothing.

"Look at this. We think we got the son of the bitch."

Lankford pressed PLAY. The image on screen showed a lone male, longish hair, making his way back toward the restrooms. "He never comes out. The girls were already in there."

"Did it capture his image earlier?"

"Still checking, but it looks like he was sitting in the camera's blind spot at the bar. We're going to be grilling everybody about who was sitting where, and when. I'm sure we'll have a description within a few hours. I'll make sure you get it to your contact."

"Thanks," Dark said.

Lankford looked to the side, then back at Dark. "Look, I know I'm not supposed to ask—but who the hell are you with, anyway? And why the interest in this?"

"That's a good question," Dark said. "I wish I could give you an answer."

Lankford nodded slightly. "Fair enough."

Dark asked if he could spend some time with this videotape—it could help him fix on the scene. The investigator said he didn't see a problem with that. Especially with the kind of credentials he was holding.

Though he hadn't slept at all during the past twenty-three hours, Dark settled in to examine the footage. This killer was probably too smart to show his face, but there were plenty of other ways to identify someone. He hit the REWIND button.

"We have him."

The voice jolted Dark from his reverie. For the past two hours he'd watched the videotaped bar footage, repeatedly, to the point where the real world faded away and Dark felt like he was actually sitting inside the bar. He could smell the cigarette smoke—outlawed, but nobody was going to say shit to anybody. He could hear the soul music on the jukebox. He could feel the ancient stool groaning under his weight; the condensation rings of the beer on the bar top.

And he watched the same man leave his seat at the bar and walk back to the ladies' room, again—

And again.

And again.

How long did you plan this?

You had to have planned this. The ropes, the locked door, the quick, methodical way you took them out, bang bang bang, *until they were yours.*

Was it this bar, or was it the women?

How long had you been watching them? Who were they to you?

Why three of them? Were they snubbing you? Did they flick their hair, turn their pretty noses up at you? Tease you with the way their sleek dresses hung to their curves?

Why did you keep the three cocktail glasses in their hands? Are you trying to tell us they were lushes, that they deserved this?

The voice behind Dark had brought him back to reality. Which was just as well. He couldn't hang around here forever. The clock was ticking; Special Circs could be on the scene at any moment.

"His name's Jason Beckerman. Construction worker up from Baltimore," Lankford said. "We put it together from a bunch of patrons. Someone chatted him up about union stuff. Another identified a tattoo, and someone else noticed what he was wearing. Didn't take long."

"Is he in custody?" Dark asked.

"Yeah. We found him sleeping it off in his apartment. No sign of the clothes he'd been wearing in the bar. Wherever they are, they've gotta be soaked with blood, so no wonder he ditched them. The techs are going through the apartment now, and he's being grilled in the box down at the station. You want to observe?"

Dark nodded. "Let's go."

chapter 24

Johnny Knack stood outside the sports bar, cold wind whipping at his body, wondering if the tip was real or somebody's idea of a joke.

The tipster claimed to be a member of the Philly PD's homicide squad, and was a fan of his work. (Lie #1, right there. The tipster wouldn't be doing this unless it benefited him somehow.) He said that he'd been called to the scene of a weird triple homicide that he thought was just like the killings Knack had been writing about. (Lie #2, most likely. The tipster was trying to sound working-class, loquacious. Homicide cops considered themselves neither.)

So either somebody was tipping him off for real, or this was somebody fucking with him. The caller ID pinpointed the caller's location as Philly. And so far, other details had been right—the name of the bar, the approximate time of the attack. Still, Knack had this feeling he was being played.

He'd driven up I-95 from D.C. and immediately started working the fringes—neighbors, people hanging on the scene. After a while he had enough to file a question-mark piece to his editor at the Slab: "Has Green's killer struck again?" Nobody, however, would speak to him on the record. It was all guesswork and innuendo. So he held off filing. At least until he got something resembling an official peg to hang everything on.

Knack also needed a handle for this guy. All of the cool serial killers had names. The BTK Killer. The Beltway Sniper. The Hillside Stranglers. Sometimes the easy names came from the location. But this guy was hopping all the hell over the place. And if it was the same killer, he was also changing up his methods something fierce. Torture one dude. Push the next off a roof. Then take out three girls at once. Couldn't he stick to one method, like most serial killers?

A while later Knack saw someone bleary-eyed tumble out of the front of the bar, led by someone who was no doubt Philly homicide.

Now who was this mystery man? Jeans, button-down shirt. Based on the reactions from the uniformed officers who watched him go—Knack knew he wasn't Philly PD. Knack pulled out his phone, snapped a series of photos. The guy looked naggingly familiar. Then again, Knack had seen so many faces over the years, he tended to think *everybody* looked familiar.

When Knack holed up in a coffee shop to cobble together an update, he called up the photo on his cell. Maybe that mystery guy was someone important. Maybe another Special Circs guy.

Knack studied the images, then hit an image search engine. Not Google or commercial ones. The Slab subscribed to a big news-agency photo pool. Knack typed: SPECIAL CIRCS AGENT. Approximately 0.347 seconds later, Knack realized that holy shit he'd just been looking at the most famous Special Circs agent of all.

His name: Steve Dark.

Five years ago, his wife, Sibby, had been abducted, tortured, then finally murdered by a contortionist freak who dressed up in a body condom, hiding under people's beds before he emerged in the middle of the night, and then had fun with your sleeping body. Later it turned out that this contortionist—"Sqweegel," the Feds called him—had been obsessed with Dark, taunting him in the days before the murder.

Rumor: Sibby Dark had a baby while held in the maniac's basement lair.

Rumor: In retaliation, Dark snuffed Sqweegel, but Special Circs covered it up.

Not a hint of this appeared in the mainstream press. This material was relegated to a bunch of serial-killer-fan Web sites, the most active being Level26.com. There was a ton of chatter about Dark, and even more so, Sqweegel. Like Elvis, ol' Sqweegs was believed to be alive, curled up in someone's attic, waiting to take his bloody revenge. The more rabid conspiracy theorists believed Sqweegel had even once struck in Rome, poisoning dozens of people and leaving behind one of his telltale suits . . . only this time, in black.

No matter what, Steve Dark being involved made this case all the more interesting. Especially because of the most recent set of rumors:

That Dark had been forced out of Special Circs.

Knack had to get into that crime scene and figure out what the fuck was *really* going on. But first, he pulled out his phone. Time to file another update . . .

chapter 25

Jason Beckerman stuck to his story. He said he'd come home around eight P.M. and cracked open a few cold ones—blowing off steam after a long weekend of work. But he hadn't gone near any bar in West Philly. He'd stayed in his room and passed out early. "I was in my cups, I admit that much," Beckerman said. "But is that a crime? C'mon, guys. I just want to go back to my room and sleep. I've got work tomorrow. No rest for the perpetually laid off. If you're lucky enough to get work, you go to work."

No, Beckerman didn't see any girls. Christ, that would be all he needed. His wife, Rayanne, would strangle him if he fucked around on her with some little college bitches.

Now Beckerman just wanted to sleep everything off. It was his only day off—he had an early-morning shift the very next day. He complained that his hangover wasn't worth the few measly beers he'd sucked down the night before. "My head's Goddamned killing me."

"Does it check out?" Dark asked. He stood with Lankford in a room adjacent to the box. A row of video monitors showed the inside of the room at three angles.

"A neighbor saw him coming home a little after eight P.M., just like he said. But then another neighbor swore it was more like nine."

"How about the job? Is he really working construction?" Dark said.

"Yeah. Beckerman's on a crew working on a building downtown. Lives in Baltimore, but took a cheap room here six months ago for the gig—work had dried up there. Everything checks."

"Think he could have done it?" Dark asked.

"Sure. He's strong enough. Grumpy enough. Clearly, he's not a card-carrying feminist. But there's one thing missing."

"Motive."

"Right. Nothing at all to tie him to those women. Yet, eyewitnesses place him there at the scene—one of the victims, Katherine Hale, walked up to the bar, talked to him about something, then quickly walked away. Nobody caught the exchange. But could you piss off somebody that fast that he kills you and your girlfriends, then strings your bodies up in the bathroom like you're freshly killed game?"

"Not likely," Dark said.

They stood and watched Beckerman for a while as he told his story again, and again. The interrogator was good. He was patient, yet exacting when it came to details. He had an icy calm. Beckerman looked hungover and desperate for a nap. His only request was a Diet Coke, to stop his head from throbbing. "I don't deserve this kind of headache, man."

Lankford looked over at Dark. "Think he's your guy?"

"My guy?"

"Yeah. Whoever you're here for."

But Dark was already somewhere else in his mind, turning Beckerman's words through his head. Something struck Dark as odd. How had Beckerman said it? *I was in my cups, I admit that much.* An old-fashioned way of saying drunk. Beckerman probably heard his old man say it, so he grew up saying it. *In my cups.*

The girls were holding three cups.

"Shit," Dark muttered.

Lankford turned. "What is it?"

"I need to borrow your computer."

Minutes later Dark typed THREE OF CUPS into Lankford's browser. An image popped up—the exact match to the image he'd snapped on his phone. Dark cursed under his breath and typed in more search terms: HANGED MAN. THE FOOL.

Tarot cards.

The killer was staging his scenes like tarot cards.

chapter 26

Riggins's cell buzzed: WYCOFF. Fantastic. Just what he needed.
"Are you ignoring my e-mail on purpose?" the secretary
of defense barked.

Oh, that Wycoff could be a charmer. Riggins sighed and tapped
through until his e-mail box emerged from the tangle of files and
boxes on his computer screen. Sure enough, Wycoff had sent an e-
mail, marked URGENT with three exclamation points next to his
name. Gee, guess this was important. The e-mail included a link to
a Slab column. The headline:

RETIRED MANHUNTER BACK ON JOB
TO AVENGE HIS PROTÉGÉ!

Byline: Johnny Knack—the fuckhead reporter who'd called him
the other day. And below that: the image of Steve Dark, cell phone
pressed to his ear, clearly leaving the scene of the triple homicide in
Philly! Riggins didn't want to believe it, but the image didn't lie.
That was Dark all right. Familiar look on his face—the look of a
manhunter, deep in thought, blocking everything else out except

for one thing: the crime scene. It was a look Riggins had seen a hundred times on Dark's face.

"Fuck me," Riggins muttered to himself.

"So tell me," Wycoff said. "What was your boy doing in Philadelphia?"

"I have no idea. It's a free country, though."

Wycoff ignored the comment. "When you said Dark was out, you swore he would stay out. He can't just come and go to crime scenes as he pleases."

"I'll look into this, but it's probably bullshit, and you know it."

"Bullshit?" Wycoff asked. "I'm looking at his picture online right now. What, you telling me he has a twin brother running around somewhere? Who just happens to be near the scene of a triple homicide?"

The thought had crossed his mind, actually. Riggins was the only man alive who knew the secrets of Dark's family tree. Every last twisted, rotted root of it.

"This is on you, Tom," Wycoff said. "I'd like you to personally take care of it."

"What do you mean, take care of it? Am I supposed to have Dark followed?"

"Hey, I'm doing you a favor here, coming to you first. Either you take care of it, or I know some people who'd be more than glad to do it."

The words sparked an instant association in Riggins's mind. Wycoff's secret goon squad—off-the-books killers who dressed in black and had a thing for needles. He'd stared them down more than once. Riggins almost hated them more than the monsters he chased. At least monsters were clearly on the side of evil. These fuckers, these faceless black ops jackoffs, they did their creepy killing in the name of the U.S. government, and probably received handsome pensions for it.

"I'll talk to him," Riggins said, then threw his phone on the desk.

Why was Dark sticking his nose in this? And how the hell had he made it to the scene in Philly so quickly? Maybe he had someone on the inside here at Special Circs, still helping him out? Wouldn't be the first time.

Riggins sighed, resigning himself to the unpleasant task ahead. Dark had always been stubborn as fuck—even as a punk kid cop. Dark had spent a year sending application after application to Special Circs, but received rejection after rejection.

One day he showed up to ask Riggins about it. Riggins tried to puncture his balloon quickly, save him the grief, telling him that the job would eat him alive. *Go out, fall in love, get married, have a kid*, he'd told him. Have a life.

Dark had refused to accept that answer. *I want to catch serials, Riggins*, he'd said. *I want to catch the best of the worst. I want this.*

A man like Dark just couldn't turn off the "manhunter" part of his brain like a light switch. No matter how much he insists otherwise. From the moment Dark supposedly "quit", Riggins knew this day would come. He just didn't know it would be so soon.

He picked up the phone and chartered himself a flight to L.A. Five years ago, he'd flown to L.A. to bring Steve Dark out of early retirement. Now Riggins was headed back to L.A. to make sure he stayed retired.

chapter 27

"Stop busting my balls, Knack. You know I can't say anything."

Knack leaned against Lankford's door frame. "Come on, Lee. Why was Steve Dark here?"

Lankford shook his head. "I don't know who you're talking about."

"Right. Like I didn't see you escorting him from the crime scene."

"You're seeing things."

"I saw him walking next to you, Lee. Talking to you. So come on—why are you denying it? Fill me in here or I'm going to have to make something up."

Knack knew Lankford from a series he'd written last year about a Philadelphia cop who'd gotten loaded late one night and decided to take his service revolver and clean up his neighborhood, one thug at a time. The only problem: This cop considered a bunch of thirteen-year-olds playing a rowdy game of pickup to be "thugs." One dead kid, two wounded, and a media shitstorm that followed. Knack, looking for a contrarian angle, focused on the insane stress on the average inner-city cop. The piece made him a lot of cop pals, including Lankford, and had resulted in a surge of goodwill that Knack was still riding.

None of that seemed to matter now. Lankford wasn't giving up a damn thing.

And now the detective was standing up, stuffing a bunch of papers inside a manila folder, and pushing his way past Knack. "Look, Jon—you're a nice guy. Maybe I can give you an update later, okay? Just not now."

Knack nodded, pretending to be hurt. Not too much. Just a little.

Not too hurt to step into Lankford's office and poke around his desk a little.

If Dark were here officially, there had to be some paperwork to that effect, right? Maybe Lankford left it out on his desk. Knack got his cell phone ready in camera mode, just in case he needed to snap something on the fly, then sat down in Lankford's chair. If the detective happened back in, Knack could just claim to be making a call. Reception was better over here, his legs were tired, blah blah blah.

After a quick minute of flicking and pushing papers, Knack saw nothing of real interest on Lankford's desk. But his browser on the other hand . . .

People never erased their browser histories. Knack credited at least three major scoops to a quick look at some CEO's or cop's Internet usage. He clicked on the history and his eyes went wide.

Knack had his serial killer handle.

chapter 28

When Dark returned to the airport just before noon, he was mildly surprised to see that Graysmith was already waiting for him on the plane. She sat on a plush creamy leather seat with her legs crossed, pile of manila folders and loose papers in her lap. Graysmith must have followed him out East on another flight while he was analyzing the scene in the bar.

"You get everything you need?" she asked.

"It's a start," Dark said.

"What do you think about the suspect the police have in custody—this construction worker?" Graysmith asked.

Dark sat down in a seat across the aisle from her, let his head tilt back, stretched his fingers, closed his eyes. They burned from lack of sleep. "Jason Beckerman? Doesn't feel right. Wrong guy in the wrong place at the wrong time. Maybe even a fall guy the real killer put in our path. Philly doesn't have anything to hold him on. Plus, Beckerman seems to have a solid alibi for the night of Jeb Paulson's murder."

"So who's doing it?"

"I don't know. Don't have enough to work with yet. I didn't

126

see the first two crime scenes, and I didn't have much time with this one."

"I think you have some ideas."

Dark looked at her, hesitated, then said: "The killer might be imitating images on tarot cards."

Graysmith's eyes lit up. "I *knew* you had something. Okay, walk me through it, starting with Green."

At first Dark seemed to ignore her. He took a laptop computer from the seat next to him and opened up a browser. After a few keystrokes, he turned the screen so Graysmith could see. "The Hanged Man," Dark said. "Martin Green."

"Jesus. It's just like the crime scene."

More tapping. Another tarot card image appeared.

"The Fool," Dark said, "Jeb Paulson."

"I'm not seeing it."

"Rewind the murder scene a few seconds," Dark said. "Imagine him up on the roof, ready to take a step out into the unknown, white rose in his hand . . ."

Then Graysmith seemed to understand. "So he's mocking Special Circs. Calling them fools?"

Dark shook his head. "I don't think so. The little I *do* know about tarot cards is that they're never meant to be taken literally. The Fool doesn't mean idiot, according to this Web site. For a lack of a better term, I think it means newbie."

Graysmith nodded. "As in, new to Special Circs. Eager, ambitious, headstrong, hungry."

"And the girls tonight were . . ."

Dark tapped, then showed Graysmith the screen. The Three of Cups card appeared. "Celebrating. Drunk with life."

"Goddamn. How did you figure this out?"

Dark shrugged. "The girls holding their drink glasses at the crime scene was too forced, too on purpose, you know? It was a detail screaming for attention."

"If this killer is screaming for attention," Graysmith said, "why not make it easy and leave a copy of the card or something?"

"The victims take the place of the cards."

"But the victims themselves don't make sense. Take these college girls—why them? What's the connection? First Green, then Paulson, the agent who was investigating Green. But where do these college girls fit in? What's the next logical step?"

"I don't know," Dark said. "I'm not an investigator anymore. I have no idea what you want from me."

Graysmith smiled, then moved across the plane and sat next to Dark. He looked up at her, breathing in her perfume—fresh and intoxicating. The animal part of him wanted to take her in his arms and fuck her, then sleep for days, only waking when he wanted another fix. He suspected she knew this.

She leaned forward, almost whispering in his ear. "You've seen, firsthand, what kind of resources I can offer you."

"But what do you want in return?" Dark asked.

"I want you to catch the monsters."

"Special Circs does that."

"But Special Circs isn't as good as you. And they're not able to follow the job through—to give the monsters out there what they deserve."

"Which would be what?"

"Death."

Dark looked away. The plane was already beginning to taxi onto the tarmac. Lights streaked across the windows. Everything was beginning to make a little more sense now.

Graysmith wasn't interested in law and order or due process. Which was why she didn't funnel her considerable resources through the usual channels—even a division like Special Circs. No matter how clandestine, you always have to account to someone for your actions. Histories, even secret histories, had to be compiled.

She could give Dark the keys to his old life. Make him a manhunter once again. Only this time, he'd have unlimited access and a blank check. All Dark had to do was say yes.

Dark turned to face Graysmith. "What do you get out of this?"

Her eyes bored into his. "The monster who tortured and killed my sister is sitting in a climate-controlled room, eating three meals a day. He is clothed and given medical treatment, dental care. He has access to books. Writing implements and paper. He is allowed to exercise. To think. To dream. Meanwhile, my sister's scarred body is decomposing in a cemetery somewhere. Believe me, not a day goes by that I don't think of sending someone into that prison to slaughter that son of a bitch."

"Why not?" Dark asked. "Maybe it'll help you feel better."

"It would be a selfish act. If I'm going to sell my soul to the devil, I'm going to make it worthwhile."

"Have you made the deal already?"

"Look," Graysmith said, "I'm simply offering you the chance to do what you do best. You found the boogeyman once, and you erased him from the face of the earth. You can do it again. And again. And again."

"Until when?"

"Until the world is safe for your daughter."

"I can't stop the evil."

"Maybe not, but you can make a difference. One killer at a time."

Dark wouldn't admit it out loud, but that was *exactly* what he wanted, too.

"So what's your answer?" Graysmith asked. "Are we in this together?"

"Yeah," Dark said quietly, trying to push the image of his daughter out of his mind. "We are."

IV

ten of swords

To watch Steve Dark's personal tarot card reading,
please log in to Level26.com and
enter the code: swords.

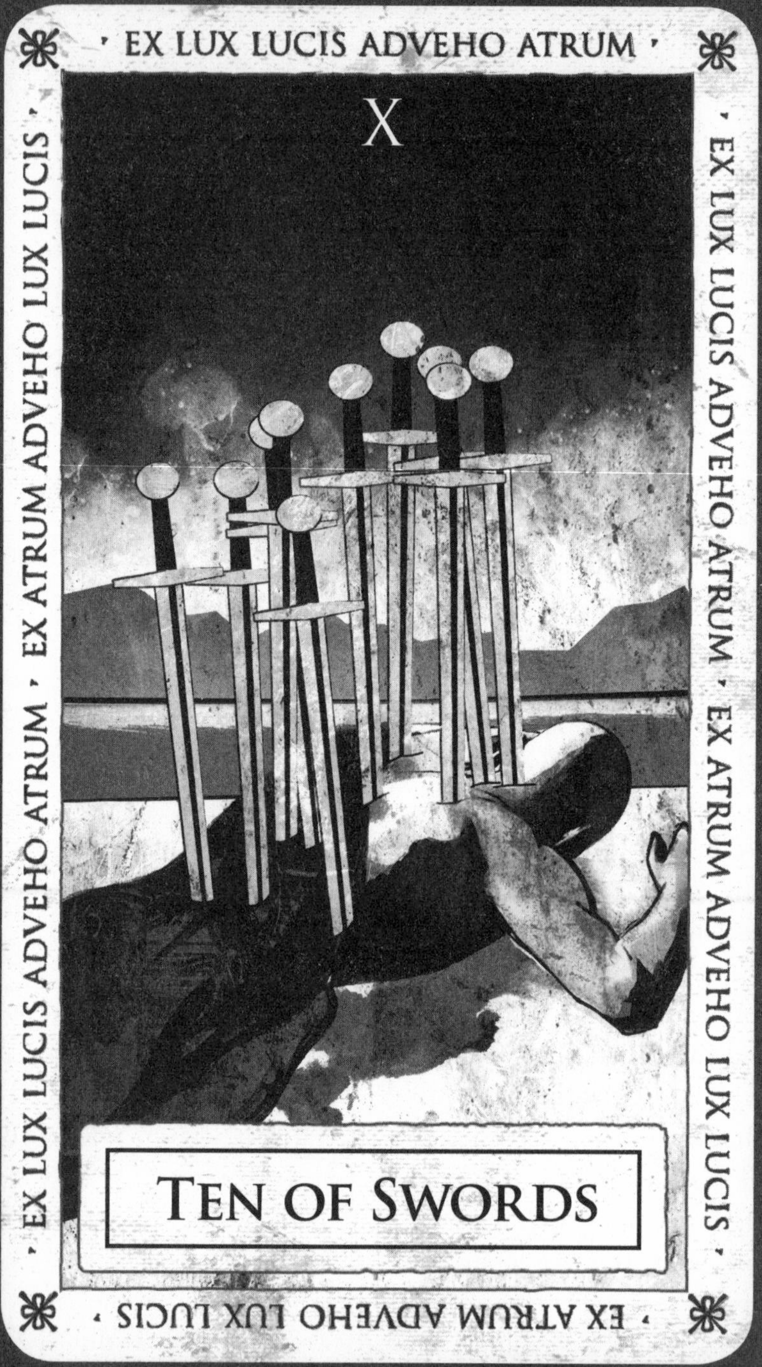
EX LUX LUCIS ADVEHO ATRUM
X
EX LUX LUCIS ADVEHO ATRUM · EX ATRUM ADVEHO LUX LUCIS
EX LUX LUCIS ADVEHO ATRUM · EX ATRUM ADVEHO LUX LUCIS
TEN OF SWORDS
EX ATRUM ADVEHO LUX LUCIS

Myrtle Beach, South Carolina

Sure, the guy was deep into middle age, but there was some muscle beneath a layer or two of fat. His skin scarred in places, like he'd been in combat, but strangely pale in others, like he's had time recovering in hospitals. He was facedown on the table, and soon he would have no secrets from her.

Nikki liked that.

She liked hanging on the poles above her clients, like a nightmare goth fuck angel descending from the secret basement of heaven, ready to make their dreams come true.

This was her little theater; she was the star.

Friends would ask her, *How can you touch gross old men like that?* And yeah, that was the typical clientele for this place—gross, old, disgusting, rich white men, away from their wives, wanting a little rubdown from a near-model, complete with happy ending. But Nikki's friends didn't understand. She wasn't out on some street, offering hundred dollar handies. She was in complete control. For thirty minutes, she totally owned these old saggy bitches. They kept no secrets from her. Not on their bodies. Not in their minds.

Discretion was highly prized at a "retreat" such as this one—a few minutes outside Myrtle Beach. Management made it clear that if one breath of what happened inside these walls made it to the outside, the penalty was instant termination, with the veiled threat of criminal prosecution.

That was okay. She liked to keep these things to herself anyway.

In return, her regular clients would reward her with lavish gifts—glittering chokers, expensive perfume, rare liquor. Nikki loved to sit up late, jacked up on cable TV, watching C-SPAN of all things. It was a strange kind of power, knowing what a U.S. senator's face looked like when he shot off a load. Or which ones liked fingers inserted in certain orifices.

She was part of the secret power structure of the United States, the way she saw it.

And now it was showtime.

Nikki looked at herself one last time in the mirror. She loved how the kimono hung from her body, accentuating her tits and hips and promising everything, yet revealing very little. The revelation could come later. She loved when her men, lying facedown, turned their heads to steal a glance. Their reaction was priceless.

The door behind her opened. A woman stepped inside the dressing room.

"Hey, you can't come in here."

Nikki turned and saw that the woman was completely naked and wearing a gas mask. Long dark hair flowed down to her shoulders, and big inquisitive eyes stared through the slightly fogged-over lenses of the mask. Nikki barely had time to register the bizarre sight before the woman lifted a can and sprayed something. The mist was cold and wet on Nikki's face and began to work immediately.

On the floor, Nikki was paralyzed, fading fast. She stayed conscious enough, however, to feel the horrible sensation of her silk robe being stripped from her body, *leaving her completely naked* . . .

U.S. Senator Sebastian Garner, naked on the table, prepared for the only moments of bliss left in his miserable life. The only place he could relax. He breathed in the warm musk of the lit candles and waited for his girl. She always wore a silk kimono—one he bought her, in fact. Reminded him of the war. The girls of the war, that is.

Garner heard the door open behind him and smiled. He wished he could freeze time and live in the next thirty minutes forever. Let everything else fade away. The Muslim holy warriors were promised an afterlife of milk and figs and virgins. Didn't a tireless holy warrior of Almighty Capitalism deserve something similar?

The door clicked shut. Here we go. Turn your mind off, you old fool, Garner told himself, and focus on the moment. Enjoying the living hell out of this session. He waited for Nikki's warm smooth fingers to work their way up his back, dancing along his tired spine, working the muscles into a state of blurred relaxation.

"Hi, Nikki," he purred.

He could hear the gentle flapping of the silk robe as it slid down Nikki's body and fell to the floor in a soft heap. Oh, that was the best. The anticipation drove him wild. Right now he was naked on the table, and she was naked just a few feet behind him. In a matter of seconds they would come together. No need for begging, or coy bullshit like *gee, my inner thighs are sore, would you rub them?* Garner and Nikki had a long-term understanding. She knew what was expected of her, and he knew exactly what to expect.

Garner waited for the first touch between them.

Instead there was a pinch at the top of his neck, like a bug bite.

Garner instinctively tried to lift his hand to swat away whatever it was that had bit him, but found that he couldn't. His right arm felt thick, rubbery, lifeless. This made no sense. He couldn't move his right arm at all. The first frenzied thought that went through Garner's mind: *stroke.* A motherfucking stroke, here of all places! How was he going to explain this? He tried his legs, his toes . . . nothing. No, no, no . . .

"Shhh," someone whispered.

"Nikki" was the name he wanted to say, but he couldn't bring his lips together. Not in any way that could form a syllable. If he could, he'd be screaming right about now. *Nikki, what the hell are you doing? Can't you see I can't move? Can't you see I need help!?*

Garner could still see, though. Not much. Just a tiny sliver of peripheral vision.

He saw a flash of silver. And the blur of a robe—not a kimono. This wasn't Nikki here in the room with him. Was it a medic? Had he passed out? What was going on?

Why couldn't he move, damn it?

Hands touched him. Rough hands. He could feel that much at least. Someone trying to help him. Thank God. Because Garner couldn't move a muscle. He felt like a slab of beef on a butcher's steel counter.

Where was Nikki? Who'd moved him? Garner tried to squint, to clear his vision, but he couldn't move his eyes, either. Everything was too bright. Too loud.

Fingers moved along his spine. Poking. Searching. Pinching for a moment, then releasing. Finally the fingers seemed to find the spot they wanted.

"Hold still," voice said. It wasn't Nikki.

No! he wanted to scream. But couldn't.

The first jab was brutal—painful. His muscles and bones may have been locked in place, but Garner could feel everything. The sharp tip of the dagger. The steel as it slid past his skin and muscle and worked its way deep into his body. His own warm blood bubbling up and running down the sides of his back, along his ribs.

The thing standing next to him seemed to be laughing. And it had another dagger. The thing showed it to him, sweeping a slender hand beneath its sharp tip, as if to demonstrate. "Ready?"

No, no, NO.

The fingers began searching again. Poking. Prodding. Tapping. As if counting the vertebrae.

Please no . . .

Garner heard a soft laugh. He tried to claw at the table, but couldn't. His pain—off the charts. He was helpless as a baby. Goddamnit, why didn't his mouth work? Why couldn't he scream? At least a scream would be some kind of release. But there was no release. There was no escape. Only the steel pushing its way into his helpless body.

No. No more. He couldn't take this anymore. Garner willed his eyes to move. Not much. Just a fraction of an inch to the left. If nothing else, he wanted to see who was doing this to him. He knew it couldn't be Nikki. Not his sweet angel Nikki. Someone else. Some evil bitch who'd lost her damn mind, got off on this kind of thing. Garner blinked hot tears from his eyes and tried to focus, his eyeballs straining in their sockets.

He couldn't see who was torturing him like this.

But he could see a small table, on which rested a clean white towel.

And on top of the towel were *eight more daggers*.

chapter 29

Dark tore off the plastic wrap, opened the flimsy cardboard box, and shook the glossy tarot cards out onto his kitchen table. He'd picked up a set at a bookstore in Westwood on the way back from LAX. If the killer was working with tarot, then fine. Dark would immerse himself in its language. He hated working blind.

The instruction book included with the deck made great pains to state that tarot was "not fortune-telling, nor religion." It was merely a symbolic language.

Still, the choice struck Dark as odd. Usually, leaving a tarot card was the kind of thing teenagers did at vandalism sites to panic authorities—to be all *spooky*. You draw a pentagram, you stab a cat, you leave a tarot card. Kid stuff. Still, Dark knew that some serious killers had tarot on the brain. He could recall two major cases. The infamous Beltway Sniper—John Allen Muhammad, along with his underage partner, Lee Boyd Malvo—left tarot cards for investigators at the scenes of his attacks. One of them was the Death card, along with a message scrawled on the back:

For you Mr. Police.
Code: Call me God.
Do not release to the press.

This card was found where Muhammad had shot a thirteen-year-old boy as he was walking to school in Bowie, Maryland. The media quickly dubbed the sniper "The Tarot Card Killer," but it became clear that Muhammad had his fevered mind on jihad, not fortune-telling. In essence, Muhammad was acting exactly like a teenaged kid trying to be spooky.

A few years later there was the so-called Hierophant, who named himself after one of the Major Arcana cards of the tarot. He didn't leave behind tarot cards. Instead, he took on the moral crusade of a hierophant, finding "sinners" and then executing them so that they would be discovered along with their sin. Tax cheats were found sliced up and surrounded by paper evidence of their misdeeds. Adulterers were found butchered together, in their hotel rooms. Pedophiles were found with DVDs and printouts of kiddie porn. The Hierophant killed himself before he could be apprehended. Predictably, the killer on a moral crusade was covering up for a host of his own sins, including forcible detention, domestic abuse, and embezzlement.

This series of murders, however, was different.

The victims were the cards.

A story was being told.

But what?

Dark drank another beer as he pored over the details on the cards. On the surface, the images appeared simple. One central image, many of them obvious. But the closer you looked, the more the smaller details jumped out at you.

The Hanged Man, for instance. The twelfth card in the Major Arcana, according to the guidebook. The scene could be considered ghastly, but the look on the man's face was one of calm, of relaxation. A halo of light burned behind his innocent head. The implication was that this man was at peace.

So go ahead and speak to me, Hanged Man, Dark thought. *I know what it's like to be left dangling. Why are you so calm?*

Dark went down to his basement and projected the Martin Green crime-scene photo on the wall again. Then he dragged an image of the Hanged Man card into the projection program. After doing a little resizing, Dark made the card image slightly opaque, then dragged it over the Martin Green image.

They matched.

Exactly.

From the crooks of his elbows to the position of his head (turned slightly to the right) to the precise angle of his bent left leg . . . everything matched, down to the centimeter. The killer had clearly obsessed over this card, committing every detail to memory, then sought to re-create it with the hanging body of Martin Green.

The killer was not just some creep using the tarot card for shock value, Dark thought. The killer had a deep connection with the symbolism and ritual of the cards. The killer respected the cards and chose them to make these grand gestures.

Jeb Paulson's body position wouldn't match, of course. But for a moment in time, as he was most likely forced to take that step off the roof, he did. Maybe the killer didn't need others to see the moment. Maybe it was something the killer wanted to keep to himself and savor in his mind's eye.

The three girls in the bar, however—they had the same attention to detail as the Martin Green murder. All of that effort to bind them and hang them and slice their throats and keep their cocktail glasses upright . . . again, it showed a slavish devotion to the tarot.

But what was the killer trying to say?

Dark admitted that the answers he needed wouldn't be in some Wikipedia page, or the instruction book from a pack of cards.

Then came a knock at Dark's front door.

chapter 30

After recovering his Glock from its hiding spot under the floorboards, Dark paused at the entranceway to his basement lair, then made his way to front of his house. He slid along a wall cautiously. The door had one of those old-fashioned magnifying peepholes mounted in the middle, but Dark never used it. Peepholes made it too easy for someone on the other side to fix your position. And even though Dark had selected the door to be thick enough to withstand a point-blank shotgun blast, the peephole was merely glass. A bullet could smash through it easily. Good-bye, brain matter. Good-bye, everything.

So instead Dark looked through a peephole hidden on the left side of the door. This gave him a line of sight to a set of mirrors mounted on the porch roof. The mirrors revealed a familiar face.

Tom Riggins.

What the fuck was *he* doing here?

Dark took a moment to control his breathing. More knocking. A little louder this time. Tucking the Glock into the back of his jeans, Dark flipped the brass lock and opened the door.

A few minutes later Riggins was twisting the top from his bottle of microbrew. He strolled through the house as if he owned the place.

That was the trick; you didn't ask, you just moved. His Sig Sauer hung heavy on his belt, his shirt untucked. It had been a long flight, on top of an even longer day. Tuesday morning in Virginia, Tuesday evening in West Hollywood, gut churning the whole way. Riggins wished he could have sent somebody else. God, anybody else. But he knew it was up to him to read Dark. No one else could.

"You know what I saw on the way here from the airport?" Riggins asked.

Dark, who had already drained half of his beer, trailed behind him, trying to act casual. "No. What?"

"Mobile hookers. I thought they were an urban legend, but no. They're real. Ladies of the night, driving down Sunset, looking for business. One tried to get me to pull over. Would have, too, if I wasn't in such a rush to see you."

"I'm touched. How do you know they were prostitutes?"

Riggins stopped, turned, and gestured with his bottle. "Well, either she was scratching the inside of her mouth with an invisible cucumber, or she was making an obscene gesture."

"Maybe she just liked you."

"Have you looked at me lately?"

"You look like you've lost weight."

"Oh, fuck you."

Riggins hadn't laid eyes on Dark since he left Special Circs. On Dark's last day there were no promises of calls, visits, or e-mails. Both knew their relationship—close as it was—existed solely within the context of the job.

The strange effect of this was that now, face-to-face again, it seemed like no time had passed at all. They picked up where they'd left off, as if they had just decided to meet up for beers after a four-month hiatus.

But as the banter flew back and forth, Riggins busied himself examining Dark's house. From what Riggins could gather, Dark was keeping up the pretense of a "normal" life. Furniture from a big-box chain. Basic bachelor staples in the fridge. Some movie posters on the walls—some of Dark's favorites from his teenage years: *The Hitcher. To Live and Die in L.A. Dirty Harry.* But that was just for show. Trivia shit.

And that was the problem. Where was the *real* Dark in this house? Where were the case files? The books on forensic science? His journals? His serial-killer book collection? Riggins didn't even see a computer, which was like seeing the pope without a cross. It just didn't happen.

Which meant Dark was hiding something. Hiding what he was *really* doing here, way out on the other side of the country.

Meanwhile Dark trailed behind Riggins, studying him. His ex-boss had walked right in, not giving Dark a chance to tell him it wasn't a good time, or suggest they head to Barney's Beanery for a beer or something. Riggins was a bulldog who wasn't going to wait for an invitation. Beer in his hand; large, muscular frame strolling through the house. Like Riggins was nothing more than an old friend, out on the coast for a couple of laughs, checking out his buddy's new place, maybe eyeing early retirement and looking for a new place to hang his hat.

Then again, that was the peculiar genius of Tom Riggins. He was very good at making you underestimate him. He looked like a guy who would knock back a basket of wings and a six of Bud with you at the corner bar, the kind of blood brother you spill your guts to, the kind who would help you move furniture. Riggins was a curious blend of menace and good-ol'-boy friendliness, which is how he had disarmed countless perps over the years. Just like he was trying to disarm Dark right now.

Riggins must have seen the photo on the Slab. Why else would he be here? But so far he hadn't mentioned it. Dark knew it was better to wait him out. Sooner or later, Riggins would get to the point. Which might be as simple as a warning. Or might be as dramatic as an arrest.

After all, Dark had noticed a van parked outside that didn't belong in this neighborhood.

"What're you up to these days?" Riggins asked, pausing in the kitchen, leaning his large frame against a tiled counter. Not much in the way of food in here. Not that Dark was a gourmand—as he recalled, Sibby had been the one with taste in that department. Still, the kitchen looked more like a television studio set than something you actually used to cook or eat. Like it was for show.

"I've been teaching," Dark said.

"Yeah. Heard about your gig with the kids at UCLA. How's that working out for you? Got any celebrity kids in your class? Like one of those . . . what do they call them, the Jones Brothers?"

"I enjoy it, and no, not that I know of."

"Any promising Special Circs material?"

"These kids are twenty, Riggins."

"You were that young once," Riggins said. "In fact, I think you were just as young when we first met, isn't that right?"

Dark drained the last of his beer, then held up the empty bottle, foam cascading down the neck. "Want another?"

Riggins stared at him—hard. "All right, fine. We could dance around your kitchen forever, but I'll admit, my feet are getting tired. What are you *really* up to?"

Dark returned his glare. "Why don't you just cut through the shit and tell me why you came all the way out to L.A. for a couple of beers? Considering that just a few days ago you wouldn't even talk to me on the fucking phone."

Riggins gestured to the tarot cards on the kitchen table. "Well for starters, you want to tell me about those?"

"Intellectual curiosity," Dark said.

"Right. *Professor Dark.* I forgot."

Riggins slammed his bottle down on the kitchen countertop.

"Look," Riggins said. "I saw the photos online, and you know I did. You were in West Philly at the murder scene. Pretty sure you've been in Falls Church, too. What I want to know is, what the fuck do you think you're doing? I thought you'd had enough of this man-hunting stuff? Enough of the bureaucracy? I thought you wanted to reconnect with your daughter."

Dark said nothing.

Riggins grunted. *Okay. Fine. Don't tell me. I'll know soon enough, either way.* And he would. Outside, Riggins's field techs, on loan from the NSA, were busy sweeping the house and the dozen others in the immediate vicinity.

chapter 31

Riggins knew that if there was an upside to working with a suit supreme like Norman Wycoff, it was the access to his toy box. And the secretary of defense had a lot of shiny toys at his disposal. Such as an Econoline van full of state-of-the-art surveillance equipment, which was parked across the street from Dark's house. This was NSA-level surveillance gear—able to pick up not only audio and video through concrete walls, but also to scan the hard drive of virtually any computer through foot-thick concrete walls. At such close range, the techs in that van would be able to lay Dark's entire house bare.

If Dark was hiding anything, Riggins would find it.

And once his team confirmed that Dark had stuff he shouldn't, Riggins could take Dark into custody with a clear conscience. Papers had been signed, agreements had been made. Dark would have to understand that, right? Besides, Riggins would honestly feel better with Dark somewhere safe. Maybe he needed to talk to somebody.

"Tell me how you got access to the crime scene," Riggins said.

Dark just stared at him.

"I can't figure it out. Not only do you have some kind of magical fucking access, but you were there even before anybody from my team could make it. Who tipped you off, Dark? What's going on? Just talk to me, man. Set my mind at ease."

Dark said nothing.

The cell in Riggins's pocket buzzed. Exactly the sensation he didn't want to feel. No doubt, the team in the van had found something. Would Dark fight him? If so, Riggins steeled himself for a long night. A man like Dark had to have more than one escape route. A gun, possibly two, stashed somewhere. Glock 22, .40 caliber. Dark's favorite. A fast car—probably that cherry Mustang that Riggins saw parked out front, pointed on the downward slope. The cell buzzed again.

"Got to take this," Riggins said, fishing the phone out of his pocket.

"No problem," Dark said.

But it wasn't the surveillance team outside. It was a text from Constance.

CALL ME NOW . . . WE HAVE ANOTHER ONE

chapter 32

Dark was surprised when Riggins stood up, slid his phone into his pocket, drained the rest of his beer, and announced that he had to leave. Was this a ruse? Was Riggins trying to lure him to the front door so a team could cuff and hood him? This wasn't the man's style—but then again, these weren't the usual circumstances. They were both in uncharted territory.

"I've got to go—but this isn't over," Riggins said. "You owe me some answers."

Dark nodded, eyeballing the outside of his house. He looked for shadows. Noises—the scrape of a rubber sole on pavement. Tells of any kind. He knew he could outrun Riggins, make a break through the backyard. There might be a team out there, too, if Riggins was serious about this.

"Thanks for stopping by," Dark said.

"Fuck you for making me worry about you," Riggins said.

"You know, there's an easy solution," Dark said. "Don't worry about me."

Riggins gestured around the room. "Is this what you think Sibby would have wanted?"

"I don't know, Riggins. She's not here to tell me. Say hi to the team in the van for me. Anybody I know in there?"

Riggins grunted once, shoved his empty beer bottle into Dark's hand, then left.

Inside the van, Riggins looked at the techs. They were hunched in front of the most sophisticated eavesdropping gear currently available. Riggins felt a little like Gene Hackman from *The Conversation*—that is to say, a stone-cold pro about to be fucked hard from every conceivable direction. The lead tech, a freelancer named Todd, lowered his headphones down to his shoulders and shook his head.

"Nothing," Todd said.

"You can't find anything?" Riggins asked.

"Far as we can tell, he's totally clean," Todd said. "No computer, anywhere. No security cameras. No cell phones. The guy doesn't even have a television. Just a single landline, and we have that tapped. It's like he's living in 1980, or something."

That didn't make any sense to Riggins. Dark was security obsessed even *before* the Sqweegel nightmare. Why would he live in a place with absolutely no visible security measures? Was he trying to tempt the monster into attacking—kind of a "come and get me"? No. Dark was clearly hiding something. Maybe this place wasn't really his house. Maybe it was a shell, and he was keeping his real shit elsewhere.

"Does he have any other property in California?" Riggins asked.

Todd said, "We checked. Nothing, other than an old address in Malibu, under his wife's name. And the old foster family's residence, but that's been sold long ago."

Riggins thought about it. "Hang on. The Slab photo showed Dark with a cell phone pressed to the side of his head."

"Well, there's no sign of cell phone activity here. That's the easiest thing to trace, even if he pulled the battery, dumped the thing inside a bucket of water. We'd get a hit. Maybe it was disposable, and he tossed it?"

"Damnit."

Riggins couldn't spend any more time here. Constance was busy arranging him a flight from LAX to Myrtle Beach. There had been another freaky ritual slaying, and this time the target wasn't just a bunch of MBA students. It was a fucking U.S. senator, stabbed to death in a high-class rub and tug somewhere near the beach. While he'd been dicking around here on the West Coast, this killer was gleefully making stops all up and down the eastern seaboard.

Wycoff would be up his ass about Steve Dark, but priorities were priorities. The killer first. Dark could wait.

chapter 33

After he was sure Riggins's van had pulled away, Dark headed down into his basement lair to continue studying the crime scene evidence. A short while later Graysmith arrived, letting herself in the front door without a word.

"There's been another one," she said.

Before traveling out to join Dark in Philadelphia, Graysmith had made some modifications to his home security system—the one she'd called "Fisher-Price."

"I gave it a security sweep," she'd explained. "Now it will be like someone threw a lead blanket over your entire house. No one will know what you're doing, who you're calling, what Web sites you're looking at—nothing. I won't even be able to look."

Somehow Dark doubted that. Graysmith didn't seem to be an *explicit trust* kind of person. But apparently her modifications had saved his ass, because Riggins had brought along a complete mobile surveillance team, which was a lot of manpower for a friendly couple of beers.

But Dark decided to worry about that later. "Tell me about the murder," he said.

"U.S. Senator Sebastian Garner. Hardliner, conservative. Made a lot of headlines last year defending Wall Street, especially at a time when his constituents were begging him to punish them. Vietnam War hero. Family man. So it should come as no surprise that they found him at a sex spa in Myrtle Beach. Naked, and stabbed to death with ten daggers."

Daggers. Dark immediately remembered the suit of tarot cards that were swords. Ten of them, plunged into a prone man's back.

"Was this trip general knowledge?" Dark asked.

"No," Graysmith said. "Far as the media knows, Garner was attending an economic think tank session in the area. I'm sure his handlers are scrambling as we speak, trying to fabricate some kind of chronic back pain that would give Garner a reason to be there. It won't last, though. The facts are the facts. Somebody's going to have a field day with this story."

"Do we know anything about the daggers?"

"One of the first responders said they looked like something you'd buy at an occult shop down by the ocean—ornate, and elaborate designs. I should be able to scoop up some images soon, but rest assured they weren't steak knives."

Dark leaned over Graysmith, did a quick Google search. "Look at this."

On-screen was the image of the Ten of Swords. In the foreground, a man is lying facedown on a sandy beach, dressed in a vest and white shirt. A red robe or shroud of some kind is draped over his buttocks, covering his legs. Beneath the man's head appears to be a small river of blood, the same color as the shroud. In his back: ten long swords, the first stuck in his head, and the rest following a rough path down his spine, past his buttocks, and down along one of his thighs. His head was facing a black horizon. Fingers dead, motionless on the ground.

Dark closed out the window, leaned against the table, and rubbed his temples. "I suppose I should get on a plane now," he said.

"No," Graysmith said. "Let Riggins and your girl Brielle work the scene. This is not the death of some hooker in an alley. This is a senator. They're going to err on the side of obsessive-compulsive when gathering evidence. I've also got a lock on Riggins's phone now, and Brielle's as well. Plus my usual backdoor sources at Special Circs. Whatever they get, we'll get."

Something about that unsettled Dark. Like he'd betrayed his friends, led them right into a compromising security situation. But he pushed the thoughts aside. Wasn't as if he'd invited Riggins here.

"So what then? Dark asked. "Do we wait around for this guy to deal another card strike again?"

"No," Graysmith said. "You do what you do best. Put together the clues into a narrative. We have four cards now, six victims, all within a period of five days. The killer chose these cards for a reason. Get inside his mind. This is what you do best."

"No," Dark said. "It's not. I don't do *random*. There's no deduction here, intellect doesn't apply. He might as well be spinning a roulette wheel and killing people according to the numbers that pop up. No matter how hard I think about it, I'm not going to be able to guess."

Dark suddenly felt claustrophobic, wondering who he'd let into his house. What had he been thinking? She could have installed anything in his house—a security override, pinhole cameras, *anything*. He decided to spend the rest of the night scouring his own basement to find out what she'd done. Maybe he'd even have to move. Take just what was essential . . . no. Take nothing. He deserved nothing less for his stupidity.

"Hey," Graysmith said. "Sit down, take a deep breath. You look like you're ready to crawl out of your own skin."

"I just need to think."

"Let me help put you at ease."

"What do you mean?"

Dark looked at her. She gave him no obvious tells. She didn't play with her hair, or purse her lips slightly, or tilt her hips. There was nothing. But just the same Dark knew what she was offering, matter-of-factly, as if she'd suggested giving him an espresso.

Instead, Dark told her: "You'd better go."

chapter 34

mazing how so simple a concept—say, a tarot card—could unlock the keys to the media kingdom.

MEET THE TAROT CARD KILLER

He's already dealt six victims. Will *YOU* be next?

Knack knew that the whole tarot thing was a gift straight from heaven; with a media-friendly handle like the Tarot Card Killer, his series would finally get the attention it deserved. Even people who wouldn't know a crystal ball from a basketball knew what a tarot card was. The whole thing was custom-made for the masses.

Even the killer's name could be boiled down to a tight little market-ready brand: TCK.

Knack was almost beside himself with glee. There was even implied momentum in the name, like a clock ticking (or, TCKing, as it were) down to another murder.

But Knack had no idea that within a few hours of dubbing this psycho "TCK" he'd be on the set of a remote studio in D.C., some tech running a mic wire down his shirt, waiting for Alan Lloyd—yeah, the Alan Lloyd of *The Alan Lloyd Report*—to start asking questions via satellite. The whole thing had come together with amazing speed.

The circus had already started without him. All of the major networks had a steady rotation of tarot experts and clueless callers, all of them offering their opinions and interpretations, and trying to guess the killer's next move. Knack even heard some Vegas bookmakers were offering odds on the next card to be referenced. The killings had captured the public imagination, and everybody wanted in on the action. Some were terrified by the very idea that a freaky killer was picking off people at random, all over the eastern seaboard. Others couldn't wait for the next grisly report.

And the mania had all started with Knack's Slab posts. Even better: Knack already had a main character in Steve Dark, legendary manhunter. That was the missing piece. If he could somehow get to Dark, get his cooperation, nobody would be able to touch him on this.

"Ready?" asked some pretty network assistant.

"Yeah," Knack said, trying to breathe slowly and take a moment to celebrate. He'd done it. He owned this story.

"You're on in three . . ."

Now that Knack thought about it, this wasn't just a story. This was a Goddamned book. A career-making book.

"Two . . ."

God bless you, TCK. Wherever you are.

"One . . ."

Alan Lloyd wore a look of dire concern. "Mr. Knack, many people are worried that this so-called Tarot Card Killer could suddenly show up on their front doorstep. Is that likely? Should people be afraid?"

Knack had to play this one right. You don't want to sound like an alarmist, but you also don't want to cut the legs out from under your own story. Keeping people in a mild state of unease was the goal. If they were uneasy, they'd want to watch and read more until they felt a little better about themselves. Every new victim was a relief because . . . well, the killer hadn't killed *you.*

"Alan," Knack said, "that's a very good question. What has law enforcement alarmed is that they truly can't figure out TCK's pattern. He could literally strike anyone, anywhere, anytime."

Crap, Knack thought. Too much, too much. Plus he'd used the word "alarm." Damnit. He began to sweat a little.

Alan Lloyd, however, was loving it. "So what should people do? Stay indoors and avoid all human contact? That seems a little unreasonable, don't you think?"

"Of course not, Alan," Knack said. "You're more likely to win the Powerball lottery than find yourself in the TCK's crosshairs. But people should know that this killer is uniquely brazen. He took down an FBI agent, Alan . . . consider that for a moment, the *FBI* . . . for his second kill. The second one we know about, anyway."

Lloyd nodded gravely, then opened up the show to viewer calls. First was Linda from Westwood, California.

"Yes, Linda, you're on."

"I would like to know if Mr. Knack thinks the Tarot Card Killer is worse than the Son of Sam or the Zodiac."

"Too early to tell, Linda," Knack said. "Comparatively, though, the Zodiac was a bit of a coward, picking on couples in remote locations, hiding behind letters. The TCK is not afraid to take the fight to the enemy."

Knack cringed a little when the words came out of his mouth; he just equated law enforcement with the "enemy." Word choice, you stupid bastard, word choice . . .

"Scott from Austin. Fire away."

"Why is this loony using tarot cards? Is he just trying to be spooky?"

Knack shook his head. "Scott, this goes beyond spookiness. I'm not an expert, of course, but from what I've seen at these crime scenes, the TCK is trying to re-create actual scenes from these cards. To what end? We have no idea. And I don't think we'll know, sadly, until he turns over the next card."

"Drew from Champaign-Urbana, Illinois. Do you have a question for Mr. Knack?"

"Yeah," a timid voice said. "You said not to be afraid, but the thing that scares me the most is how random it is. Could I be the next victim?"

"That's a great question," Knack said. "I wish I could tell you what the TCK is thinking. But none of us can. Not even the FBI."

chapter 35

West Hollywood, California

After Graysmith departed, Dark headed out, too. He brought nothing but his keys, wallet. He picked up his cell phone and looked at it for a moment before throwing it back down onto his kitchen counter. Dark didn't want to hear from anyone. That would mean he'd miss Sibby's nightly call—*again*—but he couldn't just sit here, either. Sibby would understand. She was a tough little kid, just like he'd been. Besides, he'd make it up to her. Maybe he'd pay a surprise visit tomorrow. Just drive up the PCH to Santa Barbara and spend a couple of hours with her, playing on the floor. He couldn't remember the last time he did that.

Now Dark just needed to drive, undisturbed.

He climbed into his Mustang and blasted down Wilshire, past the two- and three-story shops and restaurants and bars of Santa Monica, all the way to the end of the road, where Eugene Morahan's white Art Deco statue of the city's namesake saint stood, surrounded by gnarled trees and a patch of grass shaped like a heart. On sheer impulse, Dark turned left on Ocean and raced past the Santa Monica pier. Bad move. Too many memories on that pier. As he zoomed by, he glanced down, half-expecting to see Riggins there, staring back up at him, hurt look on his face.

Dark thought about hopping on the 405 South all the way across the border to Ensenada. Buy a cheap bottle of something that would help him turn off his mind and sit on the beach and lose himself in the night—

Then he saw her, walking up the block from Neilson Way.

Couldn't be . . .

The same way she moved her hips. The hair, cut just like always. The curve of her back.

Dark's foot slammed into the brake pedal, causing his Mustang to fishtail a little. He jumped out of the car, temporarily losing sight of her. Where had she gone? Up the street? He jogged in that direction, looking for his dead wife's long, black hair.

No. It wasn't Sibby. The rational part of Steve Dark knew that. She'd been gone five years, and though the memory of her was still alive in his mind, he knew her body was resting in Hollywood Cemetery. Dark had held their daughter and watched them lower her into the earth. It was like watching a group of strangers bury his own heart.

But this random woman on the street seemed so much like her. He couldn't help himself. He had to look at her, just to put the irrational part of himself at ease.

Dark's sneakers slapped the pavement frantically. Cool ocean air blasted across the back of his neck, freezing the sweat that had suddenly beaded there. The woman, this *Not Sibby*, couldn't have disappeared so fast. There was nowhere for her to go, to hide. And why would she hide? After a few moments Dark found himself in front of St. Clement's Church—a modest building off the main drag. Its doors were still open; the last Sunday Mass had wrapped up a short while ago.

Maybe *Not Sibby* ran in here.

—————

A young priest was still inside, picking up the stray hymnals and wilted flyers from the seats of the pews. Dark looked around, from the modest altar and wooden cross back to the small confessionals. Nobody else was here.

"Can I help you?" the priest asked.

Dark was about to ask if a woman had stepped inside the church, but realized how insane that would sound. Especially if the priest was to ask if the woman was his wife, or a relative.

No, Father, total stranger. But she reminded me of my dead wife, so I thought I'd chase her through the streets of Santa Monica just to make sure that she, in fact, was not my dead wife.

"Sorry," Dark said. "I just wanted a moment of quiet. Is that okay? Or are you closing up?"

The priest smiled warmly. "Not for a little while. Knock yourself out."

Dark shuffled into the nearest pew, lowered the kneeler with the top of a sneaker, hit his knees. Being in churches reminded him of his foster parents. *As long you pray to God, everything will be okay,* his foster father had once explained. Of course, that was before he'd stood over the dead bodies of his entire family. Dark believed his foster father had been praying in his final moments, hands bound behind his back, utterly helpless. Not praying for himself, though. Praying for the souls of his family. Including Dark.

He interlocked his fingers, made a tight ball with his hands, lowered his forehead to his knuckles.

Dark tried to recite the Our Father, but for some reason he couldn't bring the words to mind. Which was ridiculous. He'd grown up with those words practically tattooed on the inside of his skull. But now Dark could only recall fragments.

dark prophecy

Our Father
Thy Will
Deliver Us

You leave a city for a long enough period of time, your mind puts your map of the place in deep storage. Was that the same with prayer? If you stop saying the words, does your mind file it all away? Dark couldn't remember the last time he prayed. He remembered many drunken nights cursing God. Maybe God had responded by wiping the words clean from his mind.

Enough of this. Dark stood up.

"Are you okay, my friend?" the priest asked, slightly stunned by his movement.

No, Father. God's erased part of my mind. Maybe that's his idea of mercy.

"Yes, Father," Dark said, then left the church.

chapter 36

Santa Monica, California

Dark wasn't sure how long he'd been walking the streets of Santa Monica. He'd wandered out of the city limits and was somewhere near Venice Beach now. Skateboarders and beach cruisers milled around him. At times he had the creeping sensation that someone was watching him, but Dark chalked it up to paranoia. First he sees a woman he thinks is his dead wife. Then he thinks unknown agents are observing his every move. Hell, maybe he was being followed. Graysmith could have put a tail on him from the very beginning.

The wind grew stronger, fiercer. The palm fronds at the tops of the trees swayed violently. Dark finished the last of his smoke, then flicked the butt away into the sand. Sibby would have yelled at him for that. She would have also ribbed him about leaving his car in an illegal zone. Then again, why should he worry? If Graysmith could sneak him into any crime scene in the world, Dark was sure she could fix a parking ticket and have his Mustang pulled out of the impound lot.

Maybe if he kept looking, he'd run into that Sibby lookalike. If he didn't, Dark knew he would sit up all night, wondering. Wondering how someone could look and move just like Sibby, only *not be* Sibby. Maybe this was more of God's work, too.

An obese homeless man who smelled uncomfortably like antiseptic and vomit hit Dark up for money near the ocean walk. Dark reached into his pocket and realized that in his haste, he'd left his wallet in the car. He pulled out a ten and five singles; Dark gave the man the larger bill and kept the singles for himself. The bum mumbled thanks, half-stunned at his good fortune, shuffling away.

Down to five bucks. Dark thought he should probably start walking back, see if his car was still around. If not, it would be a long hike back to West Hollywood.

And that's when he saw it—the tarot card shop. PSYCHIC DELIC, the large painted sign over the doors read.

Dark looked up at the sign and couldn't help but smile. Clearly, he was going about this all wrong. If he wanted to catch the Tarot Card Killer, he needed a tarot card reading, right?

He remembered this place. Sibby once tried to drag him inside, just for fun. Dark passed.

Come on . . . it'll be fun.

No, no. Not for me.

Please . . .

I don't believe in that shit. No.

But now Dark looked up at the sign and wondered—what if he had gone in with Sibby that time five years ago? Would he have been able to see any of the horrors coming? Could he have changed both of their fates for . . . what, five bucks?

No. This was ridiculous. Dark knew he should head back to his car, get himself home. Bad enough he missed his daughter's nightly phone call. He needed to go home, prepare for tomorrow's lecture, try to get his life back in order. Dark was good at knowing what he *should* do.

Of course, he didn't always do it.

The proprietor of the shop sat at a circular reading table. She was younger than he expected. No moles, no tattoos, no wrinkled skin, no stiff black hairs poking from her chin. In her mid-forties, majestic, and deep in her demeanor. Her skin was a smooth brown, her eyes calm, youthful and friendly. She contact-juggled four glass balls in her hand, spinning them round and round and round . . .

Dark was about to turn on his heel and bolt when she spoke up.

"Steve Dark," she said.

"How do you know my name, lady?"

The woman smiled.

"Read about you in the papers. You catch him yet? TCK. The Tarot Card Killer."

"You *do* read the papers."

"It's my job to know a little something about everyone. I'm Hilda." She showed him a chair near a small table. "Have a seat."

As Dark lowered himself into the chair, Hilda began to shuffle the tarot cards, her fingers like snakes working the deck. Dark, meanwhile, scanned the surprisingly spacious shop. There were lamp stands, lit candles. A glass counter where you could buy occult ornaments, incense, jewelry, herbal treatments. Statuettes of Buddha and Jesus. A painted scene from *Alice in Wonderland*. The moment you stepped through Madame Hilda's dimly lit threshold, you were no longer in sunny, funky Venice Beach. You were in a timeless pocket of magic, where anything could happen. At least, that was the point of the decor, he supposed.

"This is all bullshit, right?" Dark asked.

Hilda was unfazed by the question. "No more bullshit than what's out that front door."

Dark had to admit—she was good. He supposed you had to be, to make a buck in a shop like this in the middle of crazy Venice Beach, relying on tourists who were busy deciding between SPIRITUAL ADVICE and a temporary henna tattoo they could show their coworkers back in Indianapolis.

Hilda pushed the cards across the table. "Cut the deck any way you'd like."

Dark paused, then lifted a pile of cards, put it to the side, and repeated the process a few times.

"Have you ever had a reading before?" Hilda asked.

"No," Dark said. "I came close once. This joint, actually, but . . . didn't happen."

"Maybe you weren't ready."

Dark didn't reply. He thought about Sibby. Her beautiful eyes, squinting in the sun. *Come on. It'll be fun.*

"Here's how it works," Hilda said. "I'll deal ten cards face up. I'm not a fortune-teller. I'm a *reader*. The cards aren't meant to make predictions or offer false promises. They're only meant to guide you. Add clarity. You can draw from it what you will. So . . ."

Hilda took a small stack of cards and pressed them to her chest.

"What do you need to know?"

Dark sighed, then decided to cut through the bullshit. He didn't have to get himself wrapped up in the mysticism. This was no different from a cop talking to an informant.

"I need to know how it all works. If I can get a better understanding of your world, maybe I can catch him."

chapter 37

Now Hilda smiled again, but it was a weak, uneasy smile. "I don't know if I can help you, but I suggest we start with a personal reading. See where it takes us."

The last thing Dark wanted was a *personal* reading. His whole career was an unholy mix of the personal and the professional, and it had taken everything important away from him. But before Dark had a chance to reply, Hilda began dealing the cards in the shape of a cross. First:

The Hanged Man

Followed by:

The Fool

And:

Three of Cups

Dark stared down at the table. He couldn't breathe. Someone had siphoned all of the air out of the room. Even the flickering lights seemed to writhe around on their candle tops, gasping for oxygen.

Hilda noticed his discomfort and stopped the deal. "Something wrong?"

Three of the murder scenes, in the *exact order*. Either this was a setup, or this woman read the papers *really carefully* and was fucking with him. The odds of these specific cards being dealt, in *this* order, was . . .

"These cards match up to the murders so far," he muttered, then looked up at Hilda. "What'd you do? Rig the deck?"

Hilda leaned back in her chair. No smile now. Either she was a skilled actor, or she truly didn't realize the importance of the three cards on the table.

"I'm not a magician, Mr. Dark. You cut the deck. All I did was shuffle the cards. Now it's up to fate to tell the story."

Hilda finished forming a Celtic cross with three more cards:

Ten of Swords
Ten of Wands
Five of Pentacles

—before placing four more on the table:

Wheel of Fortune
The Devil
The Tower
Death

Dark quickly committed them to memory. Ten, five. Wands, pentacles. That was easy. So was the final sequence: Wheel, Devil, Tower, Death. He put together a quick word association to cement it in his mind. *If you spin the wheel against the devil, you'll end up in the tower where you'll meet your death.* Also easy enough.

But now Hilda was the one with the stunned expression on her face.

"Something wrong?" Dark asked, mocking her a little.

"Look at this Celtic cross. Six Major Arcana and one from each Minor. In all my years of doing this, I've never seen that before . . ."

Dark stared at Hilda. "What does that mean?"

Hilda paused before she answered. "You were meant to be here."

chapter 38

The reading lasted until sunlight broke over Venice the next morning. As promised, Hilda gave him a personal reading, taking care to explain the meaning behind each card to Dark before moving on.

But the session took all night because each card seemed to trigger an explosive memory. With each card, Dark became convinced this was no sleight-of-hand card trick. These ten cards were tied into his life in a very real and fundamental way. It felt more like a counseling session than it did an occult reading. At first Dark tried to dismiss the cards, joke their implications away. *The card means all that, huh?* But Hilda held firm, taking her time, asking simple questions that opened the floodgates in Dark's mind. *At what key moment in your life were you the Fool? When you finally got into Special Circs, how was it? Celebratory? Are you prepared to discuss your worst memory?*

The cards also, chillingly, provided insight into the first four murders.

The Hanged Man, Hilda explained, represented the story of Odin, the god who scarified himself to gain knowledge—which he then shared with humanity. His suffering was for a greater good. So Martin Green—a member of a high-level think tank—had gained some kind of knowledge. His death, presumably, was for the greater good as well.

The Fool was embarking on a new journey, his worldly possessions slung over his shoulder, the sun of enlightenment shining down upon him, white rose of spontaneity in his hand. But the dog at the Fool's side is the voice of reason, urging him to be careful. If not, he may walk off the edge of a cliff . . . or his own rooftop, in the case of newly minted Special Circs agent Jeb Paulson. What was the voice of reason trying to tell Paulson? Had the killer attempted to warn him away from the investigation? Did Paulson ignore the warning, and end up paying the ultimate price?

The Three of Cups and the murders of the MBA students in West Philly came into sharper focus, too. The card about celebration, exuberance, friendship, camaraderie—forming a bond for a common goal. However, Hilda explained, the cards can be reversed, and the celebration can turn to self-absorption and isolation.

And finally the Ten of Swords represented the futility of the mind, a failure of the intellect to save you. A man like Senator Garner thrived by his intellect, brokering deals and changing the course of the nation. But in the end his intellect had failed him, because his base urges had stabbed him in the back. The pleasures of the flesh versus the logic of the mind.

Just as the sequence of cards fit Dark's life, they fit each of the murder victims perfectly. The victims and killing methods were not chosen at random. They were perfectly suited for each other. There was a pattern, a story being told.

But what linked them all together? And how would it end?

For that matter, what linked Dark's life to this string of murders? Was it merely fate that caused his life to intersect with these killings?

Or something deeper?

———

A while later Dark found himself at Sibby's gravesite. Even though it was just a few miles away, he'd hadn't been here in a long, long time. Sibby always had the uncanny ability to pull Dark out of his own head and help him see things more clearly. His wife soothed his soul like no one else. And ever since Sibby died, looking at her grave was a painful reminder of how utterly lost Dark felt without her.

But things felt different now. Dark lit a smoke and thought about the events of the night. About how much Hilda had opened up inside of him, how much he'd been forced to confront. Then Dark smiled ruefully.

"You knew all along, didn't you," he said softly.

The grass stirred around her headstone.

"I know, I know . . . I refused to go. You pleaded with me to at least try it, and I acted like a stubborn ass. I was pretty good at that, wasn't I?"

Sibby—if she was listening somewhere—declined to respond.

But it was true. Dark should have listened to her all of those years ago and followed her into that tarot shop. Maybe he would have taken a good look at his life a lot sooner. Maybe he could have saved himself a lot of suffering . . .

Dark flicked away his smoke and crouched down, touching the top of Sibby's headstone. It felt warm from the sun.

"I'm sorry," Dark whispered.

Sibby never liked what Dark used to do for a living. She was creeped out by all of the serial killer books in his apartment, and she never wanted to hear about old cases. But Sibby also knew that he was the best at what he did.

Dark looked at his wife's name etched in the marble.

Had she nudged him into Hilda's shop? Was she giving Dark the reassurance he couldn't give himself?

If so, that was all Dark needed.

The knowledge that he could catch this killer without losing himself in the process.

chapter 39

Myrtle Beach, South Carolina

By this point Riggins was working on practically zero sleep, so the last thing he needed to see was some dead senator's flabby naked pale ass. Especially a senator like Garner. Riggins never liked him much when he was alive, and it was hard to work up sympathy for the man now that he'd been found butchered in some high-end "spa" in a resort town. The man looked like a chicken roll left out on a deli counter too long.

Yet, that was precisely what Constance was asking him to do—stare closely at the man's ass.

"Stoop down so you can see this," she said.

"Can't you just tell me?" Riggins said. "This job's given me enough psychological scars to last me a second lifetime."

"Will you just stoop down and stop being a baby?"

So yeah, sure, Riggins stooped down. They had managed to clear the room of the local police for a few minutes, which was fortunate. They wouldn't do their usual banter in front of anybody else. And the banter sometimes did a lot to keep their emotions in check, their heads clear. Constance took Riggins on a tour of the daggers, starting at the head, working its way down the senator's spine, and ending in one of his tough old thighs. Of the ten blades, the first nine were buried in the senator's body up to the hilt. The last one, in the thigh, had been rammed through a tarot card first—the Ten of Swords. You know, just in case they couldn't figure out the reference, Riggins supposed.

"Look at the blade itself," Constance said, wonder in her voice.

Above the blood-flecked card, you could see about an inch of the blade and the elaborate designs on the steel.

"I'm guessing that's not Ginsu," Riggins said.

"This isn't something you pick up at any old occult shop. Look at the artistry, the detail."

Of course Constance was right. The detail was intricate and elaborate as the tattoos on a Yakuza gangster. Clearly, their perp hadn't gone rifling through a silverware drawer for the murder weapons. These were unusual, which was a good thing—because it meant they would be traceable. You want to kill someone and get away with it? Go to Target or Walmart. Don't get cute with exotic knives or drugs like this killer did. The problem was, the killer didn't seem to give a shit about being traceable. He—or she—had taken out six people in five days in four different cities. Given all of the time in the world, sure, they'd find out where these daggers were made. But in the meantime, this nutcase could take out a half dozen more people. From all indications, the killer was escalating. Three college girls in a dive bar is one thing; taking a stab at a U.S. senator, with a complete, armed, taxpayer-funded security detail, puts you in a whole new league.

Riggins pulled his face away from the senator's corpse. "Who found him?" he asked.

"Nikki. Real name's Louella Boxer. She says she stepped into the other room to prepare for their session, to *get into character*, as she explained, and someone walked in."

"Could she give a description?"

"Sort of," Constance said. "Boxer claims it was a woman, naked from the neck down. Olive skin, athletic build."

"And what was from the neck up?"

"A gas mask. And that was the last thing Boxer remembers. When she woke up, she came screaming into the room and found the senator like this."

"You know, I was turned on until the gas mask part," Riggins said. "How long was she out?"

"She has no idea."

"The killer's using his fancy knockout shit again," Riggins muttered. "What, did he find this stuff on sale? We need to have Banner check the tox screens for that military stuff he found in Paulson's blood. See if we can trace it back to a military base somewhere."

"You mean she," Constance said.

Riggins nodded. "Gas mask and tits. Right. And I thought the freak in the full-body condom was strange."

V

ten of wands

To watch Steve Dark's personal tarot card reading,
please log in to Level26.com and
enter the code: wands.

*T*ranscript from Flight 1015, private charter plane from Denver International Airport to Southwest Florida International Airport.

PILOT: This is Captain Ryder in the flight deck. Sorry, folks, it looks like on our approach to our final destination we've encountered some bad weather. If I had a magic wand, I'd make it go away, but alas, I don't. Please return to your seats.

PILOT: And why don't you go ahead and fasten those seat belts.

PILOT: And while you're at it, I'd like you to think about your lives. The people you hurt. The policies you enacted. The schemes you hatched.

PILOT: The actions that brought you here, now, to meet your fate . . .

Confusion spread throughout the small cabin:
"What the hell is he talking about?"
"Is this somebody's idea of a joke?"
"Did he just say *fate?*"

A few minutes ago, life had been pretty damned fantastic for the ten passengers of Flight 1015. They were headed to a corporate retreat on a secluded playground on the golden Fort Myers coast. On the official agenda: brainstorming the future of the company and reintegrating the core values of Westmire Investments. (Hey, it sounded good on paper.) On the unofficial agenda: sex, booze, coke, massages, more coke, and quite possibly an orgy, depending on the amount and quality of coke at hand.

Tiffany Adams had been to these "retreats" before, so she knew how they could run hot and cold. Sometimes, the newbies wanted to focus a little too much on work, which totally killed it for vets like Adams. Fortunately, this flight contained six vets (herself, Ian Malone, Honora Mouton, Warren McGee, Shauyi Shen, Corey Young) and only four newbies (Maryellen Douglas, Emily Dzundza, Christos Lopez, Luke Rand). The retreat could go either way, but Adams liked the odds. She also liked how the morning was unfolding. It was friggin' seven in the morning, and already the kids were at it.

Emily Dzundza, she of the ample chest and blow-me lips, was already on her second bourbon—and she'd seemed like the biggest stick-in-the-mud. Maryellen Douglas was off somewhere with Warren, and Christos Lopez was holding forth on a recent bottle-service binge he'd gone on at his last company, racking up a $135,000 tab within a matter of hours. Atta boy. Just what Tiffany liked to hear.

When the pilot started talking about fastening their seat belts however, it made no sense. Crystal blue skies, no turbulence whatsoever, calm, flat brown flyover country beneath them. Was this a joke? No. Pilots didn't joke. Not in the post–9/11 world.

But then, without warning, the horizon tilted violently, and the plane began to nose-dive. Drinks were spilled. More of her coworkers screamed. None of this made sense. You didn't get this kind of crazy maneuvering on a commercial flight, let alone on a private luxury jet where the pilot's job was to make the trip so smooth; none of them were supposed to realize they were even in the air.

Some pilots, however, were assholes on purpose. Maybe he didn't like rich people. Tiffany wasn't going to sit back and let this pilot fuck around with them. She should march up there, pound her fist on the door, and tell the pilot to knock this crap off.

And she intended to do so. Only now, suddenly, Tiffany felt lightheaded. Probably the sudden change in pressure. Goddamn this pilot. She wanted to knock his teeth in, but she also wanted to ease back into her seat, just for a minute. Just until her head cleared . . .

A bump woke her up. As did the breeze across her face.

A breeze . . . inside a jet?

Tiffany felt dizzy and nauseous. She saw that everyone else was still passed out in their leather seats. Nothing made sense. What, were they all drunk? Tiffany unbuckled her seat belt, stood up on shaky legs, and started to move toward the front of the plane. Ahead, weird, wild patterns of light and shadow danced across the tops of the empty seats and the door to the cockpit. The wind was stronger, as if the pilot had somehow cranked up the AC to full blast. A few steps later, Adams saw where the light and rushing wind was coming from.

The passenger door of the plane was open.

Oh, fuck me . . .

She grasped the tops of the seats closest to her and craned her neck to look outside. The tops of trees whizzed by, far too close to be real. This plane couldn't be flying this close to the ground?

Getting closer with every second . . .

Tiffany swallowed hard, then propelled herself forward, aiming for the cockpit door. Don't look outside, she told herself. Don't even think about what's going on out there. Get to the pilot. Ask him what the fuck is going on.

Once she reached the door, Tiffany pounded hard. She was going to open this door, FAA rules or not.

To her surprise, the door popped right open.

The next few seconds were a blur to Tiffany. She stepped into the cockpit to see a rush of green and brown filling the front windows, the array of instruments and flashing lights on the control panels, the empty pilots' seats, chairs gently rocking back and forth, a pair of headphones dangling from the stick. And a playing card of some kind, jammed onto a metal switch.

Tiffany was about to yell when the plane hit the first tree and then her body was flung forward, into the instrument panel.

He watched the crash from the ground a few miles away. All of his meticulous planning had paid off. There was the exhilaration of the perfectly timed jump. The recovery of the ATV, hidden in the brush. And a few moments later the plane went down, all according to plan. The fireball was beautiful as it bloomed out of the lush, green mountains.

chapter 40

Someone was already inside the basement lair by the time Dark returned home.

Probaby Graysmith. But Dark didn't want to take any chances. He recovered his Glock 22 from its hiding place under the floor, unwrapping it from oily rags and tucking it in his back waistband.

After pressing the button that opened the hatch in the floor, Dark aimed his Glock down the entranceway.

"Lisa?"

Weapon still in hand, Dark descended the stairs. After all—fresh insights or not—paranoia was still his friend. Graysmith was probably just sitting down there, working. But she also might have a gun to her head, held by persons unknown. Or Graysmith might be the one holding the gun, and it would be pointed up at Dark—even though there were far easier ways for her to take control. In his efforts to secure his home, Dark realized he'd practically invited in the biggest security risk of all: a member of U.S. intelligence.

Graysmith looked up from the laptop on the autopsy table. No gun to her head. No weapon in her hand. She blinked.

"You keep wanting to shoot me," she said. "I think there's something Freudian at work here."

Dark lowered the weapon, but didn't put it down. Not just yet. "Make yourself at home, why don't you."

"Where have you been?"

"Out."

"Not at Venice Beach, by chance?"

Dark said nothing.

"Hey, I'm just looking out for you," Graysmith said. "My goal is to keep you safe. Besides, it's not too difficult to track a man in a Mustang tooling around L.A. in the middle of the night. I still have some friends in LAPD surveillance."

Dark didn't reply. Somehow Graysmith knew he was at Venice Beach, but she made no reference to Hilda or the tarot card shop. Maybe she'd slipped some kind of GPS tracker onto his clothes, his wallet, his car. Could be anything, really, and short of stripping down and scrubbing himself under a hot shower, he'd probably wear it as long as she wanted him to. Fine. She could do what she wanted. But he intended on keeping Hilda—and her amazing, dead-on reading—to himself for now. Graysmith already had enough of his life on a microscope slide.

"Come here," Graysmith said.

Dark moved around the autopsy table that doubled as his desk to find that Graysmith was wearing a T-shirt . . . and nothing else. "Tell me what you're thinking," Graysmith said.

"About you being here in my house, uninvited, pretty much all of the time?"

Graysmith ignored the comment. "The first four cards. Where's this going? What's the killer's next move? Take a look at this."

As he moved closer to Graysmith, he could smell the fresh scent of her hair. She'd recently showered. Had she used his shower? Dark peered over her shoulder at the screen, which showed a map of the U.S., pinpointing the murders so far: Green in Chapel Hill. Paulson in Falls Church. The cards and killings made sense individually. But what connected them? As he stared at Graysmith's computerized map, Dark's brain started to force the pieces together.

Chapel.

Church.

A religious connection there? Was the killer mocking religion?

Then there were the three MBA students in Philadelphia. City of Brotherly Love. The Quaker City. Founded by people fleeing religious persecution. More religious themes. Then you had the senator in Myrtle Beach. No obvious religious connection, unless you consider it a sin to enjoy a special massage at an ocean-side resort.

Forget religion for now. Think about the locations.

"So . . . what are you thinking?" Graysmith asked. She turned to watch him, her eyes transfixed on his face as he worked things through. Her mouth opened slightly. Dark ignored her. He had to ignore her. Focus on the task at hand.

The locations were all within driving distances . . . to a point. There seemed to be no central hub. The murder trail climbed north, but then made an abrupt turn back south again. Why? Not convenience. It would be a pain in the ass to drive or fly back down to Myrtle Beach within hours of killing the three girls in that bar.

"I don't think we're dealing with a single perp," Dark said. "This is an organized team."

"Keep going," Graysmith said.

"Clearly there's a lot of planning involved. Surveillance and staging, at the very least. A lone killer would space these things out. Give himself enough room to operate. But that's not what's happening. Maybe one killer does Green in Chapel Hill, and the next is ready to strike in Falls Church. Then the first killer—or a third—travels up to Philadelphia. And so on. They all follow in close sequence, except for the second murder. Paulson. That was a wrinkle in their plan. They had to adjust."

"And now they've started leaving cards at the murder scenes,"

Graysmith said. "According to the Special Circs report, a Ten of Wand card was found on the tenth dagger in Garner's back. That's a big fuck-you, killing a senator and leaving a literal calling card."

"It's also a big change," Dark said. "Serials don't usually vary their signature. They have their patterns, and they live inside them. There were no cards found at the scenes of the first three murders. The crime scenes took the place of the card, the living embodiment of the cards. So why be crass now and leave a card? What's changed?"

Graysmith didn't respond at first. She chewed on a knuckle, typed in a URL, then turned the laptop to show Dark the screen.

"The media attention," she said. "This guy at the Slab, Johnny Knack, broke the story after the three girls in Philadelphia. Gave the killer—or killers, as it were—a name. TCK. Real cute, huh?"

"So they like the attention," Dark said. "Maybe that's what they wanted all along. Maybe they're not speaking to law enforcement. They could be trying to send a message to the world."

"So what's the message? What are they trying to say?"

Dark didn't respond. His mind drifted back to his personal reading with Hilda and how she'd compelled him to face the truth about his past. The message in the cards cut to his very soul in a deeply personal way. But how could that same message apply to anyone else?

She reached out and touched his face. "It's okay, Steve. You can relax. Like I told you before, I'm here to support you. To give you whatever you need."

Maybe if he hadn't been out all night, maybe if Hilda hadn't given him that tarot reading, maybe if his heart hadn't felt lighter than it had in years . . . maybe then Dark would have turned away, continued to seal that part of himself off from the rest of the world. But he stood still as Graysmith leaned into him.

"I'm hurting, too," Graysmith whispered in his ear.

chapter 41

There was no prelude, no foreplay, no conversation whatso-ever. Dark quickly pulled her shirt—actually *his* shirt, he quickly noted—up over her head before beginning a fren-zied exploration of her body. Graysmith tore at his clothes, too, commenting about the faint scent of incense on his shirt as she ripped it open. *So where were you in Venice Beach?* she tried to ask. But Dark smashed his mouth against hers, cutting off the comment mid-syllable. She quickly fought back, pinning him against the au-topsy table with her legs, unbuckling his pants, sliding them past his hips.

"I know all about you, Dark," she said. "I know what calms you. I know what excites you. Brenda Condor filed detailed reports."

"Don't," Dark said, feeling the anger in his blood. "Don't say that name."

"I'm sorry."

"Just don't."

Oh, Brenda Condor had fucked him good. He'd been vulnera-ble after Sibby's death—jonesing for the physical connection they shared. If Sibby was his narcotic, then Dark was a junkie, and Condor had exploited this when she was keeping tabs on him for Wycoff. She'd even told him: *I'm whatever you want me to be. Your psycholo-*

gist. Your stand-in girlfriend. Your fantasy wife. Your partner. Your slut. Whatever it takes to keep you focused. After that fiasco, Dark promised himself he wouldn't let it happen again. When he needed sex, he would seek it with anonymous professionals—not with anyone close to him, or who could potentially be close to him.

Like Graysmith.

But Dark told himself this was different. She wasn't fucking her way inside his mind; Dark was trying to fuck his way into hers. She kept everything hidden beneath a layer of confidence and arrogance and hurt and flirtation that all seemed scripted—too studied to be real. He wanted to reduce her to her real self and watch what came slithering out.

At least that's what he told himself.

Afterward, as they lay on the naked concrete floor, their bodies covered in each other's sweat, Dark remembered the last time he'd lost control like this, feeling his blood boil and allowing every moral inhibition to fall by the wayside. The last time he let reason slip away, and the animal part of his mind take over.

It had been the night he butchered Sqweegel.

A little while later, Graysmith finally broke the silence. "I know what you were doing."

"Do you?"

"Trying to break through to the real me, right? Look, the people in my field practically invented it."

Dark said nothing.

"It's not a criticism," she continued. "Believe me. It's welcome. My job is full of power plays and deceit and mistrust—and that's just on the surface. You have no idea the depths of some agendas and grudges. So any chance to break through all of that and reduce human interaction to something primal, something basic, something raw . . . well, I fucking get off on it. No matter your intentions."

Dark said nothing, which prompted Graysmith to laugh.

"Yeah, welcome to my fucked-up version of pillow talk. You don't even want to know the conversations I have in my head at night. Like right around this time, the middle of the night—what do they call it? Night terrors? The time the primitive part of our brains tells us we should be afraid, be very afraid, because there are predators out there in the night."

"Or inside, lying next to you."

"True enough," she replied.

At some point he relaxed enough to let himself drift into a low-level state of consciousness. He was still aware of his surroundings, and Graysmith's naked flesh next to his, her smell, the sound of her breathing. But he was able to turn off other parts of his brain enough to call it *rest*.

Something beeped. Graysmith bolted upright, scrambled for her phone, then climbed up to the laptop on the autopsy table.

chapter 42

Dark looked over her shoulder at the screen. The headline:

10 DEAD IN PRIVATE PLANE CRASH

The site: the Appalachian Mountains. He immediately thought of Hilda in her shop, flipping the fifth card: Ten of Wands. Ten victims. As Graysmith read through the initial reports—the same reports sent to Special Circs—she started making the connections.

"It's the Tarot Card Killer," Graysmith said. "Or one of them, if your theory of a team of killers is correct. According to a transmission picked up by the flight controller, the killer was on that plane, taunting his victims. Telling them exactly what was going to happen, what it would feel like to die."

"So he was on the plane with them?" Dark asked.

"According to this, yes. Right in the cockpit. Either he was the one flying the plane, or he had some kind of control over the pilot."

"And the plane crashed."

"That's the report at least. The aircraft was smoking. Why?"

"What kind of plane?"

"Pilatus PC-12, single-engine turboprop."

"You can't just eject out of a plane like that," Dark said. "Unless the killer wanted to commit suicide, he'd have an escape plan. Some way to parachute out." He considered this for a moment, ran a few scenarios through his mind. "Can you get me to the crash site? I mean, before Special Circs shows up?"

By air, Los Angeles was at least four hours away from the Appalachian Mountains. Comparatively, the crash site was practically in Special Circs's backyard—in the same state, no less. But Dark watched as the wheels in Graysmith's mind spun like crazy, making frenzied connections. Who did she know who had what she needed; how could she reach that person within the next sixty seconds; what would she have to do in return?

"Don't shower, don't even brush your teeth," she said. "Put on your pants and haul ass to LAX. By the time you arrive I'll have something arranged."

"Full access, like I had in Philadelphia?"

"Of course."

"Can you get me a weapon at the site?"

"I'll see what I can do. Now go."

Dark hesitated, unsure of the gesture he should make. Would she want a kiss? Would she want to even acknowledge what had happened? It had been so easy with Sibby. No thought required. It was as if they could read each other's minds. With Graysmith— God, listen to him, even referring to her by her last name. *Lisa. Her name is Lisa.* Fuck a woman, you really should start using her first name.

Graysmith looked at him, then nudged him in the side with an elbow.

"I'm not leaving," she said. "I promise you. Go. Now. Do what you do best."

chapter 43

Riggins and Constance were buying a couple of turkey sandwiches on the way to the Myrtle Beach airport for a ten A.M. flight when both of their phones buzzed. Two different Special Circs assistants were calling with the same grisly piece of news: private charter plane crash in the Appalachian Mountains. Ten dead; pilot missing. But most disturbing of all: It appeared to be the work of the Tarot Card Killer.

The first responders had discovered something on the plane that had clinched it. After exchanging glances, Riggins and Constance knew they'd heard the same things.

"This son of a bitch is on an accelerated schedule," Riggins muttered.

Constance held the phone to her ear. "I'm calling the airport now. We'll get as close to the crash site as possible. The fact that the pilot is missing says it all. He probably bailed mid-flight."

"Yeah," Riggins said. "And he could be anywhere now. Just like D. B. Cooper."

"True, but he may have left some of himself behind in the

cockpit . . . yeah, this is Special Agent Brielle, I want to speak to the pilot please. We need to be wheels up immediately."

While Constance made their travel arrangements, Riggins shoved his hands in his pockets. Nothing in them to fiddle around with. Not even a coin to flip. Nothing to do except wait. Wait while this sadistic bastard planned something else—God knows where. Maybe he should just bag the airport and go the nearest psychic shack. Had to be one in a tourist haven like Myrtle Beach, because that's where you find the best marks. Yeah, maybe he should march in there, slap down a twenty, and demand an emergency reading. Fuck the tarot cards, lady. Fire up the crystal ball. Show me everything like I'm fucking Dorothy in *The Wizard of* Oz. Or maybe you've got a Ouija board handy? It'd be nice to consult some of my ex-partners on this one, if they're not doing anything special in the afterlife. Then again, the way he treated some of them, Riggins expected their pale ghostly forms to go take a flying fuck at a doughnut.

The whole *occult* thing bothered him. People who hid behind mysticism were nothing more than con men, in Riggins's view. Smoke, mirrors, cards, thunder, light, all of that bullshit to obscure the truth: They were thieves who wanted to steal from you.

Only difference was, this thief wanted to steal *your life*.

Once they were buckled into their seats, Constance stole a glance at Riggins. When in these kinds of moods, the man was practically unapproachable. Gruff didn't even cover it. But now Riggins seemed positively lost in his own mind. Riggins had been this way since . . . well, if she was honest, since Steve left.

Constance didn't think Riggins—no matter what he said—trusted her in the same way. Riggins had plucked Dark from obscurity in the NYPD, brought him to Special Circs, where they'd worked closely together for nearly two decades. What did she and Riggins share, really? An awkward couple of months as partners? Constance knew Riggins would never see her as an equal. To him, she'd always be the assistant who got a promotion. Nothing more.

Still, Constance swore to always put the case first. Steve had taught her that. Put aside the personal bullshit, the politics, the jockeying, the brown-nosing, the interoffice politics . . . and focus on the work. Catching monsters was all that mattered.

Which was why she felt confident enough to turn to Riggins and say: "What about Steve?"

Riggins didn't react at first. He continued to stare out of the tiny oval window at the wet black tarmac.

"Riggins, I'm serious. We should call him in on this."

He turned, anger flashing in his eyes. "Dark? No fucking way. He made his choice."

"Doesn't mean you can't reach out to him."

"Wycoff's already freaking out about Dark being at these crime scenes. You want me to bring him back now, of all times?"

"Come on—when were *you* ever one to play by the book? He's practically begging to be involved. Why not use him as a resource? Off the record? We do this all of the time."

"Not with Dark."

What pissed Riggins off the most was that he knew Constance was right.

Part of him *ached* to bring Dark into this. Hell, Dark's mind was already on the case. Riggins had seen the tarot card pack at the house, and that was long before Knack had broken that connection in the media.

And if Riggins knew anything about Constance, it's that she wouldn't give up. She might seem to give up in the moment. But she'd find ways to keep picking at him, wearing him down, trying to scrape away at a *yes*. But Riggins couldn't tell Constance the truth. How could he?

The Steve Dark she idolized shared a genetic link with the worst serial killer they've ever encountered.

This wasn't hearsay, or a rumor, or even casual evidence. Riggins had run the test himself, lifting up Sibby's cold dead hand, running the stick under the nail as gently as he could. Sibby had fought for her life and the life of her newborn daughter with everything she had. She'd ripped through the freak's latex suit and gouged away a tiny piece of flesh. DNA, now at the end of the stick.

Originally, Riggins intended to rule out one horrible possibility: that Sibby's infant daughter had actually been fathered by this maniac.

But he'd ended up confirming something even more horrific.

He'd run the sample personally in the trace lab. If the monster had any relatives who'd ever had their DNA entered into the system, it would be revealed. The results arrived with a *ding*: seven of thirteen alleles were a match. *To Steve Dark.*

Riggins still loved Dark like a son. But he knew the violence the man was capable of. He watched it once, in that basement. Why had he left Special Circs?

Because he knew that, sooner or later, Riggins would discover the truth?

chapter 44

The sound of a girl screaming woke him up.

Johnny Knack bolted upright and saw something trembling beneath a stack of papers. The scream was his cell phone's e-mail alert. After the slaughter in Philadelphia, he'd assigned a Janet Leigh *Psycho* shriek to the alarm clock app. Yeah, it was juvenile, of course. But it kept his eyes on the prize.

Funny thing was, Knack hadn't even realized he'd fallen asleep. He'd spent a good part of the night working on a book proposal. Timing was everything. The murders were still ongoing; he knew that much. This Tarot Card Killer was just getting warmed up. Hell, how many cards were there in a deck? This guy, whoever the fuck he was, had staying power.

So Knack wanted to be ready to go. Book publishing was different now. Back in the old days you could putter around with an *In Cold Blood* or *Helter Skelter* or *Zodiac* for years and readers would happily wait. Not today. They wanted to be reading about a serial killer while the bodies of his victims were still slightly warm, and they wanted the cable movie already cast. Publishing had finally caught up and had become very good at producing insta-books, especially now that you really didn't even need paper or binding glue anymore. A friend of Knack's had knocked out a fifty-thousand-word quickie e-book about a tween star's sex-and-booze weekend binge at an Aspen resort that made it sound like *Fear and Loathing in Las Vegas 2: Loathe Harder*. The wretched thing had 130,000 downloads (and rising) plus a movie option, all for a weekend's worth of work. Sorry, Capote, old chap. You had it wrong.

Knack was determined to go one better. He wanted to publish a book while the murders were *still ongoing*. Four cards, six dead bodies—fuck, that was more than enough. Pack the thing with blood-soaked detail, add plenty of speculation here and there, plus some bullshit background on the cards themselves, and boom, you've got a book. Sequels unfolding live.

So maybe this e-mail was from one of the book editors he'd blitzed last night, teasing the project. Which would be awesome.

Knack reached for his phone with one hand, his breath mints with the other. His mouth was so rank, it even offended him. He popped a mint, thumbed the app. Nope, not a publisher. Message from someone called TCK.

"No fuckin' way . . ."

Knack opened it. Of course this was somebody screwing around with him, right? Had to be. Maybe even one of those fucking editors.

The message:

> I enjoy your work. Don't bother going to the mountains. The story there is a dead end. You want to be ahead? Go to Wilmington. Send a blank reply for more.

Mountains? That didn't make a lick of sense. Nor did Wilmington. But that's what creeped Knack out. This wasn't someone playing a joke—and if it was, the prankster had a predilection for the obscure. He should check the news sites, run a keyword search for "mountain" and "murder" and see if anything popped.

Knack didn't have to bother with a search. After he woke up his laptop, his home page—the Slab, naturally—already had the story, posted early this morning in its usual sensitive style:

MOUNTAIN: 10, BANKING INDUSTRY: 0

Westmire Execs Headed to Sybaritic "Retreat" Killed
in Freak Plane Crash in Moonshine Country

Knack skimmed the article with a nasty yellow ball of unease in his belly. If someone else was on this fucking tarot thing, he'd be ripping heads from neck stumps. But no. No mention of tarot cards, or any occult links. Just a weird rumor that the pilot was missing, and a joke that he probably bailed because he couldn't take his passengers' obnoxious coked-up behavior anymore. Maybe it was totally unrelated to the TCK.

But what if it wasn't? And what did he mean by "Wilmington"?

Knack picked up his phone, thumbed the REPLY button, and hit SEND.

chapter 45

Airspace over the Appalachian Mountains

D ark sat in the plush belly of a modified Gulfstream G650, the fastest business jet in the world. He overheard the pilot bragging that while the official top speed was somewhere around Mach 0.925, he'd personally flirted with Mach 1 on a few test runs. And while this $60 million plane had room for a dozen passengers used to luxury travel, Dark was alone. God knows how Graysmith had arranged the services of an aircraft like this on such short notice. Come to think of it, he didn't want to know. Strange enough that he was speeding to the site of a plane crash.

Mach 1, 2 or whatever—Dark didn't think it would be fast enough. Riggins was going to beat him to the crash site. Sure, his old boss would have to negotiate official channels—the FAA, the National Transportation Safety Board, Homeland Security, and the rest of the alphabet soup outfits who jumped all over a plane crash. But if Graysmith came through for him on the ground—like she did with this insanely fast plane—he might be able to sidestep all of that and take a look at the scene unimpeded.

Secondhand photos and reports were fine, but they weren't the same thing.

This might be his best chance at picking up the killer's trail.

As the Gulfstream landed at Roanoke Regional Airport, Dark imagined the Ten of Wands card in his mind.

The next card from his personal reading.

And yet again, the next card dealt by the killer. Or *killers*.

The Ten of Wands depicted ten long sticks in a bundle, held by a man eager to carry them to some unknown destination. Hilda told Dark the card implied a burden, requiring an almost superhuman effort to complete. The nearby village implied that the end of the task was at hand, as well as the sense that there can be no breaks, no rest at all, that the load must be carried.

According to Hilda, the man in the illustration was a symbol of oppression. A single man's will played out to the end of its strength and deprived of its magic. Someone had set this burden upon him.

Did the killer imagine himself as this man, carrying these ten souls to the afterlife? If so, he would have blinders on, focused only on his task, nothing else. There would be a clarity of purpose, a simplicity to his life. He would eat and breathe and sleep only to carry out his mission: to kill.

So even as Dark was transported by a white van to the crash site, he knew that the killer wouldn't be among the dead.

Maybe he jumped out of the plane. If so, he would have waited until the end, so he could watch the crash himself. All of the murders so far had been hands on; he wouldn't have done it by remote. He needed to be there.

As promised, Graysmith had delivered on the weapon, too. After they arrived at the scene, the driver wordlessly handed him a black hard case containing a Glock 22 with three extra magazines of .40 bullets—Dark's gun and caliber of choice. If he did encounter the killer out there in the wilds of the Appalachian Mountains, he didn't want to be caught defenseless.

The credentials sent to his cell phone got him past the perimeter and among the NTSB investigators and Virginia K-9 units. Dark saw that Special Circs was already here, as predicted. He recognized the vehicles, the license plates. Definitely from their auto pool.

Dark knew he'd have to stay on the perimeter. Which was fine. From even this distance, the plane looked intact, as if it had landed instead of crashed. The ground in this area was flat enough for such a landing—risky as it was.

After Riggins saw the wreckage of the crash site, he knew he needed a belt of whiskey. Maybe three. Instead, he'd have to settle for a smoke. A unit of NTSB investigators freaked out when they saw him reaching for his lighter. Riggins nodded, hands up, *fine, fine,* and moved farther away from the scene, lighting up and taking the tobacco smoke into his lungs, hoping to erase the taste and smell of burned flesh.

As Riggins lit up, he thought about the killer. This guy managed to parachute out of the damn plane . . . and what, none of the passengers said anything? They just stayed in their seat belts as the nutcase made his getaway?

No. That didn't make sense. He had to be using his military-grade knockout drugs again, just like he'd done with Jeb Paulson and the others. Once his victims were out, then he could take his time leaving the scene of the crime. Which would be obliterated by a massive fireball not long after, leaving no trace of his exit.

Or was there?

Riggins looked at the chopped-up brown earth and wondered if he followed it out to the edge, would there be footprints? No. You can't cover that kind of ground on foot. He'd have some kind of vehicle. A car. Motorcycle maybe. He needed to be looking for tire tracks.

And then he saw the skinny figure in the jacket, off in the distance.

About a hundred yards away from the crash site, Dark saw the first blood splatters in the dewy emerald grass.

Is this you? Dark wondered. *Did you injure yourself carrying your burden?*

He pulled a field collection kit out of his jacket pocket and quickly swabbed some samples. Maybe this killer had finally screwed up and left a piece of himself behind.

Riggins thought he was seeing things.

That couldn't be . . .

Dark?

chapter 46

Riggins darted forward, his feet sinking into the soft, wet mud. Somebody screamed his name—maybe Constance. He didn't care. S Dark was here, on the scene. There was no denying it now.

But how? The last time Riggins had seen Dark, he was still in Los Angeles. Unless Dark had developed precognitive abilities, there's no way he could have made it here, to the scene of the accident, so quickly. Hell, the plane had crashed only what—five, six hours ago? The only other explanation was that Dark *knew* it was going to happen, and was here waiting for it. Maybe even helped plan it . . .

Riggins didn't want to think about that. Push that shit aside, and focus on the important thing: taking Dark into custody. Lock him up in some concrete cell until Riggins got a handle on the situation. His only regret was not bagging him back in L.A.

The moment Dark saw someone running toward him, he knew it would be Riggins. The man wouldn't send anyone in his place. Not on a case like this. No matter that Riggins had just Ping-Ponged from coast to coast. His ex-boss would insist on being here, working the evidence, bagging the shell casings and spraying the carpet and escorting the bodies to a makeshift morgue nearby. Riggins was relentless. In that way, the man was still his role model.

Not now, though. Now, Riggins wouldn't understand. Wouldn't tolerate his presence.

Riggins would take him off the playing field without even blinking.

Dark quickly tucked away the last swab in a test tube, jammed everything into his pockets, then pulled out his cell phone from his other pocket. He speed-dialed Graysmith as he darted for a line of shrubs and trees about a dozen yards away. Probably the same path the killer took. Away from the plane, and out of sight.

"Graysmith, I needed to get the hell out of here. Where's the driver?"

Fast as he ran, the years of beer and poor eating and smokes and everything else Riggins jammed into his veins caught up with him. The guy vanished into the trees, leaving Riggins with his palms on his thighs, hunched over, struggling to breathe. Damn near vomiting, if he was going to be honest about it. Guy was younger, faster.

Guy. Right.

Just say it.

You know it was Steve Dark, don't you?

Now Riggins had a tough decision to make. Either sound the alarm on Dark, send a team of men and dogs out into those trees, and have him chased down and cuffed immediately. Or do nothing, knowing that he possibly let a killer go.

Riggins thought back to the day Dark quit Special Circs the first time, not long after the slaughter of his foster family. They'd been standing together in a parking garage when Dark told him:

"I'm on the brink. I'm walking a fine line. If I don't get out now,

I'm gonna be going to the dark side, and you're going to be out catching *me* at nights."

Riggins had nodded, told him that he understood. But clearly, he hadn't.

Because now Dark's own prophetic words had seemed to come to pass . . .

Riggins stopped himself. Was that what he *really* believed?

If Dark was a killer, would he really linger around the scene, watching everyone work? Why not watch from the trees?

When Riggins reached down for the cell clipped to his belt, fate made the decision for him. The phone buzzed.

chapter 47

Washington, D.C.

Johnny Knack loved the stack of hundred-dollar bills in his jacket pocket. But when it came down to it, journalism was still about connections.

If he could somehow trade what he knew for access, he'd finally have the lock on his book proposal. No one else would be able to claim exclusive access to the files of Special Circs. Never mind that Tom Riggins would never agree to that in a billion years, but even the slightest hint of official cooperation could be spun a lot of interesting ways.

"The killer's been in contact with me," Knack said.

"Knack," Riggins said. "Leave me the fuck alone."

"You're at the crash site now, aren't you?"

Silence on the other end. Knack knew he'd stunned him with that one.

"You're there because it's the Tarot Card Killer, only nobody knows it's him. Far as everybody else is concerned, just another sorry group of rich people bit the dust. But I know the truth. And how would I know the truth if the killer hadn't told me?"

"I'm not confirming anything."

"You don't have to, Agent Riggins. I don't want anything from you. I'm calling to *give* you something. Because I think the killer told me where he was going to strike next."

"Where?"

"Happy to tell you . . . but just promise me one thing."

"Fucking knew it."

"Nothing major, I swear," Knack said. "Just promise that we can keep talking. Or at the very least, you can keep up your stony silence while I run things by you. If something's way off, grunt. If I'm on to something, sneeze. Come on, you know what I mean—*All the President's Men*–style. Flag in the potted flower on the balcony, and all that."

Knack listened. The silence thrilled him. Riggins believed him! He was considering the proposal . . .

"Where you right now, Knack?" Riggins asked.

"At home."

"In Manhattan, right? Same Village apartment you've rented for the past three years? Well, listen up, shithead. In about five minutes a couple of Federal thicknecks with buzz cuts are going to be walking through your front door and seizing your laptop, your notes, your files, your underwear and sticking it into little plastic . . ."

"Wilmington, Delaware."

Well, Knack had gone for it; Riggins shot him down. This wasn't the first gamble he'd lost.

"What's that?"

"Where the killer told me he was going to strike next."

"He, huh?"

"Well, I don't know. He . . . or *she*, whoever, started texting me this morning."

"I want copies of everything," Riggins said. "And I want a tech there to look at your laptop."

"Whatever you need, buddy."

"We're not buddies."

Knack thumbed the red button. Fucking *ass*.

That's okay. It was still a free country. And Knack felt a trip to Wilmington, Delaware, coming on.

VI

five of pentacles

To watch Steve Dark's personal tarot card reading,
please log in to Level26.com and
enter the code: pentacles.

EX LUX LUCIS ADVEHO ATRUM

FIVE OF PENTACLES

Wilmington, Delaware

Too much, too little. That was Evelyn Barnes's life.

Like tonight—a unit of sick kids filled to capacity, and three of her nurses calling out sick. If it were up to Barnes she'd fire them all. This wasn't the first time. But there was still a severe nursing shortage, and replacing these three meant Barnes might be stuck with three newbies with poorer training and an even bigger sense of entitlement. That was the real problem: the next generation, the twenty-somethings. Indulged by their parents, given nothing but treats and straight As despite their actual performance, and with this strange idea in their heads that they should all be paid outrageous salaries for barely adequate work. Worse yet, they would hold out for better paying positions, even if it meant not working for six months or a year. Why not? Mom and Dad would still take care of them at home.

Barnes knew the story firsthand—her own daughter was a nurse. She hadn't worked in a year.

Meanwhile, too little sleep had taken its toll on Barnes's face. She used to be the pretty one—the petite, chesty, funny blonde ev-

211

eryone bought drinks. Even better when she'd finally admit to being a nurse (as if the scrubs weren't a dead giveaway). Working with kids? Even better. Men were apparently still very much suckers for the whole nurse-patient fantasy.

It had been a long time since someone offered to buy her a drink. Men in bars (as if she ever saw the inside of a bar these days) were more likely to suggest a vacation or, at the very least, some Advil. Her dirty-blond hair was nothing more than something to be pulled back and clipped so it wouldn't hang down in her face. Her tired, puffy face, her weary eyes completely drained of life. What the hell had happened to her?

Too much, too little. Same old story.

There was a small bodega across the street that catered almost exclusively to the doctors, nurses, and hospital staff. Barnes slid her money across the counter, the owner slid back a pack of her favorite smokes. The habit was growing more expensive by the day, and it flew in the face of the advice she gave every young person she met—*and you're never going to smoke, right, Josh?*—but what the fuck. Everyone needed an outlet. Barnes tapped one out of the soft pack, lit it, and looked over at the hospital. The institution that had sucked away more than two decades of her life.

Not that she regretted it. She'd helped a lot of kids, held a lot of worried parents' hands. She wouldn't trade that for anything. Still, she wished the stress would let up, just for a little while.

As she stood and smoked, a bracing wind cut through Barnes's body. The sky was a dark gray. Looked like snow up there. Weird for late October. She should have worn her coat out here.

All too soon her smoke was finished. Back to the floor. Barnes flicked the stub to the ground, smashed it with a foot. *Don't smoke, Josh, and never, ever litter,* she thought to herself. Then someone grabbed her from behind.

A thick forearm was suddenly around her neck, choking off her air. Christ in heaven, Barnes thought. A drug addict? The more she squirmed, the angrier she became. God, even this neighborhood was turning to shit. Who the hell would mug a nurse outside a children's hospital?

But then Barnes heard a clear, calm whisper in her ear. The voice sounded muffled, as if speaking from behind a hollow mask:

"Shhhh . . . How does it feel to be helpless? To have your life slip away from you, no matter what you do to hang on to it?"

This was no addict. There was no trembling, no stink of the streets. This person was huge, strong.

As Barnes struggled, the white nurse hat fell from her head. Barnes tried to cry out but then she inhaled and saw gray, and then nothing at all. This was it.

No. There was more.

She was in a hard bed. Stiff sheets. Was it over? Was she a patient now? No. She couldn't be. They wouldn't have put her in one of the beds in the children's hospital. Why was it so dark in here? And cold. So, so cold. She reached out into the darkness and her knuckles immediately smashed against a hard surface.

What was going on?

Her fingertips tried to make sense of it. A cold, hard surface was directly above her, just inches away. Now that she groped around in the dark, she realized she was pinned in from the sides, too. When Barnes felt the bed beneath her, she realized that there were no sheets or mattress. It was the same cold surface.

All at once she realized where she was and why it was so cold. . . .

She was locked in a morgue freezer.

Evelyn Barnes screamed and pounded at the roof and thrashed her tired legs trying to make as much noise as possible, praying someone would hear her before she froze to death. She tried to stay calm but couldn't. Who would? Oh God, please let me out of this; I promise I'll do whatever you want; I don't want to die like this; oh God, who's going to take care of my daughter; please, God, LET ME OUT OF THIS FUCKING BOX . . .

But no one could hear her screams. It was growing late, and the morgue—like the rest of the hospital—was horribly understaffed.

chapter 48

Constance couldn't imagine the horror of being left to freeze to death in a morgue body locker.

Yet the Tarot Card Killer had done just that to Evelyn Barnes. Abducted the veteran nurse right from her own hospital. Drugged her into unconsciousness. Placed her body on a sliding tray. Then he'd locked her in tight, knowing that at this hour, no one would hear her cries for help. Not in this tiny morgue, buried at the bottom of the hospital.

And Constance knew that Barnes had cried, screamed, kicked, punched, and clawed at her cold steel prison. Her hands, elbows, knees and feet were horribly bruised. She had fought to the very last . . . knowing exactly what was happening to her.

She couldn't imagine.

Why punish someone so severely? What had Evelyn Barnes done?

Or was this murder like the others—horribly random?

Riggins had sent Constance to Wilmington alone. At first she thought it was punishment. But then Riggins explained the tip Knack had received, and that he wanted his "best" ready to pounce if something happened. That made her feel good. The smallest scrap of praise went a long, long way.

Especially when faced with a nightmare like this.

And there was little doubt that this was the Tarot Card Killer at work again, barely a day after the plane crash. He'd placed a Five of Pentacles card beneath Barnes's back, the one place where it wouldn't be disturbed no matter how much she thrashed and kicked and punched. The logistics worked, too; it was easy to imagine him bailing at the plane crash scene and traveling up to Wilmington. The drive would be six hours, maybe.

Constance called to mind the card: two sick people, an adult and one child, making their way across a snowy field. Their bodies are bandaged; their clothes inadequate for the weather. They are poor people. The childlike figure hobbles along on crutches. The adult wraps a shawl tightly around her frame, her back to the child—ignoring him and his obvious difficulty. Behind them: an ornate window of stained glass, with five pentacles arranged in a treelike shape, fiercely yellow and glowing.

So the nurse—Evelyn Barnes—was supposed to be the woman? So who was the child? No child had been reported missing from the hospital. Thank God.

Like Martin Green, there was torture involved. The same couldn't be said for all of the killings. Paulson was taken out quickly. Same with the three MBA students. Their bodies were arranged, but there were no signs of torture. With the senator, there was a methodical stabbing—definitely torture. The passengers in the plane, however, were knocked out, asphyxiated, burned. Methodical. Impersonal.

Constance realized: *With some of the murders, the killer had a personal stake.*

Some were examples, impersonal: Paulson, the students, the passengers.

But the killer had a personal reason to hate Green, to hate Senator Garner, to hate this nurse here.

So what tied them together—an economic expert, a politician, and a nurse in a children's hospital?

chapter 49

Dark returned to California. At long last, he had a piece of hard evidence in his possession. Now it was just a matter of making sense of it.

Over the years he'd collected spare pieces of gear from the Special Circs crime labs—outdated incubators, centrifuges—and built his own thermal cycler and sequencer from mail-order kits once he quit the job. The makeshift setup was a far cry from what some crime labs had at their disposal, but it would give Dark what he needed. There was no court of law, no chain of evidence to preserve. The DNA would merely fill in another piece of the story.

After isolating the samples, incubating them, separating the DNA from the debris, expanding the sample, Dark loaded it into the sequencer. While he waited for samples to finish the analysis process, Dark thought about the killer's seemingly random strikes.

That was the thing: Ninety-nine point nine percent of the killers in the world did not choose their victims at random. There was *always* a reason.

Movies and crime novels were always showing you assassins who let you live or die at the flip of a coin or card, heads or tails, red or black. But that's not how it worked. Somebody wants to go through all of the trouble to take your life, they're going to have a good reason. They're going to have a plan.

They're not going to leave it up to a deck of fucking tarot cards. Right?

Dark couldn't shake the idea, though, that larger forces were at work. Let's say the killer woke up one morning and decided, *Okay, going to give myself a reading, and then I'm going to kill a bunch of people according to that reading. I'll find people who match the cards, and it'll freak people right out . . .*

Even if that was true, then the killer was still engaged in the action of *selection*. Of all of the men in the world you'd want to hang, why Martin Green in North Carolina?

And surely he chose Jeb Paulson because Paulson introduced himself into the killer's world.

If Jeb hadn't shown up—if, say, Riggins had gone in his place— what would have happened? Would the killer have targeted Riggins just the same? No. Couldn't have been Tom Riggins, who was many things, but he was no "fool," in the sense of the tarot cards. He was no fresh soul awaiting rebirth. Christ, you couldn't get more battle-hardened if you tried.

Again, it was *selection*. Not a random flip of the card.

But then how do you explain the three girls in the bar? Utterly random, no connection whatsoever to Green, other than their field of study: business. Just like the plane crash victims—execs at a lending company. And just like the senator, who was involved in banking and regulatory information. A little bit of a stretch, but not too much. You could draw a nice clean line through all of the victims, except for Paulson.

There was a digital *ding* from the sequencer. The samples were ready.

The blood was animal.

No link to the killer.

chapter 50

Dark sat in his basement staring at the ceiling in a near-fugue state, unaware of the passage of time. There were tiny fragments of fact in his head, and his brain struggled to piece everything back together again. The hard evidence was useless, just like it had been with Sqweegel.

There was a new e-mail *ding* on his laptop. A report forwarded from Graysmith. There had been another TCK killing, just one day after the plane crash. This time: a nurse named Evelyn Barnes in Wilmington, Delaware. Dark clicked open the file and knew within a few sentences that he was reading a report from Constance Brielle. Her reports were crisp, precise, and smart. If he was going to cheat from anyone's homework, Dark would pick Constance's every time.

Constance had quickly identified the tarot card being referenced: the Five of Pentacles. Then again, the killer (or killers, Dark reminded himself) hadn't been sly about it. Whoever had shoved Evelyn Barnes into that cold morgue drawer had left a copy of the Five of Pentacles card in there with her.

Again, another card from Dark's supposedly "personal" reading. What had Hilda told him about the card?

The card denoted hard times and ill health. Like the hard times after the brutal slaying of Dark's foster parents, and he told Riggins he was quitting Special Circs. *You were right*, he'd told Riggins. *I care too much*. Was that why this nurse, Barnes, deserved her punishment? Did she care too much? Or, like the image of the old woman on the card, did she blithely ignore the pain of those around her?

Stop it, Dark told himself. Focus on the case. Think about the killer. Not your own life. You've already been through that.

But everything kept returning to the cards.

How could this be possible?

Maybe life isn't what he thought. Maybe it was predetermined, and we only had the illusion of free will. Maybe the Celtic cross was a glimpse behind the façade of the machinery, giving you a glimpse into how the universe really worked.

But if that was the case, what were we but helpless pawns? Just tiny bugs, trapped in an upside-down glass, trying like hell to scramble up the surface only to slide back down. Soon, the air would disappear. We all die. We have the illusion of a vast world beyond the glass, and we gasp our last breaths thinking we'll be the ones to figure out how to escape the glass. No one does, however.

No one person in the history of the world has ever beaten the glass.

Dark picked up his cell, thumbed the number, and waited. C'mon, Hilda, answer. *Please*. Instead an automated voice mail picked up.

"This is Madame Hilda at Psychic Delic. I am unable to answer your call right now . . ."

When the beep sounded, Dark left a message. "Hilda, you helped me more than I can tell you. But I have more questions, and I really need to see you. Tomorrow morning, if you can. I'll be at your shop at nine sharp. Please be there."

chapter 51

"Tell me you're close to making an arrest on this thing."

Riggins stared at Norman Wycoff. "We're throwing every available resource at it. But I've got six crime scenes with seventeen victims in six different jurisdictions. You want to give me more resources, I'll happily take them."

The secretary of defense had shown up in his office, not content to call or send e-mails with a billion little red exclamation points next to the subject line. On television, the man looked like America's most passionate defender. His bulldog tactics were allegedly part of his charm. Such things were getting a little long in the tooth, and American citizens were tired of hearing about extraordinary rendition, waterboarding, hoods, electric shocks, dogs, and genital torture. Wycoff looked weary from constantly defending himself, let alone running his department. Sometimes he took his frustrations out on whoever happened to be close by.

"Do you understand that Homeland Security wants to treat this as a terrorist act?" Wycoff said now.

"Good," Riggins said. "Let them chase this down."

Wycoff sneered. "You don't want to avenge your own, Tom? That's not like you at all. I think you're losing your edge."

"Like I give a fuck what you think?"

Wycoff turned a strange shade of purple that Riggins couldn't quite identify. From the look on his face, you could tell he wanted to strike back with something. Anything. He'd even go for the testicles. Finally, he spat out: "Maybe Steve Dark was the only member of Special Circs who knew what the hell he was doing."

Riggins twitched. He couldn't help it, and cursed himself.

Not because of wounded pride—Wycoff didn't know shit about how Special Circs really worked. No, it was because Riggins had Steve Dark on the brain. To a man like Wycoff, Dark was like the hard steel pistol shoved inside a suburban father's nightstand. You deny you have it. Deny you fantasize about using it on home intruders. You tell your liberal friends you wish you could just chuck it in the river. But you can't seem to bring yourself to do that, either. In fact, you're glad that pistol is within close reach. Since Dark had left Special Circs, Riggins hadn't had a peaceful night of sleep.

Wycoff caught the twitch. He narrowed his eyes.

"Is he working this for some other agency?" Wycoff asked.

"No," Riggins said.

"So what's he doing sniffing around the crime scenes? I thought he was busy lecturing bratty UCLA kids."

"Yeah, Dark's a teacher now, but he's also been a manhunter for the last two decades. You just can't shake something like that aside. He told me he was just curious. I told him to fuck off, and I think he will. But last time I checked, this was still a free country. You want to stop him from traveling?"

Wycoff seemed to ignore that. He started for the door, pausing only to deliver his final thoughts on the matter:

"Just get me results. And make sure Dark doesn't get in the way. Or I'll remove him myself."

The place was Banner's favorite—a diner on the outer fringes of D.C. that served the most ridiculous pancakes ever. Pancakes with chunks of candy. Pancakes with jalapeño and habanero peppers. And Banner's choice this morning: pancakes made with little hardened morsels of pancake batter inside. Constance—who was blessed with a metabolism of a long-distance runner—ordered three fried eggs, three sausages, a double order of buttered toast, and three small glasses of vegetable juice. Riggins stuck with black coffee, dry toast. His stomach was a mess. Better to lay something basic down there to get him through the morning.

"You really should try a bite of this," Banner said. "It's like an infinite loop of pancake."

"I need your help," Riggins said. "Off the books."

"I thought a free breakfast was too good to be true," Constance said.

Riggins's head swiveled to the right. "Hey. Who said anything about free?"

"So what is it?" Constance asked.

"Dark."

"I knew it."

Banner, mouth full of a cooked and uncooked pancake, said: "You mean Steve Dark? I thought he was, like . . . gone."

"He is," Riggins said. "But I think he's not quite able to leave the job. The Tarot Card Killings have put the hooks in him. Only problem is, Wycoff's not happy he's involved. So, for our friend's sake, we need to find him, and keep him out of harm's way."

"Isn't he in Los Angeles?" Banner asked. "So, like, he'd be easy to find, right?"

Riggins ignored Banner and turned to Constance. "You remember Wycoff's special little friends, right?"

No matter how much he drank, Riggins certainly couldn't forget them—even five years later. To Wycoff, they were probably no more meaningful than his landscapers or the people who cleaned his bathroom. But to Riggins they were nightmares personified. Five years ago, Wycoff had threatened to have Riggins killed unless he performed a certain "favor" for him. He'd backed up that threat with a black ops unit comprised of men in black silk masks and sharp needles. Wycoff called them "Dark Arts." They were men who would kill upon demand.

"Yeah, I remember," Constance said. "Charming guys."

"Well, I don't want them making Steve's acquaintance. But that's exactly what's going to happen unless we rein him in ourselves."

"Right. So what do we do?"

"Find Steve. Put him in protective custody until this tarot bullshit blows over, and Wycoff forgets about him. Catch the Tarot Card Killer."

Riggins thought, but didn't say out loud: *Pray to God that Dark and the TCK aren't the same person.*

Banner paused, fork full of pancake. "So you want us to hunt the world's best manhunter?"

"That's the idea," Riggins said.

chapter 52

T he streets of Venice Beach were unusually quiet—a morning storm was gathering itself off the coast. As Dark approached the shop, paranoid thoughts raced through his mind. Maybe he *should* have had Graysmith do a background search on Hilda. His gut told him to trust her, but his gut was a weird little organ sometimes. Dark knew he might be walking into a trap.

Still, Dark opened the door and stepped inside. Only this time, a strange face waited for him inside at the circular reading table. Dark hair, haunting eyes, and a narrow frame.

Dark said, "I'm looking for Hilda."

"*Heeeelda,*" the woman repeated, turning the name around in her mouth. "I'm sorry—I don't know whom you are speaking about?"

"The woman who owns this place?" Dark asked. "She was just here a few days ago. I came in for a reading."

"Who are you?"

"Steve Dark."

The strange woman's expression changed. So did her accent, which vanished instantly. "Sorry about that. You had the look of a cop about you. Hilda called me up the other day. She didn't say why, just that she needed me to mind her shop for a few days."

"Did she leave a number? It's very important that I reach her."

"No," the woman said. "But maybe I can help you. I am very skilled with the cards. Hilda herself guided me during my earliest readings."

She took Dark by the hand, practically pulled him into the shop, guided him to a chair, sat him down, started shuffling the cards. Somehow the shop looked different without Hilda inhabiting it. The candles seemed like mere props. The counter? Full of junk to sell to tourists. Suddenly Dark was in just another tarot shop in Venice Beach. Five bucks to tell you your fortune, your future. Then you could wander back out and hit a college bar on Abbot Kinney, do some shots, ponder your fate.

"What's your name?" Dark asked.

"I am Abdulia. Don't you want a reading? I told you, I am very skilled."

"No, I don't want another reading. One's plenty. I just need answers."

"Then please, sit."

This woman wasn't Hilda. She didn't recognize him. She had no idea what he was talking about.

But Abdulia surprised him by saying, "You're wrestling with fate."

"Yeah," Dark said. "You might say that."

"I don't know what Hilda may have told you," Abdulia said, "but let me give you some advice. On the house. Many men have driven themselves insane trying to fight their fates, to change their destinies. But that's foolish. Fate is bigger than you can possibly imagine. You cannot veer from the path it has assigned you."

"So what then?"

"You do your best to embrace it. That is the only way to peace, my friend. The *only* way."

chapter 53

Dark climbed behind the wheel of the Mustang and rocketed through the streets of Santa Monica feeling more confused than ever. The peace that Hilda had seemed to have given him was shattered. Even more troubling: Where was Hilda? What caused her to suddenly bolt from Venice Beach? Dark called Graysmith.

"I need you to find someone for me. Her name is Hilda."

"Hilda what?"

"No idea."

"Do you have a phone number or a social?"

"Just a business address. She owns a shop on Venice Beach. At least I think she owns it. The place is called Psychic Delic. If you can check the lease on the property, you might dig up an owner's name, and then—"

Graysmith sighed. "Please don't tell me you're consulting a board-walk tarot-card reader on this case. Because you know, we can do a whole lot better. I can put you in touch with tarot experts at the best universities. Experts who have been studying the world of the occult their entire professional lives."

"That's nice and all, but I like to work it street level."

"Who is she? What did she tell you?"

"Just help me find her. Trust me, she's important."

Graysmith sighed, like she was disappointed, but resigned to the task at hand. Find this woman named Hilda, who could be pretty much anywhere in Southern California

"Hilda, Psychic Delic. Anything else?"

"No, that's it."

The line stayed open for a few more seconds. Dark didn't know what else to say, and apparently neither did Graysmith. Finally the cell disconnected the call. Dark tossed the phone into the passenger seat, pressed down on the accelerator. Graysmith would find Hilda. She'd no doubt compile a deep, invasive profile in no time. Which was good. Because Dark had a feeling that Hilda was the only one tapped into the real story. Graysmith may have the secret world at her fingertips, but she couldn't tell him what Hilda knew.

Dark thought about the cards she'd so casually laid down on the table. In all of the cases he'd ever worked, never had it been laid out so clearly, so simply. Hansel and Gretel were dead. Here were the bread crumbs.

Of course, he had more than bread crumbs.

He knew the next card:

The Wheel of Fortune.

Think like the killers. You've dealt the card, and you've interpreted it. Just like Abdulia said: *Embrace your fate.* So how would the killers interpret the next one?

The Wheel of Fortune, Hilda had said, was one of the trickier cards in the Major Arcana. The card about destiny, a turning point that could swing either way at a moment's notice. Like when Dark met Sibby, at random, in a Santa Monica liquor store. The Wheel of Fortune, Hilda argued, was at play there. A chance meeting that had changed both lives forever.

Did that mean trying to guess the killer's next move was as futile as trying to guess the next number on a roulette wheel?

No.

The killers were working on some kind of pattern. These were not random. These *meant* something to them.

Dark's mind went back to Graysmith's computerized map of the country, on which she'd pinpointed the murders so far. There was no discernable geographic pattern, no focal point from where the killers would strike. Dark tried visualizing the killers, whoever the fuck they were, slapping the cards down on a giant map of the United States, nodding at each other, murmuring in agreement as they—

And then it hit him. *Son of a bitch.*

Why hadn't he seen it before?

VII

wheel of fortune

To watch Steve Dark's personal tarot card reading,
please log in to Level26.com and
enter the code: fortune.

EX LUX LUCIS ADVEHO ATRUM

WHEEL OF FORTUNE

Las Vegas, Nevada

Kobiashi wanted room service *now*. He dropped enough coin in this place to have simple requests such as a pile of fresh towels, a magnum of Cristal, and a stack of pornographic DVDs to be delivered to his room *immediately*. But it had been five minutes; two minutes longer than he'd expected and three minutes away from the order becoming pointless. Kobiashi was restless. When you reach your seventies, every moment counts. He was about to pick up the room phone when there was a timid *knock knock knock* at the door.

Good. He would have someone to yell at in person.

But when the door opened, a woman was jabbing a gun at the side of his head, forcing him back into the room. She kick-slammed the door behind her.

"You're a gambling man, aren't you," she said.

Kobiashi was in shock. "Wait . . . what?"

"I said, you're a gambling man. True?"

Immediately Kobiashi understood. He'd been too public. Someone had taken note of him. He was being robbed. Oh God, he was being robbed.

"You don't have to do this," Kobiashi stammered. "I won't say a word. I can make it worth your while."

"Shhh, now. You're a gambler, yes?"

"I'm a businessman . . ."

"Who visits Las Vegas at least a half dozen times a year," the woman finished for him."

"Please."

"Do you recognize this type of gun?"

"No, no, please."

"This is a .44 caliber Smith and Wesson. An American weapon. We're in all-American Vegas, so I figured we'd need an all-American weapon."

"Please leave my room, I beg of you. You can have the cash in my wallet. I have a lot in there."

The woman shook her head. "No, no, no, Mr. Kobiashi. You don't understand. The management sent me. I'm here to help you play the ultimate high-stakes game. You like to take chances, no? That's why you attract all of those crowds. They love to watch a high roller."

"Please—"

She was moving around him, fingertips touching his shoulders, gently sliding across the area between his shoulder blades, gun still in her other hand. "You've heard of Russian roulette, right?"

"No . . ."

"Haruki. Don't lie to me."

"Yes. Yes, I have."

"Take off your pants."

"What?"

The woman frowned. Moved the gun closer to Kobiashi's face. Ran the barrel up his nose until it was pointed directly at his right eye. Kobiashi shuddered. He'd never seen something so deep, so fearsome. He knew he'd forever associate the smell of oiled metal with the smell of death. That is, if he was to live through this night.

"Okay, okay, I'm taking them off. I'm taking them off!"

As he unbuckled his pants, the woman continued speaking, massaging Kobiashi's face with the gun.

"Did you know there's a Japanese version of Russian roulette? Sounds crazy, but it's true. High school kids play it. Only it's not bullets. It's sex. The kids get together and have sex with each other—no condoms, no pills. They don't stop until each boy has done every single girl, and vice versa. Every prick in every different hole."

"Please . . ."

"Now the thing is," the woman continued, "some of the girls will be fine. It's their time of the month, or they're not ovulating, or whatever. Unless these boys have given them crabs or the clap, they're totally fine. But some of the other girls—the ones whose cycles are lined up just right . . . well, they might get pregnant. Bang. They lose. Thing is, these kids aren't dumb. They've prepared for it, actually. They all put in a bunch of yen, like five thousand each, and they call it *insurance*. If one of the girls becomes pregnant, they take some of the insurance and use it to pay for an abortion. Do you believe that? And this is your country, Haruki."

His pants were off now. "I agree, it's horrible."

"Playing stupid games with a potential life like that . . . a total innocent . . . God, it's just . . ."

"Horrible. Please . . ."

"No, it's not horrible. You know what it is, Haruki? It's cheating. That's not the way you play Russian roulette. You play for keeps. Put all of the money in the world in the pot, it doesn't matter. The ultimate gamble is where you put your own life on the line. Do you understand me?"

"Yes, I understand."

"You sure?"

"Yes, yes!"

"Good," the woman said. "Then let's play."

———

The woman guided his old, naked body into a chair, then pulled a desk chair up close so that she could sit merely inches away. She cracked open the revolver and showed him that the cylinder was empty. Kobiashi felt himself flush with anger. All this time . . . an empty gun?

But before he had a chance to react, she pulled a single bullet from a pocket in her maid uniform, slid it into a chamber, then slammed the cylinder shut and pressed the barrel up against Kobiashi's forehead.

"One bullet. Five chances to live. You ready?"

"No! Don't do this!"

But the gambler in Kobiashi weighed the odds. They were in his favor. He could strike this crazy bitch in the face and even if she managed to pull the trigger, odds were she'd click on an empty chamber.

Was he willing to take that risk?

She took the choice out of his hands.

She pulled the trigger and—

Click.

Nothing.

A million beads of sweat broke out on Kobiashi's forehead. He exhaled, and it was the sweetest, most exhilarating sensation in the world. But once again, before he could make a move, the bitch had the gun open and now added a bullet to the mix.

"You're a lucky man," she said, spinning the cylinder. "So let's up the ante."

The gun went to his forehead. Kobiashi couldn't help but freeze in terror at the gaping hole before him. Two out of six. A one in three chance of death. Those were not good chances at all with so much on the table. Namely, his life. And then—

Click.

No relief this time. Only rage and fear and a sick feeling that his life was slipping through his fingers and there was nothing he could do about it except watch as she loaded yet another bullet into the cylinder, spun it, clicked it shut.

"Now the game gets interesting," she said. "But you like these kinds of odds, don't you? You like living on the edge. But who cares what you've laid on the line? You've got plenty money where this came—"

Click.

"STOP IT, GODDAMNIT!" Kobiashi screamed. "WHY ARE YOU DOING THIS TO ME?"

As she added still another bullet, the woman said, "It's not you, my dear Kobiashi. You're just an example. Could have been any-body. You just came to our attention."

The barrel of the revolver returned to his sweat-slicked forehead.

"Four bullets now. The odds are suddenly in the house's favor, wouldn't you say? How lucky do you feel, Mr. Kobiashi? Are you in your comfort zone yet?"

"PLEASE DON'T, PLEASE DON'T, PLEASE DON—"

Click.

The adrenaline was nearly blinding him now, rendering him deaf. He hardly saw her load the weapon with a fifth bullet, barely heard the spin of the cylinder, the awful horrible sickening *click* of it snapping back into place. Hardly felt the cold steel pressed up against his face.

But Kobiashi was able to see the cylinder, and the empty cham-ber outside the gun, away from the firing pin. You didn't have to be able to count cards to know that this meant only one thing.

There would be no more clicks.

Haruki Kobaishi knew that any moment now he could die. And as it turned out, he didn't even hear the *cl—*

chapter 54

Las Vegas, Nevada

D ark looked up at the towers of the old Vegas hotel. They tried to blaze bright in the night sky, but it was no match for its brighter, gaudier, louder, slicker cousins. Dark knew that back in the day—the Howard Hughes days, the days between RFK buying it at the Ambassador and Watergate—this grand old Egyptian-themed casino was an elaborate CIA front. What better way to funnel money to various operations around the world than a casino? You had a constant drunken swirl of tourists, sex, slot machines, drugs, gluttony, and nothing but sand and mountains as far as the eye could see.

Many people thought Vegas was a glitzy mirage-turned-real, powered by cold, hard American cash and sheer can-do American spirit.

But Dark knew the truth. It was just an awfully convenient location for an amazing number of deals, white and black, overt and covert—then, just like now.

Which was why Graysmith had little trouble making a few phone calls and laying the place wide-open for Steve Dark. Her colleagues had their fingers all over the Strip; it didn't take much to gain access.

The amazing part was that Dark's hunch had been right. The Wheel of Fortune card, laid down smack dab in the middle of the American Southwest. Where else but Las Vegas? Just thirty minutes ago he'd told Graysmith over the phone: "I'm taking a charter to Vegas. I think that's where this Tarot Card Killer is going to strike next."

"How do you know that?" Graysmith asked.

"The guy's working geographically. Like he's laying the cards down on a map of the United States. He's already worked through the cross on the East Coast. Now he's headed west."

"That's shaky—at best," Graysmith said. "Even if you are right, each tarot reader uses a different layout. How can you be sure he's laying those cards down in Nevada? Maybe he'll strike next in Europe while we're dicking around in the desert."

"The next card will be the Wheel of Fortune."

"And how do you know that?"

Dark remained silent. It sounded ridiculous, even to him. *Because a five-dollar tarot card reader in Venice Beach told me.*

"Trust me."

"In my line of work, *trust me* is code for *fuck you.*"

"Just check your sources for recent murders," Dark said. "Almost definitely sure we're talking about in or near a casino. The big ones. Where the high rollers flock."

"I'll get back to you," Graysmith said.

After minutes later, Graysmith sounded almost gleeful when she called back to report: "Nothing. We've got beaten prostitutes, a full drunk tank, and a lot of meth dealers taking shots at each other, but nothing that matches the profile of the TCK."

"That just means it hasn't happened yet. Keep looking."

As the small jet raced over the Mojave Desert, Dark stared at the image of the Wheel of Fortune card he'd loaded on his phone. The crime scenes so far always referenced details in the cards. Sometimes overtly, sometimes in subtle but meaningful ways. The illustration on this card was one of the more fanciful ones in the deck: pale clouds swirling around a wheel inscribed with arcane symbols. Winged beasts and an angelic figure poring over tomes. A snake, with its whiplike tongue extended, writhing next to the wheel. A jackal-headed man—Anubis, the guardian of the underworld— either gliding along the outside of the wheel or being crushed by it. A sword-carrying sphinx resting on top, overseeing all, yet nearly faded into the background of the sky.

During the plane's descent, Dark put it together. When Graysmith called back, he didn't give her time to open her mouth.

"Something happened at the Egyptian, didn't it?" Dark snapped.

There was a stunned pause, and then:

"How the hell did you know?"

The Vegas CSI techs beat Dark to the scene by mere minutes. They were snapping on gloves and unlocking gear when Dark stepped into the room, and immediately the lead homicide detective marched over, telling Dark to get the fuck out. Dark showed him the credentials that Graysmith had sent to his phone. This only further enraged the homicide dick—a balding lifer who looked like he wanted to take a swing at Dark. But his colleagues pulled him aside. "Not worth it, Muntz," someone muttered. The Vegas guys were used to jurisdictional skirmishes; this was just another one in a long line of them. Immediately, Dark realized that alienating these guys was a mistake. This crime scene was no more than thirty minutes old; their killer was no doubt still in the city. The Vegas PD would be more of a help than a hindrance at this point.

"Look," Dark said. "I'm not here to interfere. How about walking me through what you know?"

"What, you want me to do all of your work for you?" Muntz, the homicide dick, asked.

"I'm not here officially."

"You guys never are. But let me ask you this. How the fuck did you get here so fast? We only caught the call a few minutes ago."

Because, Dark thought to himself, *I'm finally listening to Hilda.*

chapter 55

The victim's name was Haruki Kobiashi. He had checked in the night before—the first of six nights he planned to spend here in Sin City. The man was a notorious high-stakes gambler—a Japanese whale, in Vegas parlance—who made a spectacle of his time at the roulette wheel. When Kobiashi won, he roared, and the crowd roared with him. Beautiful babes would rub his bald head for luck. When he lost—which was often—it was the stuff of high tragedy, and he would inevitably need to console himself with eight-hundred-dollar bottles of Cristal, which he would share with his audience. Kobiashi's legendary spending and losing sprees were a better show than Wayne Newton's.

Such massive losses and bar tabs would be the ruin of any mortal millionaire. But Kobiashi was worth 6.1 billion yen and rising, thanks to his empire of cheap clothing emporiums. Kobiashi, of course, wore the best, and never wore the same item of clothing twice. In his philosophy, according to *Forbes* and *Fast Company*, material goods and cash were transient, and not meant to be held on to for long. He was doing his best to keep the worldwide economy humming.

Until tonight.

The economy would have to limp on without him.

Kobiashi had been found on the floor of his suite, stark naked. He'd been shot in the face at point-blank range. A steel .44 Smith & Wesson and a pair of blood-splattered dice were a few inches away on the desktop. Five bullets in all. Four still in the chamber. One inside Mr. Kobiashi's skull.

chapter 56

30,000 feet above Nevada

When the three of them agreed to keep close tabs on Dark, Constance got the idea to follow the money. Credit card transactions, car rentals, beer bodegas, everything. If Dark spent a traceable dime, they'd know when and where. She was also working on satellite surveillance of his home and car.

Meanwhile Josh Banner hit a database of traffic cameras trained on West Hollywood and LAX, entering Dark's make, model, and license plate number. Within a few minutes they had multiple hits, tracing Dark's movements down the 405 all the way to a parking garage, where a credit card transaction revealed that he'd purchased a last-minute flight to Vegas—just a quick hop over the Mojave Desert.

Their own plane was descending into McCarran now.

"Strange place for Dark to visit, isn't it?" Constance asked.

"Yeah. Dark's not exactly a gambling man," Riggins said. "Hell, he used to roll his eyes at me when I used to play the ponies."

"So why here? What kind of lead does he have that we don't?"

"No idea," Riggins said. But he was thinking to himself: *Because Dark's in league with the killer—some crazy woman with big breasts and a gas mask fetish. So of course he'd know where to strike next.* His only regret now was not putting constant surveillance on Dark from the moment he had left the man's house in L.A. If it had been anyone but Dark—if Riggins had done his fucking job and treated Dark as a *person of interest*—then maybe he could have stopped all of this sooner.

"Guys," Banner said, thumbing his smart phone. "I think I know why he's here."

chapter 57

Vegas likes to keep its eye on you, Dark thought.

They say what happens here stays here . . . but that's the point. It stays here, and *they know all about it*.

Every bet you place, every plate you take from the stack in the hotel buffet, every drink you're served, every drink you leave behind . . . they're keeping track. They know how much time you spend on the floor. They know how much time you spend in your room. They know, because they track your universal key card.

The only two people to enter Mr. Kobiashi's penthouse suite in the past twenty-four hours were Mr. Kobiashi himself and a bellhop named Dean Bosh. As a valued guest of the Egyptian, Mr. Kobiashi's suite was prepared just the way he liked it. Buckets of shaved ice, an array of flavored vodkas, and an absurd quantity of shelled nuts. According to the hotel, Bosh entered the room three times. First, an hour before Kobiashi's arrival. Then upon his arrival. And finally, about fifteen minutes before he died.

"Find this Bosh," Muntz told his team. "Now."

Within minutes they found him—bound and disoriented in a supply closet on the top floor, amid bottles of booze and toilet paper and towels and shampoo. Bosh couldn't remember who he was or where he was, or even what day of the week it was. As a result, he had no idea who'd taken his key card. Bosh apologized deliriously, then began to sob. Whatever knockout drug he'd been given, the stuff was clearly still wreaking havoc on his nervous system.

Meanwhile, Dark accompanied Muntz down to the private hotel security stronghold, located on a phantom sixth floor. The Egyptian had cameras for show, where patrons could see them. Those video feeds went to central security office on the ground floor. Dark knew those feeds would be useless. The killer had taken great precautions to avoid being caught on tape so far. Why give away the game now?

However, there was a second, more elaborate set of cameras—a holdover from the hotel's CIA glory days, recently updated and digitized. A series of pinhole cameras covered every possible public area, along with the interiors of certain rooms. Kobiashi's suite was not one of them—whales were afforded certain perks, like privacy. But the outside of his suite? That was fair game.

"Right there," Dark told the tech manning the video bay. "Bring it up."

The image showed a skinny figure with dark hair, wearing a hotel uniform. Was it male or female? Hard to tell from the angle. The figure was taking great care to avoid showing his/her face to the cameras, and that meant holding his/her body in a slightly awkward position.

"Can you pull that up a little closer?"

"Not too much," the tech said. "The cameras are small, and for that we sacrifice some clarity."

"Okay. Keep it rolling."

Just before the mystery figure reached the door, the head turned, face to the camera. The image was blurry, but now you could see the shape of the face, as well as the cheekbones. It was a woman.

Dark squinted and tried to recognize the features. There was something strangely familiar about them. At first, the hyper-paranoid voice in his brain said *Lisa Graysmith*, but that wasn't right. Dark tried to match the features against other women he knew—Constance Brielle, Brenda Condor . . . okay, now he was being insane. If he looked long enough, he'd start seeing Sibby's face in those features, too.

"Get me a copy of the highest res image you've got," said Dark. "I can get it analyzed."

"So can we," said Muntz. "Our guys are really good at this stuff, you know."

"No doubt," Dark said, "but I might have access to a different set of toys."

chapter 58

In years past, whenever Johnny Knack rolled into Vegas, it almost always meant a puff piece. Interview some vapid celebrity in a suite, or by an over-chlorinated pool, or in a dark velvety hotel bar, or some other ridiculously clichéd location. Knack hated Vegas, to be perfectly honest. Other cities were whores, but they had a quiet dignity about them. Vegas practically gave you a handjob on the way in and shook you down for a penicillin shot on the way out. There was very little a writer could do with Vegas. Even the great Hunter S. Thompson had to make shit up.

But not now. Vegas was no longer the gaudy whore. Now she had a shiv in her Gucci clutch.

Knack's phone buzzed in his hand. Another text.

GO TO EGYPT

The texts had started this morning, God help him. Little messages—all of them obscure at first. Until he tuned into their delirious form of logic. The sender was speaking between the lines.

TO FIND THE LIGHT YOU MUST FIRST SEEK THE
DARK

THOSE WHO CLAIM TO GIVE COMFORT CAN HURT YOU
THE MOST

And so on, making Knack think he had a loon on his hands.
Light and dark? Comfort and hurt? What the fuck—was this a
meth addict reading him nonsense out of a fortune cookie? But
then this anonymous texting "source" starting giving him details on
the slaughter of that nurse in Delaware, stuff that checked out later
with a few well-placed hundred dollar bills to the Wilmington
Police Department. This was either the killer or someone who
knew the killer's every move.

Abruptly, the source told him to fly to Vegas. And now here he
was, being led around by the ear. *Go to Egypt.* What the fuck did
that mean?

One look at a cheap handbill, though, clued him in. The Egyptian
Hotel and Casino. Of course.

After hopping into a cab and giving the driver a hundred dollar
bill to get him there as fast as humanly possible, Knack saw that he
was already too late. Vegas PD all over the place, with the usual
bright lights and chaos of a crime scene's outer perimeter. What
now? Did his mystery texter expect him to pull some Jason Bourne
shit and make his way into the hotel?

Knack thumbed in a reply:

IN EGYPT NOW

Then he waited. The number of his mystery texter had a 559
area code, which meant Fresno, California. Which probably meant
he wasn't hiding behind a neon sign somewhere, sniper rifle trained
on his head. Hell, Knack had seen *Red Dragon*. You start messing
around with a psycho, sometimes you ended up crazy-glued to a
fucking wheelchair, talking to a guy with freaky false teeth.

No, Fresno could mean that he was dealing with an honest-to-

God source, and not the killer himself. Who could it be, though? A concerned relative or friend? Somebody looking for a payday at the end of this all—a greedy Deep Throat? Didn't matter. As long as the information was good.

Knack's phone vibrated in his hands. A response.

SOON DARK SHALL GUIDE YOU

Fucking great. More riddles. More light and dark stuff . . .

And then it hit him. Dark. Oh God, he was so dense sometimes. He thumbed back:

DARK MEANING STEVE?

A new story bloomed in his mind. Why didn't he see it earlier? Steve Dark wasn't investigating the Tarot Card Murders. *He was the prime suspect.*

chapter 59

Graysmith opened the van door. "You don't ask a lot, do you?"

Dark squeezed in past her. "You offered."

"You won't believe how many chips I've cashed in over the past week."

"This is Vegas, isn't it?"

Dark knew his request wasn't completely ridiculous. If Graysmith was right and this was still a CIA kinda town, then it wouldn't be too difficult to scrounge up the latest Face-Tek software from some agency in the Greater Las Vegas area. Face-Tek was a program that used biometrics—the structure of your face, the shape of your irises, width of your mouth, curve of your nostrils—to identify you, even if you tried to obscure your identity. Most people didn't know that you could just as easily be identified by the shape of your ear as you could by a fingerprint. Special Circs had received a Face-Tek upgrade not long before Dark left the agency; that version had been impressive, reconstructing the sharp image of a face out of a grayish mush of pixels. He hoped Graysmith would have access to the same—or something better.

He needed to see that face.

Dark handed her the flash drive with the footage from the secret security cameras. Graysmith plugged it in, then called up the program. She hesitated for a moment, as if she had forgotten where she was, what she was doing.

"Let me," Dark said.

"I don't use this stuff all that often," she said, standing up.

"You have people for that, right?"

Dark swung himself into the seat. Again the paranoid part of his mind screamed at him: *She's hesitating because it's her on that recording. She's letting you figure it out, then she's going to shoot you in the kidneys while you're distracted.*

Using the touchpad, Dark dragged the footage into the Face-Tek window, cueing it up to the moment when the mystery woman looked at the camera. Instantly, measurements were made, processed. Extrapolations were made. Years ago, it took a skilled artist countless hours to rebuild a human face from a buried skull. Now, it took a computer a few moments—and you didn't even need a skull.

Soon, they had their answer.

There was even a hit on a national database.

Her name was *Abdulia Maestro.*

chapter 60

The police band was alive with chatter about Kobiashi and the tarot card. Another murder, right on the heels of the last. Nothing fancy about this one, though. A Japanese gambler, naked, one bullet in his head. Shit, Riggins thought. For Vegas, this was positively sedate.

Still—there was the possible Steve Dark connection.

As they sped toward the Egyptian, Riggins called Vegas PD. He was old buddies with the night-shift supervisor of the local CSI team—who immediately put him in touch with the detective in charge. Yeah, Dark had been there at the crime scene. In fact, he'd just left a few minutes ago, with a copy of the security footage, said he had a way to enhance it. What, didn't he check in? Say—didn't you guys send him out here in the first place?

Riggins couldn't ignore the evidence now. Dark had been spotted near at least four of the seven scenes—Paulson's apartment building, the bar slaying in Philly, the plane crash in the Appalachians, and now here, in Vegas—the whole time insinuating himself into the mix without so much as a plastic badge from a box of breakfast cereal.

Now he was leaving the scene of a murder, evidence in his hands, to do God knows what with. Was Dark trying to cover his tracks? Or worse, was he keeping little trophies of his Tarot Card Murders?

Riggins hated to think it, but there was a pretty good chance that Dark was not only involved in these slayings, but the mastermind behind them all.

Dark had *killer* in his blood, right down to his very DNA.

Once Riggins allowed himself to go there, and ran through the crimes in his mind, the events of the past week snapped into place with alarming ease. Martin Green's hanging/torture murder? Easy enough for Dark, especially knowing the entry and submission methods of a monster like Sqweegel. Paulson's murder? Even easier. Paulson idolized Dark. Paulson would trust him immediately. The three MBA students in the bar? Dark was a handsome enough guy to lure them into the ladies' room, smart enough to spike their beers, strong enough to string them up. The senator? Another cakewalk, with knives that Dark could have ordered—or had custommade—years ago. The plane crash? Now that was tricky. Dark wasn't a pilot, but he suddenly appeared on the scene, seemingly out of nowhere, like he'd fucking parachuted himself in. The nurse in Wilmington? Simple, with plenty of time left over for a flight to Santa Barbara, a drive down to Burbank, and another flight to Vegas. Dark had pretty much lived out of planes for the past five years since the Sqweegel murders; flights were as second nature as bus rides for most people.

What tripped Riggins up were the whys.

Why the fuck was Dark doing all of this?

On some level, Riggins understood. He'd been through a living nightmare not once, but twice. Two families slaughtered, essentially, in front of his very eyes. Anyone could snap. Let alone someone with Dark's genetic makeup.

So why?

Why wait five years to launch this spree? Was he just playing along, catching minor monsters while plotting his own masterpiece when the time was right?

All the beers they'd drunk together, food flipped on grills, late-night talks about life and God and fate and everything else . . .

Fuck it.

The *whys* could wait.

The mission now was to take Dark off the board.

Let someone else psychoanalyze him, study him, poke and prod him, whatever. The only thing he owed the world was putting Dark somewhere he couldn't hurt anybody. If you looked back at the balance of their lives together, the people they'd saved, the monsters they'd caught—it would be enough. It would have to be.

chapter 61

Dark leaned away from the image on the flat-screen monitor as if she could reach out and slice his throat.

It was Abdulia. The second tarot card reader. Five bucks, tell you your fate. *There is no escape from your fate. It's bigger than you.* "I know her," Dark said quietly.

"The killer?" Graysmith snapped, reading over his shoulder. "Who is she?"

"I think her name is Abdulia. She was in a tarot card shop in Venice Beach, but I'm sure that she's moved on by now."

"She must have been tracking you, too, just like Paulson," Graysmith said. "Your name, after all, has been all over the news."

"Damnit," Dark muttered as he realized it was true. He'd even given Abdulia his whereabouts when he called to Hilda the night before and left her a voice message. He'd even left an exact time. Dark felt a knot of unease in his stomach. By merely visiting Hilda's shop on a whim, he'd put the poor woman in the crosshairs of a psychopath. How long had Abdulia been watching Dark? Since his visit to the Appalachian Mountains? Since Philadelphia? D.C.? Apparently she had watched Dark just like she'd watched Jeb Paulson. Saw him at one of the crime scenes. Followed him back to L.A. . . .

But how? How could she follow Dark and still pull off this series of murders?

Graysmith began typing furiously on her laptop. Dark assumed she was plugging the name "Abdulia Maestro" into every secret search engine she could, and within minutes she'd have the woman's complete history on the screen—date of birth, social security, education, immunizations, voting records, tax filings, medical, dental, vision records, everything. Everything except the most important thing.

Why.

"I've got it," Graysmith said. "Finally, a real connection."

Dark turned around, snapping out of his reverie. "What is it?"

"Abdulia Maestro and the nurse—Evelyn Barnes. They met each other, at least once. Barnes cared for Maestro's sick child. A boy, terminal case of bone cancer. He died last year."

"In Wilmington?"

"Yeah. The children's hospital."

"If Abdulia believed that Barnes was to blame for her boy's death, then there's our motive."

"But what about the previous cards?" Graysmith asked. "What's the point? Why Martin Green? Why Paulson? Why the girls in that bar? It doesn't make sense."

"Abdulia's telling a larger story. Everyone she killed was for a reason." Dark remembered her words in Hilda's tarot shop. Abdulia had told him directly she was *embracing her fate.*

Then he remembered his original theory about the killer working as part of a team. Abdulia couldn't be doing this alone. There would be too many miles to cover.

Dark asked, "She had a boy—is she married?"

With a flurry of keystrokes, Graysmith started cracking open files. Indeed, Abdulia had a spouse: Roger Maestro. Graysmith downloaded sealed military records, juvenile criminal records, all based in Baltimore where he'd grown up an angry, mean dude. Construction worker. She speed-read the basics to Dark. Roger had married Abdulia seven years ago; had their only child, a boy, one year later.

"I'm pulling up everybody connected to the boy's death—doctors, other nurses, case workers, everybody."

"Did you say he was a construction worker, based out of Baltimore?"

"Yeah."

The mention of Baltimore tripped a circuit in Dark's mind. He thought about his trip to Philadelphia. "Has Roger Maestro ever worked a job with someone named Jason Beckerman?"

"The suspect in Philly," Graysmith mumbled. "Goddamnit. Let me check the union records . . ." More frenzied typing. "Yeah. For most of the past year."

That was it, Dark thought. Roger Maestro had killed those girls in the West Philly bar posing as his coworker Jason Beckerman. The two men probably had an almost identical build; Maestro could easily have hand-picked him out of the whole construction crew. Before heading out to the bar, though, he'd stopped by Beckerman's room (at around nine, just like the second witness had reported), dosed him, taken some of his clothes, then headed out. Beckerman would be out until morning. By that time, the Philly PD would be knocking down his door, and Roger Maestro would be long gone.

They had the names of the killers. They even had the next card: *The Devil.*

The image on the card was of two lovers, stark naked, heavy chains looped around their necks, both of them tethered to a pedestal, on which sat a cloven-hoofed, winged, and horned monstrosity. One hand raised in a strange split-fingered salute; the other lowered with a flaming torch in its grasp.

So if the naked lovers were Roger and Abdulia—who was their tormentor?

"Do you see any religious affiliation?" Dark asked.

Graysmith tapped more keys. "Roger was raised Catholic."

"The son's burial?"

"Catholic cemetery. Last rites given by a priest—Father Warren Donnelly."

"In Wilmington, Delaware, right?"

Dark thought about the layout of the tarot cards on a map of the United States. The Celtic cross in the East was finished; no reason for the Maestros to return. The next three cards—the Devil, the Tower, Death—would be placed out here, in the West.

"Wait . . ."

"What?" Dark asked.

"He's since been transferred—to Saint Jude's in Fresno, California."

And then the back doors of the van suddenly popped open.

chapter 62

Constance and Riggins had made a promise to each other: No matter what, they wouldn't kill Steve Dark.

Both of them had chased fugitives long enough to realize that when cornered, people could be utterly unpredictable. Not a single member of Special Circs would admit it, but the best policy was to shoot first, let the lawyers sort it out later. This unspoken policy took effect not long after the Sqweegel murders. Many suspects were brought in dead. Riggins was forced to publicly question each case, but privately applauded them.

More than five years ago, such a thing would have horrified Constance. But she had lived through Sqweegel. And to be honest—by the time Constance and her colleagues had a monster cornered, they were assured of its guilt.

With Dark, however . . .

Constance didn't know what to think.

As usual, Riggins was keeping his mouth shut. But he didn't need to say a word. Constance was good at connecting the dots on her own. The Steve Dark she knew, the man who had trained her—and for a brief while, had loved her—well, he was gone. Something else was inhabiting his body now. Maybe it had happened when he watched the monster kill his wife. Maybe a little of the monster got out of Sqweegel and made its way into Steve.

Constance held her Glock in the standard two-hand grip, playing everything according to the manual.

But there was nothing in the manual about forcing open the back doors of a van and fully expecting to shoot a man you loved

—once loved—

in the arm or leg, hoping it was enough to put him down, but not make him bleed out.

"Ready?" Riggins asked.

Constance nodded.

They found the van thanks to Banner, who'd tapped into the Vegas traffic cams and pinpointed Dark's rental vehicle, which was parked on the same level as this white van. Cameras inside the parking garage showed Dark bypassing his own rental and stepping into the van with an unidentified female. Constance couldn't help but burn a little at that. He'd found someone else to team up with him on this insane investigation.

There had been no time to call reinforcements—no FBI, no Vegas PD, no SWAT. Doing things by the book could give Dark the time he needed to slip away. Constance and Riggins had a silent understanding. He was their mess. They needed to clean it up.

Riggins did the honors. Hand on the silver handle, silently mouthing a count—

One . . .

two . . .

chapter 63

"It's over, kid," Riggins said, aiming his Sig Sauer at Dark's chest. "Step out quietly, hands locked behind your head— you know the drill."

Dark had a hard time believing what he was seeing. His ex-boss, pointing a weapon at him. Constance, by his side, her Glock 19 trained on Graysmith. He'd been on the other end of this kind of thing hundreds of times in the past. Now Dark knew what it felt like to be pinned down by the FBI, trying to explain yourself to people in bulletproof vests, fingers trembling on the triggers.

"Riggins, what the fuck are you doing?" Dark asked. "Trust me, this is not the time."

"Out of the van, buddy. Don't make this something ugly. We can talk on the flight back home. There will be plenty of time to explain."

Dark said, "I'm not going anywhere with you."

"No need for the tough guy act in front of your girlfriend here."

Graysmith put her hands up and glanced over at Dark. "Let's all calm down, okay?" Then, turning back to Riggins: "Look, we're all working for the same thing. You'll see that if you give us a chance to explain."

"Oh, you're going explain it to me?" Riggins asked. "Yeah, that'll be great. I can't wait. Maybe you'll want to start with who *the fuck* you are."

"You don't understand," Dark said. "We know the identity of the Tarot Card Killer. We traced her here to the Egyptian. She's working with an accomplice."

Graysmith glared at Dark—the look a wife gives a husband when he's said too much. Dark was genuinely puzzled. Fine, they wanted to operate without red tape or the usual departmental nonsense. But the gig was up. And the two best manhunters Dark knew were standing right here. If he could just explain the situation, the four of them could work together. The TCK would be history.

"Let's just go with them," she said.

As Dark and Graysmith climbed out of the van, Riggins and Constance kept them covered. Would they actually shoot if he made a break for it? Dark wasn't sure about Constance, but he knew Riggins would. There was hurt and sadness in the man's eyes, and Dark had no idea why. Couldn't still be about leaving Special Circs, after all of this time . . . could it?

"We don't have time for this," Dark said bitterly. "The killers are still out there."

Riggins pulled on Dark's shoulder and then shoved him against the van, cuffs already in his hand, Glock in the other.

"Yeah," he said.

Dark reluctantly put his hands behind his back. It didn't matter now. He could tell Riggins about Roger and Abdulia Maestro, and then Special Circs could call in the cavalry to apprehend them before they put the Devil card into play.

Then he heard something snapping—and a sharp cry.

As Dark turned, he saw Graysmith slam a flattened palm into Constance's throat. Constance struggled to breathe but held on to her weapon, staggering backward. Riggins turned and pointed his Sig Sauer but a second later it was flying out of his hands.

"No!" Dark screamed.

Graysmith was doing it all—disarming both of them with quick, violently efficient moves that left both Riggins and Constance on their knees, gasping for air, clawing at the ground.

Strands of hair fell into her face. "We don't have time for this," she said, as if that explained everything.

"You can't . . ."

"Let's go. There's a reason I went to *you*, Dark, and not Special Circs. They'll never catch these bastards, and you know it. Can you live with more innocent blood being spilled while you're debriefed in some conference room in Virginia? Come on."

Dark gave one last glance to his former partners on the concrete floor as the van peeled away, locking eyes with Constance. The pain she was feeling was probably bad—but it was nothing compared to the look of utter betrayal in her eyes.

chapter 64

Fresno, California

After torching the van and switching cars three times, swapping license plates each time, Dark and Graysmith drove through the night—six hours, nearly four hundred miles. South on 15, then 58 West and 99 North. Dark steered the stolen SUV in stony silence through the shadowy California desert while Graysmith used her laptop to continue compiling dossiers on Roger and Abdulia Maestro. After a few hours she finally looked up, as if she'd just tuned into his anger.

"You know, I didn't hurt them," she said.

Dark said nothing.

"Honestly. I'm not Jet Li. I just temporarily removed their ability to breathe. They'll be fine. We had to get out of there."

"You don't know them. They would have helped us."

"I believe that. Tom Riggins and Constance Brielle have done good work over the years. But this is out of their control. Special

Circs won't be able to do shit about the Maestros until this is all over, and they've slapped down their last card."

"What do you mean?"

Graysmith smiled. "Why did you leave Special Circs? Don't answer that. I'll tell you why you left. Because no matter how hard you worked, you felt like you were wrapped up in procedural bullshit and constant distractions from Wycoff and his peers, right? Sometimes you thought that if only you had a little more freedom, you could put more of these monsters behind bars. Well, let me fill you in on a little secret: It's amazing you accomplished anything at Special Circs. The moment Wycoff started waving his dick around, Special Circs became a joke. Something to trot out at law enforcement conferences."

"We stopped a lot of killers," Dark said quietly.

"You weren't supposed to. The fact that you kept taking these monsters out really pissed certain people off. Steve, there's a part of the government that doesn't want you going after some of these killers. Because they don't see them as killers. They're potential assets."

"Assets," Dark said coldly.

"I could show you a report about your nemesis, Sqweegel, that would make you want to storm the Pentagon with a sawed-off shotgun. This report talks about how Sqweegel could have been *weaponized*. Imagine an agent with his capabilities? Sneaking into any crevice, anywhere in the world? Some guys in my department were practically cumming in their pants thinking about it."

"That monster killed my wife."

"Yeah, and someone like him slaughtered my sister. Which is about the moment when disillusionment set in for me, personally. Why do you think we're doing this? *Because nobody else can.* Not even your friends Riggins and Brielle."

By the time they arrived in Fresno, it was late. No time for any rest at all—even thought Dark's entire body was crying out for just a few minutes of downtime. They had to see this priest and warn him—and figure a way to catch the Maestros in the act.

Dark agreed that he should be the one to talk to the priest. Meanwhile, Graysmith would scope the church and rectory—for all she knew, the Maestros were already here.

chapter 65

Las Vegas, Nevada

By the time the shock wore off, Knack had already e-mailed it to his editor in New York—the second biggest story of his career:

FBI STUNNER!
FORMER AGENT SOUGHT AS "PERSON OF INTEREST"
IN TAROT CARD MURDERS, INSIDE SOURCES CLAIM

The first biggest story? Well, that would be when Knack filed Steve Dark's jail cell confessions—the tell-all to end all tell-alls.

But no, the shock wasn't because of the material. It was the identity of his "source."

Tom Riggins, head of Special Circs.

Even more incredible, Riggins had called *him*. Told him he needed to spread the word about something immediately—on deep background, of course. But Riggins had promised: Help us catch him and you'll have all of the access you need. The old buzzard had seemed disturbed to discover that Knack was in Vegas, too—but for the time being, he swallowed it. Watch the tough old worm turn. The game was different now, because Riggins needed Knack.

The details Riggins wanted leaked:

That a former agent named Steve Dark—famous for the Sqweegel murders five years ago—was now wanted as a "person of interest" in a series of homicides the media (*c'mon, Tom, it was us! It was US!*) dubbed the "Tarot Card Murders." Dark is believed to be in the company of an unknown female subject, description attached, also a person of interest in the case. Do not approach. Call the tip line if you see either, mostly likely in the Southwest or California areas.

Knack also pried some more out of Riggins about the Kobiashi murder—the strange game of Russian roulette the billionaire had been forced to play. The fact that he was buck nekkid when he played it.

The big question now, though: Should Knack tell him about his Mystery Texter? Or was that a card better off left in Knack's back pocket?

And would the Mystery Texter be happy or upset with this latest development?

Knack waited for his cell phone to buzz. Any second now . . .

chapter 66

Father Donnelly was unlike any priest Dark had met before. Still in his early forties, short black hair, and with a friendly face and an acid black humor about him. God knows what his parishioners thought. When Dark had knocked on the rectory door in the middle of the night, Donnelly had taken his arrival with good humor, considering it was almost ten at night and the story Dark hurriedly told him bordered on the insane.

"So let me get this straight," Donnelly said, dressed in slacks and a ribbed T-shirt, short stub of a cigarette tucked between two fingers. "You're a former FBI manhunter now working freelance, and there's a pair of psychopaths who want to kill me—but I can't confirm this with the FBI, because they're now after you, because they seem to think you're involved with one of the psychopaths. Do I have that right?"

"That's pretty much it."

"Okay, good. Come on in. You a bourbon man, by chance? I've got a bottle of Four Roses somewhere."

Donnelly led him to a small office just to the side of the main hallway. The office would have been described as spare, had it not been jammed with books—in shelves, in great piles on the green-gray carpet. Donnelly's desk was littered with more books, legal pads, pencils, and pink rubber erasers. Not a computer in sight. Not even a phone.

"I was working on my homily," Donnelly explained. "I tend to obsess over these things, even though I suspect most people tune me out until I start leading the profession of faith."

"Then why so much effort?"

"Ever hear the story about Creedence playing Woodstock? They went on at . . . well, around *this* time of the morning, and John Fogerty noticed that everybody was asleep. All except for one guy in the back, flicking his lighter, cheering them on, saying *Don't worry about it, John, we're here with you*. So that's me. Playing for that one guy in the church with a lighter."

"A priest who listens to Creedence," Dark said.

"Better than when I wore eyeliner and listened to the Cure."

Dark couldn't help but smile.

"You were raised Catholic, weren't you?" Donnelly said. "I can tell by the way you look at me. There's still a glimmer of respect, buried somewhere deep in that brain of yours. You don't look at me like I'm going to try to rape the nearest available child."

Dark nodded. "Father, I'm serious about this threat. Your life's in danger."

"What would you have me do?"

"Let me protect you."

"From what, exactly?"

Dark explained that his suspects were Roger and Abdulia Maestro, that they had a little boy who had died in Delaware about a year ago. A look of recognition, then sadness, spread across the priest's face. The memory was painful.

"Of course I remember them. It was only a year ago. That was a horrible loss. But I can't believe they would be responsible for something like . . . well, what you're alleging."

"You know," Dark said, "I've been chasing monsters for twenty years, and that's exactly what I hear from most people after a neighbor or a friend or a boss or a family member is revealed as a vicious sociopathic killer. *I never thought they could. They seemed like such nice people. They can't be responsible.* Will you let me protect you?"

"How? Am I supposed to pretend you're a visiting monk, or something?"

"Just tell me your schedule, and we'll take care of it from there."

"We?" the priest asked.

"I'm not alone."

"None of us are, my son."

Dark stared at him.

"Priest humor," Donnelly explained, reaching down into a desk drawer. "You like your bourbon neat, or are you one of those sissies who needs ice?"

chapter 67

Tom Riggins's Rule #1 when dealing with reporters: If you're going to let them use you, then you have to make sure you use them back—harder.

Johnny Knack being in Vegas for the Kobiashi murder wasn't a coincidence. Riggins knew better. Someone had steered him this way. Could be Dark, could be his mystery woman. Either way, he'd know in a minute—once Banner finished downloading the guy's cell phone records.

For once Norman Wycoff had come in handy. The Department of Defense wasn't even putting up the pretense of citizens' privacy anymore. Every Web page you visit, every e-mail you send, every call you make, every text you thumb—all fair game. Within minutes Banner had what he needed, and began sorting through the files.

And Wycoff could barely contain his enthusiasm when he learned that Dark was the prime suspect in the Tarot Card Murders. Since June the man had been looking for any excuse, the flimsiest of reasons, to sic his black-bag kill squad on Dark. Riggins had to play this carefully. As they all agreed: They wanted Steve Dark cap-

276

tured alive. Despite appearances, their friend and loved one was still in there. He deserved a chance to explain himself. He deserved a shot at salvation.

They had gathered in a small room at the Egyptian to strategize, ice down their bruises, and, in Riggins's case, drown his aching muscles in a little whiskey. "FBI business," he'd told the room service guy. "Keep it coming and don't be stingy with the ice."

Constance watched him pour a drink, at least six fingers' worth.

"I don't feel good about this," she said.

"I'm not planning on driving," Riggins said.

"No, I mean bringing the media into this. What if we're wrong? What if we've just ruined his life?"

"More than it already is?"

"You know what I mean, Tom. This is Steve we're talking about. No matter what we think he's been up to, it's all conjecture. We're dragging the man's reputation straight into the toilet here. Would you sell me out to Slab just as quick?"

Riggins sighed. He lifted the tumbler to his mouth, then paused. "Dark's already fucked us over, remember? I flew five hours to give him a chance to come clean with me, and he didn't say jack shit. He's had his chance to explain."

"What if someone decides to shoot first, question Dark later?" Constance asked.

"I'm not too worried about that. Not with Jane Bond there, serving as his bodyguard."

Constance grimaced. She had a bruise on her upper chest that already looked like a purple and yellow storm cloud, and it hurt every time she swallowed. Just the look of that woman pissed Constance off. Smug. Superior. No matter how far you made it in your own career, life was still like high school. There were still people who would piss on you just as soon as look at you.

"I run into her again," Constance said under her breath, "I'm going to kick her ass."

Riggins nodded. "Hey, I'll hold her down for you."

They exchanged glances. The gallows humor again. Sometimes in this line of work it was all they had. No matter how desperate the circumstances.

And then Banner spoke up. "Guys."

"What?"

"Ever been to Fresno?"

chapter 68

Fresno, California

Graysmith found a hotel room not far from the church. In the meantime, she'd gathered some supplies—extra Glock 22s and magazines, surveillance gear. Dark didn't ask how. He supposed there were individuals spread all over the country just waiting for the predawn call from a CIA spook who needed equipment and was willing to pay a premium for it.

As Graysmith handed him a plastic bag full of motion detectors, she asked about the priest's itinerary.

Dark said, "After he finishes writing his homily, Donnelly says he's going to try to sleep for a couple of hours before early morning Mass, followed by the morning Mass, then the children's Mass, and then finally a Halloween parade for the parochial school children."

"That's when they'll strike," Graysmith said. "Plenty of parents. Plenty of masks and costumes. Lots of confusion."

"I thought the same thing. So let's have him cancel the parade, put him into some sort of protective custody."

"Then what? They'll just find another Devil. Look at what happened to Jeb Paulson. Do you really think he was the original Fool they had in mind?"

A good point. Abdulia's plan was adaptable. Hiding Donnelly might piss them off, but it wouldn't stop the murders.

"So what then?"

"*We* protect him."

"Just two of us? We can't even call in reinforcements. How are the two of us supposed to cover a parade?"

Graysmith called up a document on her laptop and showed it to Dark. "These are Roger Maestro's military records. He was a sniper—one of the best, taking out countless Afghan warlords and drug traffickers from pretty much a whole mountain range away. Their last few murders haven't been as elaborate as the first. They have our attention now. They're going to go for something clean and simple."

"A rooftop shot," Dark said. "Or from one of the church or school windows."

"Maestro could also blend into the crowd as one of the parents. They could come from anywhere. So let's give the priest some Kevlar to wear under his vestments. Roger goes for his shot, Donnelly lives, and we get the chance to take down Roger."

Dark called up the Devil card on his phone. "And what if he goes for the headshot on the Devil? Look at the pentagram in this illustration. The tip points to the middle of his forehead. Roger won't go for a chest shot. If what you're telling me is true, then he'll be able to hit anything he wants."

"Talk to Donnelly. See what he's comfortable doing."

"That is not a garment of the Lord," the priest said.

Dark looked down at Donnelly's shoes. "And those Rockports are what—blessed by the Vatican?"

"Hey, I have fallen arches. Am I supposed to suffer for my faith all day long?"

Dark pulled the Kevlar vest out of its plastic bag. Another score from Graysmith. It offered Type III protection, which meant it could potentially stop a round from a rifle. He handed it to Donnelly, who rocked it up and down on his fingertips.

"This is ridiculously heavy," the priest said.

"The stronger the protection, the heavier the armor."

Donnelly frowned. "Do you know how much my back kills me after chasing around these kids on a normal day, let alone during a parade?

"It's not just about you, Father. We want to catch these people. You're our best shot to do it."

"That's an extremely poor pun," Donnelly said. "Considering the circumstances."

Donnelly looked at the vest, running his fingers over the rough surface, eyebrows furrowed. Then he spun in his chair and draped it over a bookshelf packed with leather-bound religious volumes before turning around to face Dark again.

"You're not drawing them out to kill them, are you?"

"We want to stop them," Dark said.

"I understand that, and of course I want the same. But what troubles me is that you and your associate—who you won't even name, or introduce—well, you're not with any law enforcement agency. No one is holding you accountable for your actions. In fact, law enforcement seems fairly determined to stop you. Now, don't get me wrong. I believe your story. But I won't be party to a slaughter."

"That's exactly what I'm trying to prevent," Dark said.

chapter 69

The next morning Dark made his way through the swarms of masked children—comic book characters, wild animals, celebrities, angels, devils, dinosaurs, spacemen. Clowns, too. Dark had a special hatred of clowns, dating back to a case from his early career. He could do without clowns. What made matters worse was that some of the parents were costumed, too. No problem with them joining in the fun. But they made it easy for a killer to hide in the crowd.

The Halloween Morning Parade began a few years ago when concerned parents stopped taking their kids out at night for trick-or-treating. A couple of miniature candy bars and sticks of gum weren't worth the risk of being mugged or shot. And since the beginning, the pastor of Saint Jude's Parish was at the forefront, organizing the costumes, the music, the food, the drink, the prizes. With the arrival of Father Donnelly, it had blossomed into something even bigger, with local companies vowing to donate "treats" to the impoverished neighborhood in the form of grants and food-bank donations. Donnelly had been working toward this event since he was assigned to the church a little more than a year ago, and he wasn't about to hide in the rectory, no matter what Dark said.

So now Dark was strolling the streets, Glock 22 hooked to his belt, concealed under his black button-down shirt, looking for someone who could be Roger Maestro.

Or Abdulia.

The wife, the tarot reader, knew what Dark looked like. He had to assume Roger did, too. Who would recognize who first? Would they even be here?

Making matters worse was the fact that Dark's face had been all over the news this morning, telling viewers that he was a "person of interest" in the Tarot Card Killings. Dark should have been the one wearing the mask out here. At any moment he was expecting to feel a strong grip on his arm, and a Fresno cop telling him to step aside . . .

Static popped in Dark's ear.

"Anything?" Graysmith asked.

Graysmith had perched herself in the choir loft of Saint Jude's, the tallest structure in the area. A bird's-eye view might help her spot one of the Maestros before it was too late. Of course, both of them knew this was close to absurd—a two-person team trying to trap a decorated sniper.

"Nothing yet. You?"

"Just a lot of little screaming reminders why I never had kids."

Dark was feeling the opposite. Here it was Halloween and he had no idea where his daughter might be, even if she was dressing up. Sorry, kid. You can never have a normal holiday because your dad fucked up your entire life. Better luck at Thanksgiving.

And there were dozens of parents, snapping photos on their digital cameras, recording the mayhem. Father Donnelly, meanwhile, seemed to revel in it. He was a man who genuinely liked to see other people happy, took strength from it.

Dark continued to scan the crowd. He saw something that made him tense up—a man and a woman in wedding garments, connected by plastic chains. Just like the Devil card. A couple in chained bondage. Dark examined their faces carefully. The outfit was a joke, of course—a play on "the old ball and chain." But killers often hid behind jokes and smiles. The bride could have a rifle under that gown; the groom could have sharp knives up his sleeves.

Then a pair of kids—a boy and girl—came crashing into the couple, almost toppling them over, screaming, "Mommy! Daddy!" The bride and groom exploded with laughter. Dark exhaled. For a second, anyway.

Someone grabbed Dark's arm. He spun around and reached for his Glock at the same time.

A pale-looking man with curly hair looked at him. "Whoa! Didn't mean to startle you. I just wanted to introduce myself."

Dark narrowed his eyes. The guy held out a hand, but Dark ignored it.

"I'm Johnny Knack. I write for the Slab."

The receiver in Dark's ear crackled to life. "Who is that?" Graysmith barked.

Dark pulled his arm away. "I don't have time for this now."

"You don't understand. Riggins and Brielle know you're here. They're in the city right now, only they don't know you're at the parade just yet . . ."

"Leave me alone," Dark said, and darted back into the writhing swarm of children.

"Dark, what the fuck's going on down there?" Graysmith hissed.

Lifting his right wrist to his face, Dark whispered: "A reporter. The guy from the Slab. He says Riggins is here, too."

Knack caught up to him quickly, though, and practically had to shout to be heard over the screaming, laughing Halloweeners.

"I can help you! Just stop and talk to me for a moment, please."

Dark stopped, spun, and grabbed Knack by the shoulders, ready to knee him in the fucking balls if he had to. But then came a sharp cry in his ear. Graysmith. Screaming.

"Dark! To your left!"

There.

A tall man in a goat mask, lifting a rifle to his shoulder.

Dark launched himself away from Knack and began pushing aside the kids, screaming at them, plowing through them. As he ran, he followed the rifle's trajectory—which led right to Father Donnelly's face, just thirty yards away. The gunman lined up the shot. Dark dove through the air. Graysmith shouted through the earpiece—*I don't have a shot!* Dark's outstretched hands slammed into the gunman's forearm a second before he squeezed the trigger. The barrel went up in the air a few inches. The shot echoed off the façade of the church. Children screamed. Parents rushed forward to scoop their sons and daughters out of the way.

The man in the goat mask turned to Dark, who was struggling to climb to his feet. The butt of the rifle smashed across Dark's jaw, then nailed him in the chest.

At which point Dark grabbed it and refused to let go, no matter how much the goat man tried to shake him loose. Finally Dark slammed his palm into the middle of the rifle, snapping it in half. *There's your fucking weapon.*

But the man in the goat mask wasn't finished.

By the time he pulled his second weapon from a holster under his coat, the crowd had scattered enough to give him a clear shot at Father Donnelly.

He fired twice.

VIII

the devil

To watch Steve Dark's personal tarot card reading,
please log in to Level26.com and
enter the code: devil.

EX LUX LUCIS ADVEHO ATRUM

XV

THE DEVIL

PRIEST SHOT IN FRONT OF
ASTONISHED PARISHIONERS

FRESNO, Calif. (AP)—Father Warren Donnelly, pastor of a local parish in an impoverished neighborhood, was shot twice in the chest today during the annual Halloween Morning Parade.

Donnelly had been leading the parade, a decades-old tradition in the southwest Fresno area. Police say that a man in an animal mask shot twice before making his escape.

Donnelly, appointed to Saint Jude's Parish a little more than a year ago, was taken by ambulance to Community Regional Medical Center.

chapter 70

Johnny Knack had never seen a man die before, much less a priest.

And it was all his fault.

The images were still swirling around in his brain. One minute you think you're in total control of the situation. Then . . . everything is lost. Knack sat on the marble stairs of the church, phone in his hands. The story had already gone out over the wire. Nobody had made the Tarot Card Killer connection yet, but it was just a matter of time. The Slab's story editor had sent him six texts in the past two minutes:

```
NEED AN UPDATE NOW
KNACK COME ON
ARE YOU FUCKING THERE?
```

For the first time in his life Knack felt at a loss for words. He'd come to Fresno thinking he had the world by the balls. He'd find Dark—the Mystery Texter said he'd guide him all the way to him—

and then force him to tell his exclusive story. Knack would hole up in a hotel room and record Dark for days, if necessary. Journalists could offer their subjects something the cops and the courts couldn't: a chance to explain freely and uncensored. Clearly, time was running out for Dark, and Knack thought he was holding the lifeline.

Now, though, he was holding the weapon that had really killed that priest. His phone.

The texts burned in his mind:

```
DARK @ ST. JUDE'S PARADE SW FRESNO
DARK IS IN THE CROWD
APPROACH HIM NOW
```

And Knack had, just like a good little accomplice.

He had to make this right. Forget the book deals, forget the career . . . that was nothing. Just go somewhere quiet and write everything down. The complete truth, for a change.

"Excuse me, sir?"

A thin, dark-haired woman was suddenly standing next to him, a panicked looked on her face. "I can't find my son—he's only five, and . . . oh, please, can you help me?"

Knack climbed to his feet. "Of course."

They tried the parking lot behind the church, because the woman—who was actually kind of beautiful, behind the worry— thought she saw him run back here. Knack suggested they find a cop immediately, but the woman shook her head, frantic, insisting they'd be too busy looking for the gunman to stop and look for her little boy. Knack assured her that wouldn't be the case.

"You have something on your face," the woman said, then took a handkerchief out of her pocket. Before he could reach up and feel for himself, the woman was wiping at his upper lip with her handkerchief. Knack smelled almonds. Cyanide? Then he felt strangely weak, like he'd stood up too quickly. How was that possible? He had already been standing and trying to help this poor woman find her missing boy . . .

The woman who now guided him to the side of a van, leaning his weight against it and whispering in his ear:

"You've done good work so far, Mr. Knack," she said. "But there is still more of the story to tell."

chapter 71

Riggins received constant updates as they swept toward the Southwest. Dark had been at the parade. The priest was shot—but expected to live. A gunman in a goat mask was spotted—the shooter was not Dark. Eyewitnesses said Dark tried to stop the shooter. The priest was rushed away in an ambulance, but hadn't arrived at the hospital yet.

Constance drove. "Maybe we're wrong about Steve."

"We're not wrong about him being involved," Riggins said. "In fact, I'll bet he made contact with the priest."

"Let's go to the hospital then. You know Dark's long gone from the church."

"Yeah."

Dark was long gone from everything, Riggins thought.

Riggins tried the hospital, but still no contact with the ambulance driver. Which didn't make sense. The hospital wasn't all that far away, if the mapping program on his phone was right. What the hell was going on?

Unless the ambulance wasn't going to the hospital.

Riggins thought about Dark's accomplice—the chick with the fancy moves from the back of the van. He'd only had a glimpse of the gear inside, but he saw enough to know it was on par with what they had back in Quantico, maybe even better. What if Dark didn't leave Special Circs to "retire," but instead left it for another agency? Special Circs was the top of the food chain when it came to catching monsters. But that didn't mean other parts of the government weren't interested in doing the same.

If that was the case, why wouldn't Dark tell him about it? What, were they offering better medical and dental? It made no sense.

Riggins told Constance to head for the hospital anyway. Maybe he could talk to a dispatcher there, figure out how the system worked here. Narrow down the field a bit.

You can pull all the fancy moves you want, Riggins thought. But you and your weird girlfriend can't take a dying priest and vanish from the face of the earth.

chapter 72

Father Donnelly sat up on the ambulance gurney, clutching his sides. "Jesus," he muttered. "This fucking hurts."

Dark nodded, an ice pack pressed against his jaw. "I know what it feels like. You'll have serious bruising, and your muscles will be tender for weeks."

"But at least I'm alive, right?" The priest's grimace turned to anger. "Is that what you're going to say? You going to stand there and gloat, tell me you people were right? I shouldn't have been so stubborn. The looks on those kids' faces . . ." Donnelly sat up and swung his legs over the side. "What a nightmare."

Graysmith put a hand on Donnelly's shoulder. It was only the three of them in the back, with a driver and his partner upfront. They weren't real EMTs; this wasn't a real ambulance. The whole setup was something Graysmith had arranged less than two hours ago, to be on standby in case something happened. The moment the first shot was fired, Graysmith pressed a button on her phone, signaling them. Right about now there would be real EMTs showing up at the scene, wondering where their patient had gone.

"You're alive," she said, "and nobody in the parish was hurt. That counts for something."

But the Maestros would keep going. There were two cards left. The most frightening cards of all.

The Tower.

Death.

"Tell us about the Maestros, Father."

"Do you really believe that was Roger out there just now, trying to blow my head off?"

"We're sure of it," Graysmith said.

Donnelly sighed. "I prayed with the man over his son's dying body. I never met someone who seemed so utterly lost and devastated. There's really not much sense you can make to someone in that position—they're lost in their own torment, and all you can do is assure them that you're there, that you'll pray with them, that there is a light at the end."

"Did you see him after the funeral?"

"No—I was transferred a short while later. He dropped out of sight, which didn't come as any real surprise. I continued to pray for him. I suppose all prayers aren't heard."

Graysmith handed Donnelly an ice pack. "What about his wife, Abdulia?"

"She was always skeptical about my presence. I got the idea that she tolerated me being around, because praying with her husband seemed to give him some kind of peace."

"Abdulia studied the occult," Graysmith said. "She's written a few books on the history and art of the tarot. In her circles, the books were praised for their insight. Outside, she was totally unknown."

"That would explain it," Donnelly said. "But what about Roger?"

"Ex-military. Navy Seal. He received a dishonorable discharge after a friendly-fire incident. Came back to the States, found a job as a shop foreman in an auto plant, making $118,000 a year, full benefits. Lost his job not long after, though. Moved into construction. Work dried up."

"It did for a lot of people," Donnelly said.

"Yeah, but that was just the beginning. After the layoff, Abdulia tried to amp up her tarot-reading business. Someone got jealous, put the local business-affairs people after her. She was convicted of scamming people during readings."

"I had no idea," Donnelly said.

"You were gone by then," Graysmith said. "The Maestros were in over their heads, losing their house, losing everything. Victims of forces beyond their control."

Now it made sense to Dark. All of the victims were players—directly or symbolically—in the Maestros' personal nightmare. The Hanged Man, Martin Green, was a money man advising banks—the same banks that turn down loan requests from people like the Maestros. The Fool was a symbol of the cop who accused Abdulia of being a con artist. The Three of Cups were MBA students who were killed before they could blossom into greedy adults. The Ten of Swords senator was in bed with Wall Street. The Ten of Wands were fat cats who made insane profits from closing American factories—like, say, auto plants. The nurse failed to save their son, despite promising to do everything she could. Kobiashi, spinning the Wheel of Fortune, wasted money while others were unable to buy health care. The Devil priest asked God to save their boy, but failed.

But how did the Maestros—a broke couple who couldn't afford to pay for medical treatments for their son—afford this cross-country killing spree? They needed weapons. Plane tickets. Surveillance gear. All of it expensive as hell.

Maybe they financed it from the first murder—Martin Green.

He asked Graysmith to call up Paulson's notes from his visit to the crime scene. Dark scanned them quickly. Paulson had been young, but he had a good eye. He'd been asking the right questions. For one thing, he hadn't been distracted by the grisly nature of the torture-murder. He'd asked good, solid questions about motive and potential suspects. And there it was, in Paulson's own hand: *Follow the money.*

According to the local cops, Green had kept a lot of cash in a bedroom safe. Kind of ironic for a guy who made a living consulting bankers and financiers. What if Roger and Abdulia knew that? What if he was chosen to be their first victim because he had a lot of cash on hand, and because he fell within the right geographical area? The first murder covers the rest.

He made a note to have Graysmith pluck all Roger and Abdulia's financial records. In the words of Jeb Paulson: Follow the money. Because as much as they wanted to pretend this was about fate, this was also about finance.

Dark silently thanked Paulson. *If you can hear me, Jeb, I think you just helped me catch your killers.*

"So what now?" Donnelly asked.

"We take you to the hospital," Graysmith said. "The vest may have absorbed most of the impact, but you still need to be checked out for internal injuries."

"What are you going to do, then? Just drop me off and vanish into thin air?"

"That's the idea," Graysmith said. "These men will take you to the hospital. If anyone asks about the delay, tell them they said something about being new, and being lost."

"And the bullets that were supposed to have hit my body?"

"You have no idea. You were knocked to the ground. Consider it divine intervention."

"Nobody's going to believe it," Donnelly muttered.

"Why not?" Dark asked. "You're a priest."

chapter 73

When the fake ambulance finally pulled up at Community Regional Medical Center, Riggins was waiting for them.

He didn't get in their faces; he let them do their thing, which was mostly handing off the injured priest to the ER staff. Riggins watched them. The two men seemed like they were in an awful hurry to get the hell out of there, to step back into the fray. Which wasn't like most of the EMTs Riggins had known over the years. You catch a call to bring someone to the ER, you hang out, catch a smoke, a coffee, until it's your turn in the barrel again. There's usually no rush—especially on a Sunday. Even if it was Halloween.

"Constance, you talk to the priest," he said. "Get him to tell you everything. Beat him if you have to. The old Dirty Harry shoe-leather-in-the-bullet-wound trick should work just fine."

"You're a sick man," Constance said. "What about you? Where are you going?"

"Going to catch an ambulance," he said, then trotted off back to their car.

Surprise, surprise—the EMTs took their vehicle not to the closest dispatching station, but to a private garage in suburban Fresno. After parking the vehicle and peeling themselves out of their fake uniforms, they bullshitted with each other for a while, with Riggins watching them from across the street. One of them must have suggested breakfast, since it was Sunday morning, and the other agreed. They piled into a Ford Taurus and drove a half mile to a diner. Climbed into a booth, ordered some eggs, bacon, muffins, coffee.

Riggins entered one minute later, slid in next to them. Put his Sig Sauer on the table. Eased back, like he had all the time in the world, then showed them his Special Circs badge.

"Hi, fellas," he said.

chapter 74

Dark thought about Hilda's interpretation of the Tower:

The Tower card is about war, breaking apart. A war be-tween the structure of lies and the lightning flash of truth. The lightning is Thor's hammer.

A bolt of divine power, almost a cosmic course correction.

God strikes you down when you are arrogant, she'd continued, *hoping that you'll see the truth. And tap back into the heart of inno-cence. It's a divine act. A wake-up call for the rest of your life.*

The image on the face of the card was horrifying, with shades of 9/11 and the apocalypse and the Tower of Babel rolled up into one black spectacle. A proud gray edifice is struck by lightning from the ebony skies, knocking a gold crown from the roof, setting it ablaze. Two figures fall from the skies, one wearing a crown, the other not. Both stretch out their arms in stark terror. Below is noth-ing but a terribly eroded foundation, proof that you've built your entire life on unstable ground that has been rotting away beneath you. There is no escape. Everything you know is about to be struck down.

The card was about sudden change, a downfall, and a revelation.

Like every tarot card, there were positive and negative interpre-tations of the image. The Tower, to some, would be welcome, because it would mean a spectacular breakthrough, exposing the hidden truth behind a situation, or receiving an answer—like a bolt of inspiration—after months of denial. The Tower card didn't spell doom. Like the Fool, it promised a new beginning. The negative interpretation, however, meant a devastating loss of fortune, the crisis of your life, and utter chaos.

So far, every murder (or attempted murder) had been closely tied into the images on the cards.

Who was the Tower? The Maestros believed someone had built up something powerful and mighty on a ruined foundation . . . so who?

The geography of the card layout also had to be a factor. Las Vegas, Fresno, the card progressing in a northwesterly direction to . . .

Wait.

Graysmith stepped out of the shower to find Dark poring through the documents on her laptop.

"What are you looking for?" she asked.

"Tell you if I find it."

If the Maestro's financial records were right, Dark knew exactly where they were going to strike next.

IX

the tower

To watch Steve Dark's personal tarot card reading,
please log in to Level26.com and
enter the code: tower.

EX LUX LUCIS ADVEHO ATRUM

XVI

THE TOWER

S *crawled on the back of the owner's copy of a receipt from Send It Packing, a mail delivery service located in Nob Hill, San Francisco, California.*

You won't find this note until it's all over.
You may call us monsters. That would be missing the point. The fate of this country has already been written. Our path leads to death and destruction.
YOU CANNOT CHANGE YOUR FATE
EMBRACE IT

chapter 75

D ark looked up at the Niantic Tower in downtown San Francisco.

There were only two structures said to be able to withstand earthquakes: pyramids and redwood trees. The Niantic Tower kept both in mind when it was built in the early 1970s. Named for the massive whaling vessel buried near the foundation, the Niantic was a forty-eight-floor crushed-quartz rebuff to Mother Nature, built on top of notoriously unstable ground. The Niantic had a nine-foot foundation that took a full day to pour, and a base made of eighteen thousand cubic yards of concrete and enough rebar to stretch from San Francisco to Santa Barbara. The Niantic's base was also incredibly flexible; that, along with its truss system, meant it was able to withstand any seismic jolt imaginable.

The Niantic was also home to Westmire Investments, the umbrella corporation to dozens of lenders, including the particular lender that foreclosed on the Maestros' home.

The Niantic had to be their target.

But how?

What kind of lightning bolt from the sky could they have prepared—just the two of them, to topple this tower?

"You're infamous now," Graysmith said, looking at the screen on her phone. "Special Circs has a hard-on for you. Big manhunt and everything. The Slab's got the whole story."

"Great," Dark muttered.

They were close to the city now, but caught up in early morning traffic. Dark felt like there was a giant clock ticking in his brain, counting down to something horrible. But the numbers were missing from the face. The end might be any minute from now. Or it may have already happened.

"Strange," Graysmith muttered. "Does Knack usually invent things out of whole fucking cloth?"

Dark turned in her direction. "What do you mean?"

"I mean, he claims to have spoken to you at length and that you've confessed to all of the Tarot Card Murders. That you wouldn't stop until the last card was dealt, and that many more would die."

"What?"

"The whole thing's bizarre. Kind of a diatribe, making you seem like a disgruntled ex–G-man trying to outwit your former employers by committing these crimes. Point is, your face is everywhere. You're no longer a *person of interest*. You're pretty much the main interest."

Dark thought about what had happened in Fresno. Knack had approached him, tried to pin him down for something. Had he lost his mind, figuring that he could turn a fast buck on a quick-and-dirty fabrication? This caused Dark grief, to be sure, but such blatant fabrications were usually revealed. Just ask Clifford Irving, Jayson Blair, or Stephen Glass. Like bank robbers, journalists who cooked up the facts were almost always caught. Knack would be no different.

Graysmith's attention, meanwhile, had turned back to the Niantic Tower. She had access to a secret database tracking security at all major U.S. landmarks. Not long after 9/11, the fledgling Department of Homeland Security held a summit meeting of Hollywood screenwriters, best-selling novelists, demolitions experts, former terrorists, and career criminals. A list of landmarks was distributed; the request was simple. *How would you breach these?*

Apparently, a team of people had set their minds to destroying the Niantic Tower. Graysmith ran through the options.

"Think they're going to steal another plane?" she asked.

"It's possible," Dark said. "Not a commercial airliner, but more likely a private plane, just like the Westmire Investments charter. But they haven't repeated methods yet. We've had a hanging, a push off a ledge, strangling, knife attacks, a plane crash, feigned suicide . . ."

"They repeated with guns. Maestro shot at Donnelly. Kobiashi was forced to kill himself."

"True," Dark said, faraway look in his eyes.

"You don't seem convinced," Graysmith said. "What's your gut telling you?"

"They'll try something else. This is their big finale—an entire institution they blame for their family's downfall."

"So they're definitely going after the building."

"I think so," Dark said. "Can you have it evacuated? Get emergency response teams here?"

Graysmith looked at him. "How sure are you, Steve?"

"This is the place, Lisa. I know it."

"Okay. I'll sound the alarms. I'm not saying it will be easy. You had to deal with bureaucracy at Special Circs. Well, it's pretty much the same all over the government."

"Do it."

Graysmith started to punch in a phone number, then paused.

"Wait. If we evacuate, the Maestros will know it. They could abort this plan, come up with something else."

"No," Dark said. "This is their big moment. The rest of the murders were just a sideshow; this is going to be their statement. Whatever they have planned, I don't think they can just pick it up and move it somewhere else."

"But they still could trigger the event early."

Dark knew she was right.

chapter 76

Montgomery Street / San Francisco, California

Sleepy-eyed workers filed into the Niantic Tower. Just another workday, bustling with accountants, lawyers, bankers, CPAs, insurance agents, caterers, janitors, security guards, and deliverymen. It was Monday morning, first of the month. Everybody had reports to file, e-mails to send, phone conferences to set up, deliveries to make.

There was the usual flurry of FedEx and UPS and DHL shipments, backlogged from over the weekend. Free gifts from PR agencies. Catered food, for breakfast meetings. Flowers, too. Surprise romantic gestures, congrats, belated birthdays, well-wishes on new deals. Books, samples, clothes, paperwork.

Just another busy Monday morning in the city by the bay.

As he waited for Graysmith's request to make its way through the proper channels, Dark positioned himself in the lobby of the Niantic Tower, mind racing in overdrive, watching the workers come and go. People in professional gear, bike messengers in Spandex, deliverymen in crisp brown shirts and creased shorts, all streaming in and out of the revolving doors in constant flow, especially at this hour.

The stream of people made Dark see the Maestros in a different light. Roger was a former soldier turned blue-collar worker. Abdulia, a professor and card reader. A life of sweat and toil, a life of the mind. Neither one of them would ever work in a building like this—not unless Roger were working construction or repairs. Was that it? Had he managed to get himself hired on this site?

No, the Philly PD had established that he'd been working a construction job in the city for the past few weeks. Unless he'd bribed someone to fake his time sheets and actually spent his time out here in San Francisco. Roger Maestro had the cash. But you can't check into a hotel with cash, no matter how much you have. Hotels required credit cards. The Maestros' credit, Dark recalled, was shot.

Dark remembered the police report: Items were stolen from Green's Chapel Hill home. Could they have nabbed credit cards, as well? Other sources of funding?

He called Graysmith. "Quick favor."

"I'm in the middle of groveling with a high-ranking member of the U.S. intelligence world. Do you mind if I call you back?"

"This is easy. I need a credit check on Martin Green. Specifically if anyone's been using the dead man's credit cards over the past ten days. And if so, for what."

Families didn't always sort these things out right away after a murder. And from what he could tell, Green didn't have much in the way of family. The Maestros would know this. The man might have been their opening statement, but he could also function as a kind of blank check.

While Dark waited for the call, he watched the lobby of the Niantic Towers. He was a wanted man, thanks to the Knack story, which this morning had been picked up by TV and cable news stations around the world. Being out here, in the general public, was a little insane. Anyone could recognize him at any time, despite the baseball cap he'd picked up from a street vendor.

But he couldn't leave. Not when he was the only one who knew what the Maestros were up to.

They would be close to the action; they'd want to observe, first-hand, the tower falling. They might even be fine-tuning preparations inside the building somewhere. Dark should go inside, start looking for devices . . . something. That idea was also insane, of course. Even a fifty-man security team could scour the premises and not find a single suspicious device or package . . .

Dark's cell buzzed.

"Martin Green supposedly used his AmEx Black at a mail-it-yourself place in Nob Hill. Kind of odd for a guy in Chapel Hill, North Carolina. There are a load of other similar purchases in the Greater San Francisco area."

"Shit."

Package, Dark thought.

Or *packages*.

"But what—he's going to hide a bomb in a box?"

Dark's eyes swept over the lobby again. There wasn't just one delivery guy. There was an armada of them, constantly coming and going, carrying boxes and bags and trays and containers and over-night envelopes . . .

"If I were doing this," Dark said, "I wouldn't plant just one bomb, I would send multiple bombs. And I'd study the layout of the build-ing so that I knew exactly where to send them, like a controlled demolition."

"Fuck," Graysmith said.

"I'd even err on the side of overkill," Dark said, "so even if a per-centage of the packages didn't show up, then I'd still have plenty of destructive power to bring this tower down."

"And nobody screens packages—hell, we're not even screening ninety-nine percent of the shipping containers that come into U.S. ports."

Dark looked at all of the people waving their badges over the security turnstiles. Dozens and dozens headed in, almost nobody headed out. Monday morning. Everyone reporting to work, jacked up on Starbucks and thinking about the long week ahead.

"You have to get a team to this building now, Lisa."

"I'm trying. You don't understand the shitstorm I just stirred up when I told my supervisor what's been going on. The intelligence world is not too different from the Justice Department. Slow, suspicious, stupid."

"Then I'll start searching."

"You might force Roger to trigger these bombs now."

"He can't have eyes on the entire building."

All of these people, all of these floors.

"Look, can you send me credentials to get me into this building?" Dark asked.

"What are you going to do?"

"Anything I can."

"I don't like the sound of that."

"At the very least, you'll have plausible deniability," Dark said. "You can blame it all on the crazy rogue ex–FBI agent."

Graysmith didn't respond. Dark stood up and started moving across the lobby floor, weaving his way around the crowd. A few people glanced in his direction, curious. Was that because he looked like he didn't belong to any of the professional tribes here? Or because they recognized his face from CNN?

By the time Dark reached the counter, the phone in his hand buzzed. One new e-mail message.

"You've got it," Graysmith said.

"Thank you," Dark said, leaned forward on the security desk, and showed the face of his phone to three jacketed men stationed behind it.

"Gentlemen," Dark said, "I need your help."

chapter 77

T he only thing the Niantic security force could do: attempt to remove all packages delivered this morning. Every. Single. Last. One. This was no easy task. Total manpower on the morning shift: fifteen men, including the three at the front desk. (Cutbacks, the supervisor explained.) That meant fourteen men for more than forty floors, multiple businesses on some floors. And good luck convincing an administrative assistant to hand over the mail to people they perceived as nothing more than rent-a-cops. If this was a real bomb threat, then why wasn't the FBI or Kevlar-clad members of Homeland Security sweeping through the offices? Why weren't the floors being evacuated immediately?

"Once we get these packages, what are we supposed to do with these damned things?" the supervisor asked.

Dark thought about it. "Do you have mail chutes?"

"Yeah. But they're meant for envelopes, not boxes."

"Then tell your men to load whatever won't fit into the freight elevators and send them down to the basement as fast as possible."

The basement and foundation were designed to withstand earthquakes; they would hopefully absorb the worst of the blasts, just like the World Trade Center did during the original bombing in February 1993.

"Go *now*—spread the word to your men. Nab as many of those packages as possible."

"What about you?"

"I'm going to help."

Dark, along with the security team, raced through the building. In some cases, boxes were still in their metal rolling carts, waiting to be delivered to various offices and cubicles on the floor. That made it simple. Without a word, Dark took the cart, rolled it out to the hallway, loaded it onto the freight elevator, and sent it down to the bottom floor where a guard took all incoming packages and quickly shuttled them into a corner. Dark offered to take this part of the job, but the guard refused. "My building, my job," the guy said. "These terrorist motherfuckers can kiss my ass." Word quickly spread, and office managers began to voluntarily remove the morning's packages from the premises.

Instead of waiting for the elevators, Dark used the fire stairs to travel between floors. Somewhere around the twentieth floor, Dark heard a loud clanging sound, followed by hurried footsteps on concrete. As he rounded the corner, Dark looked up into Roger Maestro's face.

Maestro didn't hesitate. He immediately pulled a pistol from his belt and opened fire on Dark, who leaped out of the way a second before slugs chipped away at the concrete.

Dark tried the closest doorknob, but it was locked from the other side. Shit. Dark listened—Maestro was creeping down the fire stairs for him. Dark looked around him. Just a few water pipes above. Nothing that could be used a weapon. Nothing that could serve as a shield. Nothing to protect him from one of the most decorated shooters in recent history.

The only way to go:

Up.

Stepping on the metal support railing, Dark jumped up and grabbed hold of the water pipes, then pulled himself up, curling the rest of his body until he was as compact as possible. If he were Sqweegel, he could no doubt figure out how to squeeze his little insectoid body into the tiny crevice behind the pipes until danger passed. Dark was not Sqweegel. But that didn't mean he couldn't rip a few pages from the freak's playbook.

Maestro turned the corner, gun sweeping the area.

Dark pushed against the pipes—launching himself down onto Maestro.

The bottoms of Dark's shoes slammed into his upper back, the blow tilting him off balance and sending him into the concrete wall. Maestro moaned. The gun dropped to the concrete. Dark rolled off, keeping his body as limber as possible, then dove into him again, unleashing a flurry of dirty punches meant to shatter face bones and snap his windpipe.

But Maestro was heavier, taller, and thicker than Dark. He absorbed the blows before reaching out and seizing Dark's neck. Dark felt himself being choked, then lifted and driven into the opposite wall. Skull cracking on concrete. He lifted a knee—Maestro blocked the blow. He balled his fists, then smashed them against the sides of Maestro's chest. If any ribs cracked, Maestro gave no indication. He just continued choking Dark, the man's thick, rough fingers sinking deep into his neck.

A trained military man.

Expert in killing.

Most likely armed with more than a single gun.

Dark clawed at Maestro's body and was starting to go gray when he finally found it—the hunting knife in the sheath, hanging from the man's belt.

The moment the blade cleared the leather, Maestro realized he'd left himself vulnerable.

He released his grip and stepped back to defend himself, just like he was trained.

But Dark wasn't going for a jab—he wanted to eviscerate the motherfucker.

The blade glided along Maestro's side, slicing through skin and muscle. Maestro bellowed. Dark raised the knife to drive it into the man's chest. Maestro blocked the blow, so instead, Dark tightened his grip on the handle and drove a jackhammer punch into Maestro's face.

The blow didn't seem to faze Maestro at all, who returned with a series of punches of his own that drove Dark to the corner. He tried to the block the blows, but couldn't stop them all. After a while, they blurred together and then everything faded—the grunting, his vision, and finally, the pain.

chapter 78

After a few moments, Maestro realized his side was bleeding heavily. He took a step back, gingerly touched his wound. It would need to be patched. Sooner than later.

Then there was the matter of their pursuer, now unconscious on the floor.

Abdulia had fully expected Steve Dark on the scene. She said he was a savvy investigator; he'd followed the trail to Fresno, he'd likely follow the trail here. But she didn't expect him to be inside, scrambling to undo their life's work. All of their careful planning over the past year, all of the intricate details of their campaign . . . dashed to pieces by this lousy son of a bitch. Roger wanted to crouch down, wrap his hands around Dark's scrawny neck, and twist until he heard bones snapping. Rip the man's throat out, and squeeze the veins until his blood splatters on his dying face.

But no.

That wasn't possible now.

Abdulia had explained that Dark's life had intersected with theirs, just like that other lawman—the boy, Paulson. Now they needed Dark to finish the sequence. Killing him now would jeopardize everything.

Steve Dark would die when fate commanded.

Roger ambled down one flight, took a deep breath, then opened the door with a stolen passkey. He made his way through the elevator bank silently, passing two office workers who were flirting with each other while waiting for the next car to arrive. Roger remembered when he was that young, invulnerable, and could afford to ignore the dangers all around him. Like these two people. Early twenties and no idea that death was literally passing right by them. Why would they notice? Death was wearing a custodial uniform. If you were a janitor, it was proof you had fucked up somewhere along the way, that you deserved to be in that position.

When Roger reached the second set of fire stairs, he finally exhaled, then took the cell phone attached to his belt and pressed 1, speed-dialing a programmed number.

"It's me," he said. "Are you ready?"

"Yes, Roger. I'm across the street, waiting for you."

"See you in a few minutes. Dark was here, inside the building."

"Oh God," she said. "Is he . . ."

"He'll make it to the end, don't worry."

"Do you think he knows about the packages?"

"Doesn't matter. There are enough of them."

"Come out now."

"Soon as I can finish dialing," Roger said.

"I don't know why you can't do that from out here."

"I told you," Roger said patiently. "I have to make sure the first wave goes off. If not, I may have to do some improvising from inside."

Abdulia was brilliant in so many ways—Roger was routinely dazzled by the way her mind worked. But she hadn't been in the military. She didn't fully understand bombs, gases, poisons. Not like Roger did.

"I understand," she said. "I love you, Roger."

"You, too."

Roger had memorized the list of numbers. All of them: old-fashioned beeper numbers, assigned to defunct beepers he'd picked up cheaply a few weeks ago. Each beeper was attached to an explosive device he'd sent to certain mailrooms in particular companies. Back in Iraq, he'd helped provide security for a crew of freelance reconstruction teams. Among them were some of the best demolition men in the business. Over beers, they talked about how easy it was to bring down a building, as long as you had the right amount of explosives in the key structural places. Roger listened to that, filed it away. He spent a lot of his time in Iraq filing things like that away. Nerve agents they'd discover in some stockpile, then have to destroy. Ways to bring down buildings. Roger figured such knowledge would come in handy in the future. Maybe he could work for one of these outfits, even—stateside. He'd impress them with how much he'd retained.

Of course, that hadn't quite worked out. Roger had been left with a head full of knowledge and not much practical application for it.

Until now.

Roger dialed the first number.

Time for the tower to start tumbling down.

Somewhere, distantly, something went *boom*.

chapter 79

When the Niantic Tower explosions began, everyone in the immediate vicinity thought it was another Big One. Workers scattered under conference room tables, perched themselves in doorways, and waited for the worst. Earthquakes, though, have a unique sound. They start with a rumbling—like a planet-size tank running over an endless field of speed bumps. It's a sound unlike anything you've ever heard, unless you happened to have experienced an earthquake before. This rumbling is followed by a shaking, back and forth, back and forth, which is both longer and more severe than you'd imagine. Finally comes the desperate and fervent prayer that the building's designers were doing their job, and had indeed prepared for the worst temblor that Mother Nature had to offer.

But the occupants of the Niantic Tower quickly realized that the noise and the vibrations were not caused by an earthquake.

chapter 80

Dark's eyes snapped open when he felt the blast pulsing through the concrete floor. A few seconds later, the screaming began. God, no. Was he too late? Pressing his hands on the ground, Dark pushed himself up to his feet. Blood splatter trailed across the floor and down the stairs right to the door. Roger Maestro had made his getaway, set the charges. Dark prayed that the security team was able to remove some of the packages and send them down to the basement.

He raced down the fire stairs. On the floor below, the steel door flew open and smoked poured into the tower, followed by a swarm of frightened office workers.

"Did any of you see a strange man on your floor? He would have been cut and bleeding?"

A chorus of confused noes. Dark muscled his way through the frightened crowd to the floor proper, looking down to see if he could find any traces of blood drops. Nothing. Where the hell had he gone?

There was another loud *BOOM*. Closer this time, as if it was just on the floor above them. They'd intercepted many of the packages, but there were still some left. Dust particles fell from between the drop ceiling tiles. Lights flickered. People screamed. Dark crouched down instinctively, waiting for another blast, counting the seconds.

Five seconds later there was another rumble—somewhere else in the building. He was setting these fucking things off one by one. That meant Roger had to be inside the building. He was triggering them. His plan wasn't to bring the whole building down right away.

He'd give himself an exit strategy.

Roger Maestro leaned against drywall in the empty office and wondered what the building looked like from the outside. He remembered watching the 9/11 attacks with Abdulia not long after they first met. Roger knew he'd be deployed soon, that the life he knew would soon end. It was unfair. They held each other, lit candles, ate dinner in silence. That night, their son was conceived.

After 9/11, the world had seemed to pay attention. But only for a little while.

Roger spent nearly three years in Afghanistan and saw his baby boy only in little snatches of time. A few photographs, a halted and confused conversation over a bad cell phone connection. By the time Roger returned, the boy treated him like a stranger. When he hugged him, the boy wriggled as if he couldn't wait to pull himself free. Abdulia hugged her husband instead, consoled him, told him it would just take time.

Roger often thought of those burning towers in lower Manhattan, like candles slowly sinking into white frosting and disappearing into the cake. Was that what it would look like now?

Soon he would be outside, triggering the second set of charges. He supposed he would find out then.

Because that was the point—to duplicate the horror of that sunny September morning. First the fire and the smoke, then the jumping and the screaming and the fresh shock. And then the tower would come tumbling down.

———

Fire stairs were designed to literally be the last safe passage out of any given building. The Niantic Tower had two—east and west—from the thirtieth floor to the bottom. As the building tapered to a point, there was a single fire tower running up one side. Dark thought about it. A military man like Roger Maestro would stay below the thirtieth floor to avoid limiting his options.

And if the blood splatter led away from the east stairs, then Maestro would have to be in the west stairs, making his way down.

Roger dialed a number, but heard nothing. He knew this number corresponded to the twenty-second floor. He was on the nineteenth now, directly underneath. He would have heard something. What had happened? That accounted for the third misfire in eight strikes. Too many to be chalked up to chance. Something was wrong.

As he thought about it, he quickly dialed another number.

chapter 81

By the time Riggins and Constance arrived at the Niantic Tower, smoke was already pouring out of broken windows and people were streaming from the revolving doors. Riggins had been in D.C. during 9/11, in a Special Circs briefing room, watching the live feeds, waiting for instructions to do something, anything, wishing he could have been in front of one of those doomed buildings to help. Well, today appeared to be his lucky fucking day.

They pushed their way past the frantic crowds and made their way to the security desk. Constance had a photo of Dark ready. "Has this man approached you?" she asked.

The stunned security guard nodded his head and immediately started to worry for his job. "Yeah, he had Homeland Security credentials . . . wait, was I not supposed to let him through, or something?"

"Do you know where he is?" Riggins barked.

"He went upstairs—he told us to stop all packages and start evacuating. Wait—who the fuck are you people?"

Riggins flashed his badge. "We're FBI. Special Circs division, and yeah, we're coordinating with this guy. But his cell must be off. We need to find him immediately. How many other guards do you have stationed in the building?"

"A dozen, but they're scattered throughout the building. Your friend had them pulling packages."

"Let us through."

"Are you kidding?" the guard said. "We're trying to get everybody out."

Dark's new lady friend had led them right to San Francisco.

When Riggins squeezed the fake EMTs with the fake ambulance in a private garage—threatening to pound them with the full fury of the U.S. Department of Justice—they shrugged their shoulders and spit out a name. She's one of you, anyway, they said. Not that that was extremely curious. Riggins started making gentle inquiries, seeing what the name "Lisa Graysmith" meant. At first nobody returned his calls. Then some bureaucrat he didn't know called and made vague threats if Riggins didn't quiet down about this "Lisa Graysmith." Bingo. Riggins went to Wycoff—perhaps the first time he'd ever been *eager* to hear that prick's voice—and asked him to rattle some cages. Told him that this "Lisa Graysmith" came up as a person of interest in their Tarot Card Killing investigation.

While he waited for Wycoff to get back to him, Riggins checked his own Special Circs case files, seeing if maybe she was a loose end. To his astonishment, *she was*.

On computer, anyway.

In the actual files back in Quantico, her name didn't come up at all. Sure, there was a Julie Graysmith—a victim of the Body Double killer a couple of years ago.

According to the files online, however, "Lisa" was the victim's older sister.

But on paper, no Lisa.

What the fuck?

Wycoff called back. "Lisa Graysmith" was off-limits. Hidden behind layers of diplomatic security and the State Department. No way she could be involved in the Tarot Card Killings, as she was "on assignment" elsewhere in the world, and that would be that, fuck you very much. Which Riggins assumed would be the case. He thanked Wycoff, told him it must be a name mix-up. Weird.

Yeah.

Twenty minutes later a man who refused to identify himself told Riggins that if he wanted to talk to Lisa Graysmith, he might try the Niantic Tower in San Francisco. She'd just reported a possible terrorist attack on the building.

"Does she belong to a certain company? Can you give me a number, or even a floor?" Often, intelligence officers would operate out of false front companies.

"You are," the voice said, chuckling, "an FBI agent, are you not?"

The only thing more obnoxious than politicians on a crusade were intelligence types hopped up on their own importance.

"Thanks."

Though now that they'd arrived at the tower, Riggins could see why the man thought this whole thing was so fucking funny.

Riggins ignored the guards, hopped over the security turnstiles, and ran back behind the elevator banks. Constance followed. Once they'd reached the fire towers, they had to fight their way through even more frightened people, coughing and crying and trying to figure out how their Monday morning had gone so wrong.

"Why don't you stay with the guards," Riggins told Constance. "Maybe you can find Dark on their surveillance system."

"What," Constance said, "and have you die a hero up there so you can haunt me the rest of my life? No thanks, Tom. I'm going up."

"God, you're stubborn."

"And that's why you love me."

"Love's not even the word," Riggins said, then started to wave his beefy hands in front of him, urging the panicked crowds to make way, make way. This was crazy. This was impossible. Yet, they were doing it anyway. Welcome to Special Circs.

chapter 82

Dark wasn't even sure what floor he was on. The smoke was black and thick, burning his eyes, clotting in his mouth. Alarms and screams sounded in his ears. He crouched down to his fingertips and balls of his feet—something he'd been practicing for months. Dark took some grim satisfaction knowing that his paranoia had finally come in handy.

"Where are you?" he shouted. "Keep shouting so I can follow the sound of your voice!"

There were screams—to the left. Dark moved quickly along the carpet, staying low to the ground, looking for any traces of Roger. Give me a drop of blood. A boot print. Something. There were more screams. Dark, as always, found himself torn. On one hand, the victims. On the other, the monster. Logic dictated that if you slay the monster, you help the victims. But what do you do when the monster is running away, and the victims are screaming for help?

Constance had a spatial mind; she almost never needed a GPS. Once she fixed on the location of the elevators and the fire stairs, she was able to direct people with dead certainty—even though she'd never before set foot in the Niantic Tower. The FBI vest she was wearing gave her instant authority, but it was also the look in her eyes. This was a woman who knew the way out, who would not let you down.

"This way!" she shouted. "Follow the sound of my voice."

All the while, she kept careful watch for Dark.

Despite the strange evidence, she knew Dark wouldn't be part of something like this. He was trying to *stop* it—as always, throwing himself into fires because he felt a moral compulsion to stop arsonists everywhere. But what Constance couldn't figure out—and honestly, what hurt—was why he didn't involve them. Not Special Circs, not Wycoff. But Riggins and herself. What had they done wrong? Weren't they worthy anymore?

Constance pushed the thoughts out of her mind. She could feel hurt later. Now she needed to get as many people out of this building as possible.

She moved quickly, clearing a floor, then following the last straggler down another flight, all the while fighting the urge to flinch whenever another explosion went off. This was a slow-motion nightmare.

Then she saw something odd: a man with a phone in his hand. Not hurrying down like everyone else. Taking careful steps. Dialing a number. She watched his thumb move over the buttons. Ten digits, pushed deliberately. There was a three-second pause, and then Constance flinched again—another explosion, this one faint, distant.

By the time he started dialing again, the pieces had come together in her mind. By the sixth digit, Constance had her Glock 19 out. By the seventh she was yelling for him to freeze. He pushed another number and she let off a shot, above his head. That got his attention. Slowly, he turned on the cement stairs and looked up at her on the landing. Thumb over a digit. Which would be the ninth digit. Only one more to make a call.

"Don't," Constance said.

"Please," the man said, his face screwed up in an expression of worry. "I'm just trying to call my wife. She's going to be worried sick."

"Put the phone down."

"I don't understand—did I do something wrong?"

His lip trembled. His skin was pale, glistening with sweat. But Constance looked at his eyes. They were cold, hard. Nothing there at all.

"Final warning," Constance said, taking a step down closer.

"Okay, okay, okay . . ."

As he stooped down to place the phone on a stair, his expression changed. The coldness of his eyes spread to the rest of his face. Constance's trigger finger twitched, and then without warning he came charging up the stairs at her, two at a time, fast—incredibly fast. She fired—and missed. It was all happening too fast. By the time she took a breath and pointed a gun in his direction he was already on top of her, smashing his forearm into her hands, knocking the Glock aside. The shot ricocheted off cinder block. The man made a V with his thumb and index finger and thrust it into her throat. Constance dropped to her knees, dropped her gun. She couldn't breathe. It felt like a rock had been shoved down her trachea. Two objectives raced through her mind, both at cross purposes. One: defend herself. Two: recover the gun and shoot this bastard. Still choking, she reached for the gun. That's when he flattened her against the concrete landing by pushing a knee into the middle of her back. Once she was immobile, he grabbed her head with two large, rough, dry hands.

Constance knew what he was trying to do.

Would do, in another second.

She reached out for her Glock, which had landed on the step below. Wrapped her hand around it.

Immediately she felt one of the big hands leave her head. A second later it smashed into her elbow. Constance felt her arm break, then go partially numb.

She refused to let go of the gun.

Constance had always modeled her career after Steve Dark's. Taken her interoffice cues from him; learned how to piece together a difficult case from him. She wanted to be like him so badly, she even tried to inhabit his life in a weak moment. And now Constance knew what she had to do, because Dark would have done the same thing in this situation. Despite a six-foot-two, 220-pound man focusing his body weight onto the middle of her spine, hands wrapped around her head, arm broken in probably more than one place.

She aimed the best she could.

Then she fired her Glock down the stairs, blasting the cell phone into a million pieces.

Roger cursed himself for not thinking ahead. His commanding officers had always told him that he was a good soldier, but he didn't have a mind for strategy. Roger Maestro was someone you deploy with a specific objective. You didn't have Roger Maestro plan your war. Roger understood that, was at peace with that. Which was why he was glad to have Abdulia.

Only now, he'd failed her.

With an annoyed grunt, Roger slammed the FBI agent's head into the concrete, knocking her unconscious. Then Roger stood up and made his way down the stairs to his broken phone. He picked it up, hoping that somehow it was operational . . . but no.

There were a few options—none of them good. One was to stay inside the building, make the calls from one of the hundreds of empty cubicles available to him. But their plan depended on the tower falling, and triggering the second—and more lethal—wave of explosives from the outside, across the street. He couldn't do it from inside without it being a suicide mission.

Or Roger could make his way outside and make the calls from Abdulia's phone . . . but no. She was already away, taking care of the details of the final card. Their plan depended on him holding onto his phone.

A disposable? Not enough time . . . even if Roger knew where to buy one. They'd spent a lot of time in the city, but he never thought to notice cell phone shops. Roger had worried about many details, but not about finding another phone.

Aggravated, he slipped his broken phone into his jacket pocket and marched down the stairs.

chapter 83

Dark was running down the fire tower when he saw the body, the FBI vest. He recognized her before he gently turned her body over and looked at her face. Spend enough time with someone and your mind files away hundreds of sensory details about them. So Dark knew it was her, even before he reached the landing. Even though it made no sense—how she could be here, in this building, in the middle of these explosions.

Because she came to find you.

"Constance," he said, crouching down next to her, pressing his fingers against her neck. Dark repeated her name again, yelling this time. He felt his blood catch fire, as if he'd mainlined napalm.

Constance's eyes fluttered open.

". . . Steve?"

Dark exhaled and leaned forward, kissing her forehead in utter relief. He couldn't lose someone else close to him. Not like this. Not to these monsters.

"I'm going to get you out of here," Dark said, preparing to scoop her up into his arms.

Constance winced, then shook her head. "No. Because then I'd just have to arrest you."

Dark looked at her quizzically for a moment, but then she reached up and touched his face, reassuring him that, yeah, she was of sound mind and all of that, despite the blow to the head. She understood Steve Dark, and his gift, better than anybody else.

"Go," Constance said. "Go catch that son of a bitch."

chapter 84

Outside, Dark brushed debris from his shoulders. News media were everywhere, along with fire trucks, police vehicles, and haz-mat teams. Instead of walking with a purposeful gait, Dark stumbled around like one of the many dazed victims on the perimeter. His face was covered in ash and soot, but if someone recognized him, it was over. The Maestros had managed to make Dark look like the psycho here. It probably wouldn't take much to connect him to these blasts, too. Someone could even argue that he planted the bombs to make himself seem heroic.

Dark turned to steal a glance at the Niantic Tower. Smoke poured out of a dozen windows, and through the windows were a few visible fires. But the tower refused to fall. They'd managed to send enough of the packages down to the basement, after all. Roger Maestro had enough to spark fires and cause general panic, but he'd failed.

The Niantic Tower would needs millions in repairs, but it would not fall.

On the plaza, Dark glanced over at two men sitting in the back of an ambulance, oxygen masks pressed to their faces. They looked like they could be father and son, with the older man in an untucked white dress shirt, and the younger one in a gray coat and black jeans. Dark instantly recalled the Tower card and the two figures plunging to the earth. Could have easily been these two men, but that hadn't happened. Fate *could* be changed.

Something else on the plaza directly in front of the building caught Dark's eye. A man being carried, arms over two uniformed EMTs. At first the man seemed dead. Until he convulsed, then tore himself away from his rescuers. The man took a few steps, then stumbled to his knees and began to vomit, shaking his head and waving rescue workers away. Then, amazingly, the man climbed to his feet, and Dark recognized him. *Riggins.* He was trying to fight his way back into the building, no doubt to look for Constance. Two EMTs grabbed his arms; a third tried to slip an oxygen mask over his face. Riggins responded with a flurry of punches, pulling his arms away and tackling the EMT with the oxygen mask, knocking the guy on his ass before charging back into the building.

Dark knew why. Riggins would never rest until he made sure every member of his team made it safely home.

Every ounce of Dark's being wanted to tear after Riggins and shout *No!* at the top of his lungs. *No! Don't! You're only going to get yourself killed!*

But he knew such actions would be futile. You can't stop a man like Riggins. There would be no time to explain. Dark would most likely find himself arrested.

Roger and Abdulia were still at large. Here, somewhere, within eyeshot of the Niantic Tower. They'd be hoping for the building to come tumbling down.

So where?

Still ambling like a traumatized office worker, Dark scanned the corners, the sidewalks, the windows of street-level cafes. Would they be sitting, sipping a coffee, as they watched the mayhem across the way? No. Stop looking for pairs. Roger would still be busy. Abdulia would be the one watching, her dark, deep eyes studying every detail. She was the mastermind. Her husband was the muscle, the executioner, the pilot, the provider. But it was Abdulia who laid out the plan. Just like she'd laid out the path for Dark. The need to bring Abdulia down was urgent, almost painful.

As Dark moved, he felt a fluttering in his upper thigh. He patted his pocket, then remembered. His phone.

There were seventeen missed text messages. Several were from Graysmith. But the last few were from a strange number he didn't recognize:

HILDA HAS A MESSAGE FOR YOU

Graysmith answered. Dark gave her no time to speak.

"Tell me you've got transport," he said.

"Get to Pier Fourteen, right off the Embarcadero," she said. "I'll have a chopper waiting. So where are they? If this isn't the worst of it, where are they dealing the Death card?"

"I'll tell you once we're on board."

X

death

To watch Steve Dark's personal tarot card reading,
please log in to Level26.com and
enter the code: death.

EX LUX LUCIS ADVEHO ATRUM
XIII
EX LUX LUCIS ADVEHO ATRUM • EX ATRUM ADVEHO LUX LUCIS
EX LUX LUCIS ADVEHO ATRUM • EX ATRUM ADVEHO LUX LUCIS
DEATH
EX ATRUM ADVEHO LUX LUCIS

*T*ransmission picked up by U.S. Coast Guard, Vessel Traffic Service, Sector San Francisco. Lt. Gen. Allan Schoenfelder, Director, Operations Center Supervisor.

UNIDENT. FEMALE: Roger.
UNIDENT. MALE: I'm here.

[static]

UF: . . . so wish I could be with you, Roger.
UM: We will. Soon.
UF: Is it cold where you are, Roger?
UM: I'm a little cold. But I have my jacket.

[static]

UF: Roger?
UM: Yes.
UF: Do you remember what I told you about this last card? That this is about rebirth—the raising of our consciousness, flow of life?

UM: You told me.

UF: Good. I just wanted to make sure you understood. You're not afraid are you, Roger?

UM: I'm just tired, I guess.

UF: That's okay, Roger. It will be finished soon, and then we can rest.

[static]

Rest, just like the bodies in that tower were supposed to rest.

But Steve Dark had ruined that, just like the young agent—Paulson—had threatened to ruin their earliest efforts. You step into the path of fate, and fate will find a way to step into your path.

Abdulia wondered if the person they'd originally chosen to play the role of the Fool knew how lucky she was to have avoided her fate.

But now Dark pieced their story together too soon, laying their plans clear. The authorities were supposed to analyze the murders, write books about it . . . and most important, spread their message to all corners of the globe. Embracing your fate brings balance to the world. Fighting fate was as futile as fighting the currents of a mighty river. You try to swim upstream, and you only end up hurting yourself and others.

Hadn't humanity learned the lesson by now? The major corporations of the world were founded on the principles of challenging the natural order of things—squeezing the resources out of the struggling masses, being allowed to absorb an amount of wealth that would have shamed the Roman Empire. These same corporations were allowed to destroy the natural world in the process. Witness the growing mass of oil in the Gulf, and the corporate entity responsible shrugging its shoulders like some spoiled teenager.

The world needed a wake-up call. Abdulia would give it to them.

Everything depended on the final card.

chapter 85

Cape Mendocino, California

C ape Mendocino is the westernmost point on the California coastline, with a squat lighthouse that had been attempting to warn sailors away since 1868. One flash of white, every thirty seconds. Maintaining its lighthouse over the years wasn't easy. The area was notorious for seismic activity, as well as being exposed to the brunt of Pacific windstorms. The lighthouse, only three stories tall, was constantly broken, shifted, shattered, and at times destroyed by the worst nature had to offer. Still, the lighthouse was rebuilt time and again. The sharp rocks and sea stacks protruding from the Pacific coast were too dangerous, the risks too great. In recent years, however, modern navigation technology rendered the Cape Mendocino lighthouse obsolete. It was abandoned to the wind-swept salt during the mid-1960s, and was currently awaiting funding for renovation.

Inside its rusting hulk was Hilda. And the killers.

Abdulia's second text had been brief:

LIGHTHOUSE MENDOCINO . . . ALONE

Dark's stomach churned at the thought of Hilda being held captive by these maniacs. She had been patient with him, even when Dark had lost it and began tearing up her shop. Hilda had saved him, and she'd asked for nothing in return. Not even the price of the reading.

He couldn't let anything happen to her.

Now they raced over northern California in a Piper Tech chopper. Dark would have be to dropped somewhere within walking distance of the lighthouse, but no closer.

"That's incredibly stupid," Graysmith said. "You set foot inside that thing, you're dead, along with that tarot-card-reading friend of yours."

"If they see a chopper," Dark said, "Hilda's dead. At least this way I have a chance to bargain for her with my own life."

"Let me put together a strike team. I'm good at this."

"There's no time. And besides, Abdulia wants me. If she can't have me, she'll settle for Hilda."

Graysmith bit her lip. "I don't like it. Give me fifteen minutes and I can have a gunship up here to blow those killers off the top of that cliff."

But Dark thought that was probably what the killers wanted. After all, Hilda had explained to him that the Death card signified a new beginning as much as it did the end. *One must sacrifice oneself to be born again.*

He couldn't let Hilda go to her death with these psychos.

"No," Dark said. "It has to be me, alone. You brought me into this. Let me finish it."

Graysmith looked at him for a long moment before she sighed. "You know, I'm doing it. Letting my feelings get in the way. And people used to think I was blithe."

Before he left, Graysmith outfitted him in the bulletproof gear she'd acquired back in Fresno—as much as she could convince him to wear. It added weight, but Dark would deal with it. He checked his Glock 22, slid it into a holster clipped to his belt at the small of his back. He didn't want anything dangling from his body. For a crazy moment he wished he had a version of the Sqweegel suit that fit him.

chapter 86

Johnny Knack never wanted to be in a war zone. That was his one rule—domestic assignments only, thank you very much. Hell, he even avoided going to the UK, because of the IRA. One of his greatest fears was being plucked from the sidelines of a story and dropped right into the violent, churning *middle* of a story. One minute you're asking a question. The next you're sucking air through a fetid black hood, on your knees, not knowing if someone was going to cut your head off, or rape you with a broom handle, live on the Internet. Or maybe both, take your pick which comes first. So yeah—no fucking Iraq, no Kabul, no Korean border, no India, no Pakistan, not even Northern friggin' Ireland.

But Knack knew that if you take great pains to avoid something, you'll eventually end up confronting it anyway.

That's how life does ya.

Like right now: bound to a steel chair. Right arm behind his back, strung up in some kind of sling wrapped around his throat. If he tried to lower his arm, let the muscles breathe a little, then he'd start to choke to death.

Left arm: affixed, palm up, to the arm of the chair. At first the idea of his exposed palm and upturned wrist frightened the living fuck out of him. No worse torture for a journalist than to be forced to watch as your hands are mutilated.

But the crazy bitch didn't use a knife. Instead, she taped Knack's own digital voice recorder to it, his thumb poised so that it could easily reach the RECORD button.

"What do you want with me?" Knack asked. His voice sounded thick, slow. None of the precision and speed he liked to use. This lady had drugged the living shit out of him.

The woman—who'd helpfully introduced herself as Abdulia (which would come in handy when telling the police later, provided he lived through this experience, ha ha ha)—put her hand to his cheek.

"Don't worry, Mr. Knack," she said. "The Death card is not for you. You are to be its herald."

"Death card," he said, shuddering involuntarily. "So that's next, huh. Guess I should have seen that one coming. What was the priest? The Holy Man card, or something?"

"Do I hear mockery in your voice, even after all that you have seen and experienced?" Abdulia asked.

"No mockery. Just trying to understand."

"All will become clear if you keep your eyes open."

Knack adjusted his right arm—God, it *hurt*—and nodded his head toward the opposite side of the room. "What about her?" he asked. "Is the Death card for her, then?"

In the corner was a sleeping woman—long dark hair, kind of pretty in a hippieish kind of way. He'd watched Abdulia kneel down and shoot her up with something. Probably the same shit she'd been slamming into his veins. Keeping him nice and blissed out.

Knack heard a buzz. Abdulia put a cell phone to her ear, turned away from him. Well, it was good to know that a killer immersed in the ancient way of the tarot stayed nice and connected.

But with whom? Knack knew she couldn't be working alone.

She would have needed help stringing up poor Martin Green. Help slaughtering those girls in Philadelphia.

"Okay," Abdulia said. "I'm ready. Don't worry, Roger."

So "Roger," huh?

So much great material, Knack thought. Other journalists would kill for access like this. Imagine being able to hang with the Manson freaks as they breached Cielo Drive? *Hey, dirty hippie. Before you plunge that fork in that nice pregnant lady's belly, mind if I ask you a question or two?*

Abdulia finished her call to her husband, Roger, then crouched down and rooted through a small duffel bag. She returned to Knack's side, and he saw that she had three objects in her hands.

"Wait," Knack said. "You said Death wasn't for me! What the hell are you doing?"

"This will be uncomfortable," Abdulia said, "but it will not bring death."

In her hands: A dirty rag.

A roll of medical tape.

A pair of surgical scissors.

chapter 87

Steve Dark never thought he'd think these words in his mind. But part of him wanted to thank Sqweegel.

The monster stole nearly everything in the world from him. But he did leave one sick gift behind: *stealth*.

For many years Dark had studied this monster's movements and methods; he couldn't help but pick up the skills and methods of the monster. He thought of him every time he patrolled his house in the middle of the night, listening for the tiniest sound, the slightest hint that another monster had come for him.

Now, as he approached the lighthouse, those skills came in handy again.

Adrenaline was a factor, certainly. Dark's muscles surged with raw, nervous strength, even though he'd been through literal hell just a few hours ago. But it was Dark's ability to crawl, duck, and contort his body as he approached the lighthouse that saved him. The terrain was rocky, which was ideal for crouching and hiding as he made his approach. This made his joints and bones loose, like rubber. Dark kept the location of the lighthouse fixed in his mind so he didn't have to look up from behind a rock to see it. The structure was there, and it wasn't moving; he guided himself to it.

Finally he found a pile of rocks that served as adequate cover.

Dark used a tiny mirror on a thin metal rod to observe the light-house. Only three stories tall—about the size of your average Victorian home. He could see two figures inside the lantern room—one seated, one standing. The Maestros, alone? There was no sign of Hilda. Could she be in the watch room down below?

Dark put away his mirror, then crouched down low again, on his fingertips and the toes of his boots. Quickly, he scurried to the base of the lighthouse. The Maestros would be expecting him through the main entrance—the only way into the lighthouse. The struc-ture was built long before building codes demanding fire exits or wheelchair access. Maybe Dark could come in on their level, sur-prise them.

When Dark reached the base, he began to climb immediately. The rusted-over rivets cut into his skin, but Dark didn't care. It was something to cling to. He reached the main railing and looked into the lantern room.

chapter 88

The lens and lamp were long gone, as were many of the glass storm panes.

Reporter Johnny Knack, tied to a chair, lips around a rubber ball that was strapped to his head. The Maestros seemed to like their ball gags. His eyes were unusually wide, as if in a perpetual state of terror. Dark squinted. Knack's eyes were taped open, thick wide pieces of medical tape affixing his eyelids to his brows and cheeks *Clockwork Orange*–style. His cheeks were wet with tears.

Standing next to him was Abdulia herself, cell phone pressed to the side of her head. Dark hadn't seen her since Venice Beach, back before he knew the truth. But Abdulia seemed just as calm, at utter peace. Why were the worst monsters able to seem so cool and collected, even at the most desperate of moments?

And then, in the corner, passed out on the floor—Hilda.

Meanwhile, Roger watched Dark from fifty yards away. The shot couldn't be easier. But he had to wait. Sometimes Roger didn't understand his wife's ideas—not completely. He believed in her, he believed in the power of the cards, but he didn't understand why she had to make things so complicated sometimes. Roger thought they should have taken the money from Green and gone somewhere they could live cheaply. Instead they'd spent most of the past two weeks apart, traveling all over the country, killing and arranging. Killing and arranging.

And now he was perched in a small cave across a rocky plain from the lighthouse, rifle in hand—waiting for the final kill.

Roger's side still hurt from where Dark had slashed him. He'd managed to give it a quick field dressing, but his battered body needed rest. Sometimes when he closed his eyes, he could hear tiny explosions, and he imagined it was his veins, bursting from the stress of the past few weeks. The past few years, really.

But Abdulia had assured him it would be over by nightfall. And then they'd be together. Finally at peace, after the torment and grief both had endured.

Roger was eager for it to finally be over.

The light was so intense Knack was starting to go blind. Sensory overload. *God, this tape. This is worse than hand torture.* All he wanted to do was blink. If he ever got out of this, that's what he'd do—just spend a day blinking. Or maybe just close his eyes, tape them shut for a few days, let the moisture slowly resoak his eyeballs . . .

How did this crazy tarot lady expect him to "observe" if he couldn't see?

Then, out of the corner of his eye: a blur. Outside the window.

Dark leaped through one of the open spaces between the metal bars. As he landed he drew his Glock 22. Pointed it at Abdulia's chest.

"On your knees, hands behind your head."

He quickly scanned the room. Where was Roger? Probably downstairs in the watch room with a gun, waiting for Dark to use the front entrance.

Obediently, Abdulia knelt down in front of Dark. "Go ahead," she said. "Bring me *death*."

Dark kept his pistol aimed at her heart, one eye on the winding staircase on the side of the room. "So this is what you wanted all along? You should have called me ten days ago. You could have saved yourself a lot of trouble."

Abdulia smiled. "You know it had to be this way. Actions mean nothing unless you have the will to surrender everything. Including one's own life. And you are my dark knight. Death riding proud on a white horse."

"You think I'm Death?"

"Why else would our paths have crossed?" Abdulia asked. "The moment I saw your face . . . oh, the moment I heard your name, Steve Dark, I knew it was fate. I knew you would follow us to the end. You would never give up. Never surrender."

Dark nodded in the direction of Hilda—still unconscious on the floor.

"So why involve her? She has nothing to do with this."

"She has *everything* to do with this," Abdulia said. "You sought her counsel, and you spent all night in her shop. I was there. I watched you enter that evening. I watched you leave, blinking in the morning. Hilda brought you into the world of the tarot, and I knew she would draw you here to fulfill your destiny."

So that hadn't been paranoia—or Graysmith—at Venice Beach that night. Abdulia had started watching him from that moment. Johnny Knack here had snapped his photo in Philadelphia, bringing him to the killers' attention.

Dark glanced over at the bound reporter.

"And you have Knack here to watch me kill you?"

"The world needs to know what it means to embrace your fate. They will study my example and learn."

"You didn't need me here for this," Dark said. "You could have had your husband do it. He's killed a lot of people—he's very good at it."

"He would never hurt me. Roger loves me too much. But you're different, Steve Dark. When you stepped into our path, I read all about you. You're a born killer. Your life was meant to intersect with ours."

Dark's fingers tensed. He'd been here before—at the brink. Once again he was standing in front of a psycho responsible for the deaths of people he cared about. Once again, he held the weapon. He heard Sqweegel's voice taunting him:

It's no fun unless you're fighting. So come on. Fight! The world will be watching!

"Do it," Abdulia cooed. "Slay the monster, Dark. Collect your accolades. Your medals. Your honors. Isn't this what you've wanted all along? To prove yourself to your colleagues that you're not damaged goods? That you can do this on your own? That this is what you were meant to do with your life? So do it!"

Dark came to his senses. This was not Sqweegel. This was some fucked-up chick who believed that tarot cards were commanding her to kill. She had a killer soldier for a husband, who followed her every command. The Maestros were not monsters of his blackest nightmares; they were just psychotic people who needed to be taken off the playing field. Dark lowered his weapon.

"You think that following the cards will give you some kind of peace, is that it, Abdulia?" Dark asked.

"Fate wants me to die. For allowing my son, Zachary, to perish. I am as guilty as everyone else—the nurse, the priest, as well as the greedy, the vain, the pompous. You have a daughter. Surely you must understand the punishment I deserve."

"You're wrong," Dark said. "Can't you see that? You and Roger are in bondage, just like in the Devil card. You could easily take the shackles off, but you choose to be enslaved. It doesn't have to be that way."

Abdulia's eyes widened. Blood rushed to her cheeks. Her face seemed to explode with sheer rage.

"DON'T YOU SPEAK OF THE CARDS TO ME!"

"You know I'm right."

"YOU MUST BRING ME DEATH!"

"No," Dark said. "You're going to jail."

Abdulia charged at him suddenly, attempting something Dark had seen before: suicide via cop. But Dark quickly sidestepped, taking the cuffs from his belt, and caught Abdulia by her arm. She screamed and struggled wildly as he brought both arms behind her back. There would be no Death card. There would be a trial. There would be a verdict, delivered by a jury of her peers. There would be a sentence. *There's your fate.*

In the middle of the struggle, Dark caught a look from Knack. Flicking his open eyes to the window. Urgent. Quick. *Look!*

Two seconds later, the windows exploded.

chapter 89

When Roger Maestro saw Dark squeezing a pair of handcuffs around his wife's wrists, he was momentarily stunned. He didn't know what to do.

Abdulia had told him she would force Dark to kill himself. Dark would become the Death card, just like Jeb Paulson had been forced to embody the Fool card. Otherwise, Hilda would die. The journalist, too. And a man like Steve Dark wouldn't allow any more innocent victims to die.

But if Dark refused to do himself in, Abdulia would bow her head. And then Roger was to shoot him.

Blow his head clean off.

Bringing him Death.

Meanwhile the journalist, Knack, would watch, and then he would tell the world what he saw:

The price for refusing to accept your fate.

The last card, the last death. Finally they could go somewhere in peace. Abdulia had promised him. After this last one, everything would be all right. Balance would be restored at long last.

But Abdulia had never nodded. Instead, she rushed toward Dark, screaming as if she were in mortal pain. What had that son of a bitch said to her? What could he possibly have said to enrage his wife so? Abdulia was the model of calm, of inner peace. She relaxed the rivers of rage in his own heart. None of this made sense. Roger was momentarily numb as he watched Dark wrap his arms around her, cruelly bending her arms until her wrists were joined. This was not supposed to happen. This was not part of the plan. Abdulia had never told him this would even be a possibility.

So Roger Maestro lifted his gun, ignored his aching side, aimed, and fired.

A second before the windows exploded, Dark grabbed Abdulia by the arm and pulled her hard to the right, throwing them both to the ground. Glass burst and sprayed over their falling bodies. Someone was firing at them—Roger, no doubt. The decorated sniper. Concealing himself on a hill near the ocean, level with the lighthouse, just a like a soldier would position himself. Water at his back, enemies toward the front.

Dark quickly scrambled over to where Hilda lay unconscious. They were all too visible. Roger could have unlimited ammo. He could keep shooting and shooting and shooting—

Roger let the rifle fall from his shoulder, then picked up his binoculars, focused them. The image made no sense. Dark was down on the ground, over the girl. But so was Abdulia. He blinked, focused again. His wife trembled, like she was cold. It still didn't make sense. None of this did!

Knack would never forget the image for as long as he lived—the shots, his abductor screaming, glass bursting out of the frames, his eyes completely *naked and exposed*. Knack's face jolted, blinking involuntarily, the muscles working so hard that the tape above his left eye ripped free. He jammed it shut, but his right was still open. He couldn't look away. There was a pile of glass on his lap. The woman was down on the ground, twitching. A small trickle of blood flowed out from the side of her head. Then a *lot* of blood. Knack didn't want to look. He rolled his eye up, trying to see out in the semi-darkness. Someone was out there with a gun. Someone had just fired into this fucking lighthouse and could do it again, easily, and Knack couldn't do a thing about it unless he decided to pull his own arm down and choke himself to death first.

Abdulia cried out. Dark ignored her. He tried to rouse Hilda. What had she been given? He felt her neck for a pulse. Strong and regular. "Hilda," he whispered. "Come on, wake up. You can do it. You saved me, so now I'm going to save you."

A faint ringtone went off in the room.

Roger held the phone to his ear, still watching the lantern room through his binoculars. Come on, answer. Get up. Show me you're faking.

Dark had to get Hilda out of this room.

"Come on, Hilda. Wake up. Please."

Roger's wife didn't answer. Why didn't she answer the phone? The shot had been easy, but at the last minute Dark had flinched and moved to the right, like he'd had some kind of premonition. Roger was used to moving targets, though. In a fraction of a second he'd compensated, took the shot. He'd hit Dark in the head—didn't he? He saw the spray of blood. Head wound.

Unless . . .

No.

Not *her.*

This was unfair.

This was massively *unfair.*

Roger picked up his rifle, pressed the eyepiece to his socket.

Abdulia felt faint. She couldn't move her arms. She heard the phone, wanted so badly to push the green button and talk to Roger one last time. But she wasn't even sure if she could form the words.

This was not how it was supposed to happen. Dark was a man who slayed monsters. Well, he was supposed to slay her. Roger would see and Dark would be no more. Roger would take his own life, and they'd finally be together again in a better plane of existence, leaving behind their story for the world to study. Others had tried. None of them had her insight.

But it didn't matter, in the end. While she didn't expect to be felled by Roger's bullet, she knew Roger wouldn't let Dark leave the lighthouse alive. And then they would be together.

As the life ebbed out of her, Abdulia remembered the night she met Roger, and the reading she'd given him. He thought it was silly, at first. She knew he felt differently now. Their lives had been forever transformed by that reading.

She had been waiting for Death for a long, long time.

Dark quickly carried the unconscious Hilda to the winding stairway leading down to the watch station. The walls were thick; as long as she wasn't near any of the windows, she'd be safe from Roger's bullets. He nudged open a supply closet door with his knee, then gently lowered Hilda into it. Out of the line of fire, protected by two sets of walls.

Wait. That wasn't enough. He stripped out of his own bullet-proof vest and covered her chest with it.

Where was Graysmith now? He thought she would have been close enough to hear the rifle fire, but maybe not. Dark took his cell phone out of his pocket and pushed the speed-dial button. The tone rang six times before he gave up. Maybe she was already trying to take Roger out.

Then Dark realized that Knack was still up in the lantern room, completely exposed. Dark closed the closet door, then raced up the winding stairs.

Roger was a second too late. By the time he'd focused in on the lantern room, Dark had already taken Hilda down below. Fine. He'd use the journalist to draw him out. Dark considered himself a hero. No way he'd let an innocent man die. Placing the rifle to his shoulder, Roger squeezed the trigger.

Knack screamed. Jesus fuck almighty, the shooting had started again, glass shattering all around him, and yeah, he was crapping in his pants now. He wished he could close both eyes. He knew it was a matter of time before a tiny bead of flying glass sliced open his cornea. The sound, echoing off the metal frame of this room, was horrible. Hands, eyes, ears. Did a journalist have any other tools than these? Brains, too, he supposed. But his brain might be splattering out of the back of his head any second now.

———

Dark was halfway up the staircase when the bullets rang out and Knack started screaming. He cleared the top and scrambled across the floor. Just as he was about to tackle Knack, two shots slammed into his back, propelling him forward. Dark grunted and stumbled, his shoulder slamming into Knack's chest and tipping his chair backward. Knack's screams were the last thing he heard.

chapter 90

It was over.

Steve Dark was done.

No head shots this time; he'd put two in the center of gravity. Explode his heart, pop his lungs. Good-bye, hero.

Roger lowered his rifle from his shoulder and began to disassemble it, removing the bolt, lifting the trigger group out of the rifle, separating the barrel and receiver from the stock, removing the gas tube and piston, then packing everything quickly into his case. He liked this rifle, but he would have to destroy it.

That would have to come later. First Roger had to go to the lighthouse and make sure Dark was dead and Knack was still alive. He'd been careful not to hit him, but Dark had slammed into him hard, and for all he knew the guy might have been strangled by his own bindings. If that were the case, no big deal. Roger would retrieve the digital recorder and mail it somewhere. Maybe CNN or *The New York Times*. Some other journalist would be able to piece the story together. Abdulia had been insistent; someone had to tell their tale, or all of this meant nothing. There would be no balance. No peace.

Abdulia.

He thought of her now and nearly lost control of his emotions, but then he quickly pushed the thoughts out of his mind. Because that's what she would have wanted. It would be difficult to walk into that lighthouse and see her body on the floor, but he steeled himself. *That's not her anymore. She's on the next plane of existence, with our baby boy.*

And while Roger was still taking air into his lungs, he would honor his wife by continuing her work.

At some point he hoped to be worthy to join them.

Roger remembered their first date, when Abdulia told him that she was a reader. *Go ahead*, he'd joked, *read me*. She did. When the Death card came up, Roger groaned. *Oh great, you've just killed me.* Abdulia shook her head no, and explained that this was a fortuitous card. You are my dark knight on a white steed, she explained. Roger liked that.

Now that Abdulia was gone, it was up to Roger to flip the cards. But now he was secure in the knowledge that Abdulia was speaking to him from the afterlife. He would study the tarot, then carry out the orders.

They would tell *him* who to kill.

chapter 91

Knack stared up at the paint-chipped ceiling with one eye, marveling that he hadn't strangled himself to death. And that was about the only positive thing he could say for himself at this moment.

On top of him was the body of Steve Dark. He could feel the man breathing faintly, but clearly he would be checking out soon. Two bullets to the back—you're not walking away from that, no sir.

Knack's arm was still pinned behind him, and clearly broken in a number of places. The pain was unreal, racing up and down his arm in urgent jolts of agony.

There was broken glass everywhere.

And his friggin' eye was still taped open, no matter how much he wrinkled his face or twisted his jaw or knitted his brow. The exposed eye was driving him insane.

Downstairs, he heard the sound of a door creaking open.

Oh God.

Urgent footsteps up to the lantern room. Knack looked over with his one good eye and saw a tall man, salt-and-pepper hair in a buzz cut, weathered looking. He was carrying a rifle in one hand, a case in the other.

The other killer.

"Please," Knack said. "Don't do this."

"Don't worry," the man said. "You'll live. We want you to tell our story."

"I will!" Knack squealed. "I promise I will, whatever you want me to say."

As the man crouched down, Dark pushed himself up off the floor and pulled a knife from the sheath on his boot.

Graysmith was the one who insisted on Dark wearing Kevlar.

"I spent too much money for it to go to waste. What can it hurt?" Dark had initially objected, worried that it would weigh him down too much. But then Dark considered Roger Maestro's background, his skill with the gun. Dark would deal with the weight.

"This first," Graysmith had said, handing him a black button-down shirt, long sleeves. He took it, and was surprised by its weight.

"What is it?" Dark asked.

"Kevlar lining, front and back, nearly invisible. High protection. Can stop a .44 Magnum. Only $12,000 each, but I was able to get a discount."

Dark had worn the shirt, which felt like chain mail, and then added the vest—which, even though it was slimmed down, added even more pounds. "You got to be kidding me," Dark had said. But now he was glad he'd worn it. The shirt had displaced the impact of the rifle blasts. The impact still knocked him forward and hurt like holy fuck, but the bullets did not break his skin, nor pierce his lungs or scramble his internal organs.

A pro like Roger Maestro would come to confirm the kill. Dark would be ready for him.

The moment he was on his feet, Dark stabbed his knife at Roger's upper pectoral muscles. But Roger grabbed Dark's wrist and twisted it hard, forcing his fingers open. The knife dropped. Roger grabbed Dark by his Kevlar shirt, pulled him close, then flung him back into the metal framework of the lighthouse windows. Impossibly, there was more glass to be shattered. The impact of Dark's body shattered it. He slid to the ground, feeling a white-hot blast of pain at the base of his spine.

His Glock. Dark reached around to his back—then remembered. He'd dropped it when he pulled Abdulia to the ground. There it was, a few feet from her body, partially hidden under the rusted base of the old light source.

Roger charged forward.

Placing his palms on the glass-covered floor, Dark slammed his boot into Roger's knee. The damned thing felt like an iron pole. Such a move would have blown out any normal human being's knee, or at least given them pause. Roger didn't even seem to feel it. He picked Dark up again and slammed his body into the metal frame. Again. And again. This was going to turn out like their fight in the Niantic building. Without weapons, Dark had nothing—not against a human slab of concrete like Roger Maestro. Abdulia had been the brains of the outfit. But Roger had gone and blown them out of her skull. All Dark had was one last card to play.

"She had a message for you," Dark muttered.

Roger stopped the pounding and held him up. "What did you say?"

"As she was dying," Dark said. "She told me to make sure you understood something."

"You're a liar."

"About Zachary. Your boy."

"Don't say his name," Roger growled. "You don't have *the right to say his name!*"

"She said the last card wasn't about him, it was about you, you were Death all along. You brought Death into their lives, back from the war. You were responsible for your son's death."

"Enough!"

"Look in her pocket. It's there. She made me swear to have you look in her pocket. She said it would explain everything."

Roger slammed Dark against the frame one more time before looking back at his wife's dead body. Then he turned his attention back to Dark for a moment, then body-slammed him into the ground. Dark felt the air smashed from his lungs, and his vision go gray around the edges. Shards of glass dug into his skin. Before he had a chance to recover, Dark was being dragged across the lantern room floor, all the way to Abdulia's body. He was flipped over. Something that felt like an anchor pounded into the middle of his spine.

"If you're lying to me, I'm going to take my time tearing you apart. Then I'm going to find everyone you've ever loved and I'm going to cripple them right in front you."

"Just look," Dark said.

As Roger gingerly touched his wife's corpse, Dark reached out, grabbed his Glock, bent his elbow, and fired blind—backward over his head.

POP POP POP POP POP POP POP

Ejected brass casings rained down on the wooden lighthouse floor.

Within a second the weight on his back eased, then disappeared completely. Dark rolled over, coughing, feeling like his ribs were nothing more than a collection of hard white marbles in his chest. Part of Roger Maestro's face was gone. His mouth was open, and he was still trying to form words, but nothing came out. Roger's body weight had shifted back on his heels. Finally his eyes rolled down, but it was not Dark he was looking for. Roger wanted his wife. Dark could understand the feeling. He sat up and put five more bullets into Roger, all chest shots. The ex-soldier tipped backward and landed on the ground, his hand reaching out, fingers twitching. Seeking his wife's hand.

chapter 92

After he cut Knack free, Dark went downstairs to the closet in the watch room. Hilda's eyelids were fluttering open, her small eyes darting back and forth worriedly. Where was she? What was this heavy weight on top of her?

Then she saw Dark and a smile broke out over her face. "Seems our fates are entwined as well."

"Guess so," Dark said.

Dark pulled aside the Kevlar vest and helped Hilda to her feet. She was pale and shaky, but otherwise unharmed. Hilda explained that she remembered falling asleep a few nights ago and waking up in the custody of the Maestros. Both had grilled her about Steve Dark, the kind of man he was, where his family lived—anything. Hilda had refused, expecting to be killed for her disobedience. Instead they kept her drugged. The last few days seemed like a hazy nightmare, sparked by the set of tarot cards. *The Wheel of Fortune. The Devil. The Tower. Death . . .*

"Well, your nightmare's over," Dark said.

Hilda touched his face. "Thanks to you."

"No," Dark said. "It's entirely thanks to you. You helped me understand."

Dark called Graysmith, but received no answer. No matter. He escorted Hilda outside, called 911. There would be explaining to do, but Dark was at peace with that. Even Knack could write what he wanted. It didn't matter.

"You said to me during our reading that you felt numb and help-less," Hilda said. "You saw yourself reflected in the Devil card."

"Yeah, I did."

"Do you still feel that way?"

"No, I don't," Dark said, the hint of smile on his face. "You led me to the truth inside of me—the stuff I've been pushing away all of these years. I was lost inside my own head, and you showed me the way out. And I'll always be grateful to you for that."

But as Dark stepped through the doorway, the smile died on his face. Someone was standing there, waiting, Sig Sauer in hand.

chapter 93

"**H**ey," Riggins said.

Dark froze. Hilda looked at up at him nervously.

Riggins gestured with the gun. "I know you're not going to try anything stupid, right?"

"How did you find me?" Dark said.

"Through your silent benefactor," Riggins said. "She's in custody right now. Just in case you've been trying to reach her. I may be an old man, but I still have some moves left in me."

Riggins tried hard to sound nonchalant, but he'd practically had to sell his soul to the devil—in this case, Wycoff—to get the clearance to bring Lisa Graysmith in for questioning. She might have had deep ties to the intelligence community, Riggins had argued, but that didn't make her immune from a criminal investigation. Wycoff, to his credit, had seen the merit in the argument. He made the appropriate phone calls. Within thirty minutes Riggins was in a chopper with a SWAT team. They found Graysmith near Cape Mendocino. She went without a fight—almost without a word. Instead, she just smirked at Riggins. On the way to the chopper she told him: "You'd better go check on your boy." Creepy bitch. When Riggins heard the shots, he'd made his way to the lighthouse.

And now, for the second time in a matter of days, Riggins found himself pointing his Sig at the man he used to consider a son. They tell you that you should never point a weapon at anything you don't intend to kill. Is that what he was preparing to do? Kill his surrogate son?

That would depend on whether Dark was still the man he knew. Or whether he'd allowed genetics to take over, and he was slowly becoming a monster.

"Constance almost died," Riggins said. "This has to stop. You and your sick, crazy games."

"I'm not playing games," Dark said.

"Come on back with me," Riggins said. "You'll have the chance to explain everything."

"No," Dark said. "I'm going home to my daughter."

"You're crazy if you think that's going to happen."

"I'm not, Tom. I'm as sane as I've ever been. I think I've spent the years since Sibby's death looking for some kind of sign. For a while there, I thought these tarot cards were that sign. But no. You make your own promises. You set your own goals. You create your own fate. As long as you do that, there's hope. Even when the cards are stacked against you."

"What have you been doing?"

"My job," Dark said. "Just not for you."

Riggins lowered his weapon. He knew Dark better than anyone. He also knew serial killers better than anyone.

The psychos they chased? They all had this iron compulsion to kill, the unquenchable thirst for blood and violence. Dark had the same compulsions, the same thirst . . . only for justice. For vengeance. Special Circs had been able to channel those gifts for a while, but Dark had grown restless. He needed to do this his own way.

Mind you, this way was ridiculously illegal. The law had no room for vigilantes. Riggins knew there may come a time when he'd have to put Dark down. But now wasn't that time. For now, Dark was a force of good in the world. And it was best to let him go home to his daughter.

He'd sort it out later.

Riggins tilted his head up at the lighthouse. "I'm guessing they're both gone."

Dark nodded. "The reporter, Johnny Knack, is still alive. You might want to talk to him. He saw everything that happened up there."

"He okay?"

"A little banged up, but otherwise fine."

"Yeah, I'll talk to him," Riggins said. "But I think it's better for all concerned if you weren't here at all. Let's just say that Special Circs followed the trail here. An agent got inside, took both of them out. How's that sound?"

"The husband did the wife," Dark said. "Forensics will show that."

"We'll figure it out. Knack will tell me all of the gory details, I'm sure."

"Will he? I mean, think you can count on him to keep things quiet?"

"I eat these little pissant reporters for breakfast."

Riggins now turned his attention to Hilda, who'd observed their conversation in amused silence.

"You okay, ma'am?"

"You're just like Steve described you," Hilda said. "I'm honored to meet you."

"No offense, but who the fuck are you?"

Hilda grinned. "Have you ever had a tarot reading before?"

To watch Steve Dark's personal tarot card reading,
please log in to Level26.com and
enter the code: life.

EPILOGUE

Santa Barbara, California

"Sorry I'm late," Graysmith said.

Dark was only half surprised to see her at his in-laws' front door. "It's okay. I heard you were detained."

Graysmith frowned. "Yes, thanks to your former boss, who's a real . . ."

Her voice trailed off, mainly because Graysmith didn't seem to be able to find an acceptable word to use in front of a five-year-old. Little Sibby, who was hugging her daddy's legs, peeking from behind them.

"You must be the beautiful Sibby," Graysmith said, crouching down. "I'm Lisa."

Sibby smiled for a moment, laughing wickedly, then ran back into the house.

"She's shy," Dark said, still uncomfortable with the idea of Graysmith being here, around his daughter.

Graysmith seemed to sense the tension. She smoothed out her skirt as she stood up again. "Or she's an excellent judge of character. Look, is there somewhere we can talk? Somewhere quiet?"

Dark's father-in-law took command of the barbecue grill; his mother-in-law continued chopping a salad; Sibby returned to dressing her dolls, which Dark had finally driven up from West Hollywood. Now Dark walked with Graysmith down a path to a beach entrance. He had to admit, beaches were a place he did his best thinking. The crashing waves, the soft sand—it all calmed him. As if it took something as powerful and violent as an ocean to drown out the turmoil inside his mind.

After a few minutes of silence, Graysmith turned to face Dark. "I'm being reassigned," she said.

"Where?"

"Well, without breaking any security clearances . . . let's just say it's some other place with a lot of sand."

"Nobody knew about your extracurricular activities, I'm guessing."

"No idea. I'd told them I needed a few months' leave of absence. The gear, the equipment, the sources . . . all of that I supplied on my own. You get in deep somewhere, you learn their tricks. It's not hard to pick up."

Dark nodded. "How much trouble are you in?"

"Not enough to have me shot for treason, if that's what you mean. And apparently I'm too valuable to be fired. So the best punishment is to keep me around and keep me in constant deployment."

"You never told me exactly what you do, or who you work for."

"You're right. I didn't."

Behind them, the Pacific smashed into the golden beach, which was part of one long stretch of east-west coastline. Most of California bore the brunt of the Pacific head-on; Santa Barbara was a little haven. Ocean to one side, Santa Ynez Mountains to the other. A cradle. Dark definitely understood why Sibby's parents lived here, and felt comfortable raising their granddaughter here.

"So I guess this is the end of . . ." Dark's voice trailed off. What the hell was it, anyway? Some grieving intelligence type goes off the deep end, teams up with a burned-out manhunter, they stop two psychopaths, and what? Was he supposed to kiss her under the setting sun? Was music supposed to swell? No. That was only in the movies.

"Yeah," Graysmith said. "Unless I quit."

Dark raised an eyebrow.

"It's still a free country, last time I skimmed the Constitution," Graysmith said. "I can pick up the phone and pull the plug now. Just give me the word."

"And then do what? Catch serial killers in our spare time?"

Graysmith took his hand and squeezed it. "Yeah," she said.

Dark didn't respond for a while. He watched the white foam on the water, the families making their way back from the beach to cook dinner or play games or do whatever it was families did in Santa Barbara.

Later, at her hotel, Graysmith made an untraceable call on a prepaid cell phone she'd picked up at a drugstore. First she dialed the relay number, which recorded the incoming number. Then she waited. Poured herself a glass of chardonnay. Half of it was gone by the time her disposable cell phone rang. She picked it up and listened for a moment.

"Yes," she said. "We met earlier today and I explained the situation, just as you recommended."

More listening.

"I assure you. He's ours now."

EPILOGUE II

White roses seemed appropriate. Though Dark never understood the idea of laying flowers on top of a grave. The roses were cut, packaged, soaked in water to maintain the illusion of life—but they were already dead, or dying. *Here, death. Have more death.*

Not that he would share these thoughts with his daughter.

Dark was being morbid though. His wife, Sibby, wasn't here, in this cemetery. This was merely a marker to note that she had, indeed, lived. But his wife, *her essence*, was alive in his mind, and always would be.

"Where should I put them, Daddy?"

"Anywhere you want, sweetheart."

The important thing was that Sibby had a physical reminder of her mother, who had died the day she'd been born. His daughter had no memories of her mother; nothing to keep alive in her mind. Of all the things Sqweegel took from Dark, this was the most heartbreaking. A daughter's right to know her own mother—the smell of her skin, the kindness of her touch.

"That's good, sweetheart," Dark said, watching his daughter

place the bunch of roses right next to the grave marker, in the corner where the stone met the earth.

"Is Mommy down there?"

Dark shook his head and crouched down. He placed his hand over her chest. "She's right there. And she always will be."

West Hollywood, California

Today was move-in day. Dark had spent the previous four days finishing the paint job and assembling furniture before driving up to Santa Barbara to retrieve his daughter. Hello Kitty figured large in the design scheme—not that Dark knew what the hell he was doing. He figured Sibby would set him straight with other suggestions along the way. After the cemetery and a quiet dinner and a trip to an ice cream parlor, Dark tucked his daughter into her new bed, kissed her forehead, and wished her sweet dreams.

He waited in his living room and listened. There was the hum of traffic on nearby Sunset. Someone laughing—drunkenly. The faint *click-clack* of high heels on concrete. A car horn, muted and distant. Normal L.A. night sounds. Nothing out of the ordinary.

After he was certain she was asleep, Dark went downstairs to his basement lair.

He had a video monitor trained on his daughter's room, along with the best motion detectors available. If so much as a carpet beetle were to amble across her threshold, alarms would sound in the basement. But Dark also had another monitor displaying real-time murder stats. A system powered by experimental software and links provided by Graysmith. It was a command center that would be the envy of any law enforcement agency in the world, and it was right here. In Dark's basement.

Turned out that it was possible to be a good father *and* a good manhunter. It wasn't easy, of course. But nothing worthwhile ever was.

Over the past few days, a disturbing pattern in Eastern Europe had presented itself. A sadist who seemed to be able to walk through walls and who collected obscure trophies from his twitching, dying victims.

A few minutes later, the cell phone on top of the morgue table vibrated. Dark hit the green button, pressed it to his ear.

"I'm watching it now," Dark said. "He's going to make a mistake soon."

Graysmith said, "How soon can you be ready?"

"I'll call the sitter," he said.

acknowledgments

Anthony E. Zuiker would like to thank: First and foremost my wife, Jennifer. Thanks for cheering me on to direct. To the cast and crew of *Dark Prophecy*, thanks for continuing to make the *Level 26* cyberbridges the best they can be. To Matthew Weinberg, Orlin Dobreff, Jennifer Cooper, William Eubank, David Boorstein, and Joshua Caldwell, you guys rocked this shoot. Not to mention the pig. Oink! Oink! A very special thanks to Duane Swiercyznski. Our second book together. We rock! And last, but not least, Team Zuiker: Margaret Riley, Kevin Yorn, Dan Strone, Alex Kohner, Nick Gladden, and Sheri Smiley.

Duane Swierczynski would like to thank: My wife, Meredith; my son, Parker; and my daughter, Sarah. Huge thanks to Anthony Zuiker for bringing me back into the Darkness, and all of Team Zuiker (especially Matt, Orlin, David, and Josh), who helped me find my way. Dr. Boxer watched my back. And last but not least, Team DHS: David Hale Smith and Shauyi Tai, my longtime partners in crime.

dark prophecy

Starring

Daniel Buran as Steve Dark

Justine Bateman as Hilda

Michael Ironside as Tom Riggins

Tauvia Dawn as Sibby Dark

Aaron Refvem as Henry

about the authors

ANTHONY E. ZUIKER is the creator and executive producer of the most-watched television show in the world, *CSI: Crime Scene Investigation*, and a visionary business leader who speaks regularly about the future of entertainment. Zuiker currently lives in Los Angeles, California.

DUANE SWIERCZYNSKI is the author of several thrillers, including *Expiration Date*, and writes for Marvel Comics. He lives in Philadelphia, Pennsylvania.